PRAISE FOR **LOU BERNEY** AND ***GUTSHOT STRAIGHT***

"You don't have to play poker to enjoy *Gutshot Straight*, a highly entertaining caper novel with a title straight out of a high-stakes game. All you need do is grasp the concept of long odds, embrace the notion of noir lite, have a sense of humor, and relish oddball characters. . . . The plot [is charged] with unexpected twists. . . . Thickening the plot is Lou Berney's mastery of locale including Vegas, Los Angeles, and Panama City. . . . At the heart of the mystery is [a] briefcase. . . . What happens to the contents of the briefcase is delicious and just, enthralling and unpredictable. . . . What the hype [about Berney] doesn't mention is how well he renders characters, detailing them so vividly and deftly you can distinguish their tones of voice, even their tics. Like Carl Hiaasen, Berney delights in the cartoonish. Like Elmore Leonard, he can drive a plot. What sets him apart is how well he evokes love, making the romance at the heart of this cinematic book as compelling as the mystery." —*Boston Globe*

"Fast, funny, and smart. . . . The snappy dialogue and bad-guy stuff whizzes along and will be welcomed by Elmore Leonard fans. Grade: A-."

—*Plain Dealer* (Cleveland)

"Full of intriguing characters and violent action. . . . Highly entertaining, the serpentine novel has unexpected twists and turns. Many of the quirky characters could have just stepped out of an Elmore Leonard or Carl Hiaasen novel. Berney, a talented and experienced author, has crafted one of the most unusual and enjoyable crime novels of the year. Hopefully a sequel is in the works, with film adaptation following shortly." —*Lansing State Journal*

"A fast-paced, sexy novel packed with spine-tingling intrigue and money-induced lust. . . . Berney, an accomplished screenwriter, brings his detail-oriented expertise to fiction work in this debut novel, and the book reads like a movie. Readers can almost imagine who the actors would be portraying this lively and diverse cast of misfits as the words play out the story in their minds. In my opinion, that's a pretty good mark of a great storyteller. . . . Excellent."

—*Times Record News* (Wichita Falls, Texas)

"Virtually every character is memorable, and the chemistry between Shake and Gina is brilliant. The plot turns are constant, and the dialogue is sharp. The bad guys are wonderfully scary, and the locales are vividly drawn. Elmore Leonard might be very pleased to call *Gutshot Straight* his own."

—*Booklist* (starred review)

"A fast-moving caper . . . smoothly blends humor, action, and romantic frisson."

—*Publishers Weekly*

"*Gutshot Straight* has my vote for, among other things, best MacGuffin ever. Just when you think it can't get any weirder or quirkier, here comes the scene where . . . well, I better not give that away. Just be assured that Lou Berney's novel is so energetic, so droll, and so wheezingly funny that it accomplished what no book ever has before: It made me forget to eat lunch."

—Stephen Harrigan, *New York Times* bestselling author of *The Gates of the Alamo* and *Challenger Park*

"A literary sucker punch—surprising, funny, effervescent. It's a cocktail that won't let you off your barstool till closing."

—Ted Griffin, screenwriter of *Ocean's Eleven*, *Matchstick Men*, and *Best Laid Plans*

"An exciting read you can't put down. A definite must-read."

—Abraham Rodriguez, 2008 Dashiell Hammett Award finalist and author of *South by South Bronx*

"I was curious to read Lou Berney's take on the dark, intriguing personality of my favorite town. And I wasn't disappointed. . . . Berney, an accomplished screenwriter, brings his detail-oriented expertise to his fiction work in this debut novel, and the book reads like a movie. Berney deftly captures the grime and the tension-induced sweat of being on the run. . . . [An] excellent novel."

—*Las Vegas Review-Journal*

"*Gutshot Straight* zigs and zags more than enough to hold readers' attention, and Berney is an able hand at the sort of cons that drive solid caper fiction, and interested in examining why those cons work so well. Shake and Gina . . . develop in believable, occasionally surprising ways, and their growing commitment to each other is sweet without ever compromising either character. . . . The dialogue is clever without being glib, and the ending ties it all together just perfectly enough to be a little messy. Whether Shake and Gina manage to find love amid the chaos always comes across as a question worth asking; it's just too bad that finding the answer means reaching the last page. A-."

—*The Onion's A.V. Club*

"[Has] a fast-paced style apropos of [Berney's] title character Charles 'Shake' Bouchon. . . . With comparisons to Elmore Leonard, it's apparent Berney is not simply riding out the success of his acclaimed short *The Road to Bobby Joe and Other Stories*."

—Daily Beast

"The [cover] features names like Elmore Leonard and Carl Hiaasen, and the comparisons are apt. . . . Berney is a skilled writer. . . . He has obviously spent some time in Las Vegas, because the scenes set here resonate with accurate observations and details. . . . Fortunately, the same attention to accuracy and detail continue when the story moves to Panama. . . . Mixed with smart dialogue, nonstop plot twists, and palpable chemistry between Shake and Gina, the locations and historical elements make for an exotically wild ride to an ending that satisfies. . . . *Gutshot Straight* is vividly visual and cinematic. The novel seems to cry out for translation to the silver screen. . . . I like Berney's up-to-date portrayal of Las Vegas, and I'll be happy to follow his characters to Panama."

—Living Las Vegas

"Has a cinematic feel to it; as with the best of books, you can see each and every scene unreeling in your head as sentence after sentence flies by. . . . Comparisons between Berney and Elmore Leonard are perhaps inevitable, with Berney more than adequately holding his own. There are plot twists that are wondrously and skillfully navigated; one of the most unique MacGuffins I have encountered recently; and, perhaps most importantly, Gina, a strong, smart, attractive, and dangerous woman who you won't soon forget. Nor will you forget *Gutshot Straight*."

—Bookreporter.com

"Awesome debut novel by Lou Berney, everyone needs to read this book. Look for it later this year on awards nomination lists."

—*Crimespree Magazine*

© J. D. Merryweather

ABOUT THE AUTHOR

LOU BERNEY is an accomplished writer, teacher, and liar. He has written feature screenplays and created TV pilots for, among others, Warner Brothers, Paramount, Focus Features, ABC, and Fox. He is the author of *The Road to Bobby Joe and Other Stories*, and his short fiction has appeared in publications such as *The New Yorker*, *Ploughshares*, and the Pushcart Prize anthology. *Gutshot Straight*, his first novel, was written during the 2007–2008 film and TV Writers Guild strike.

www.louberney.com

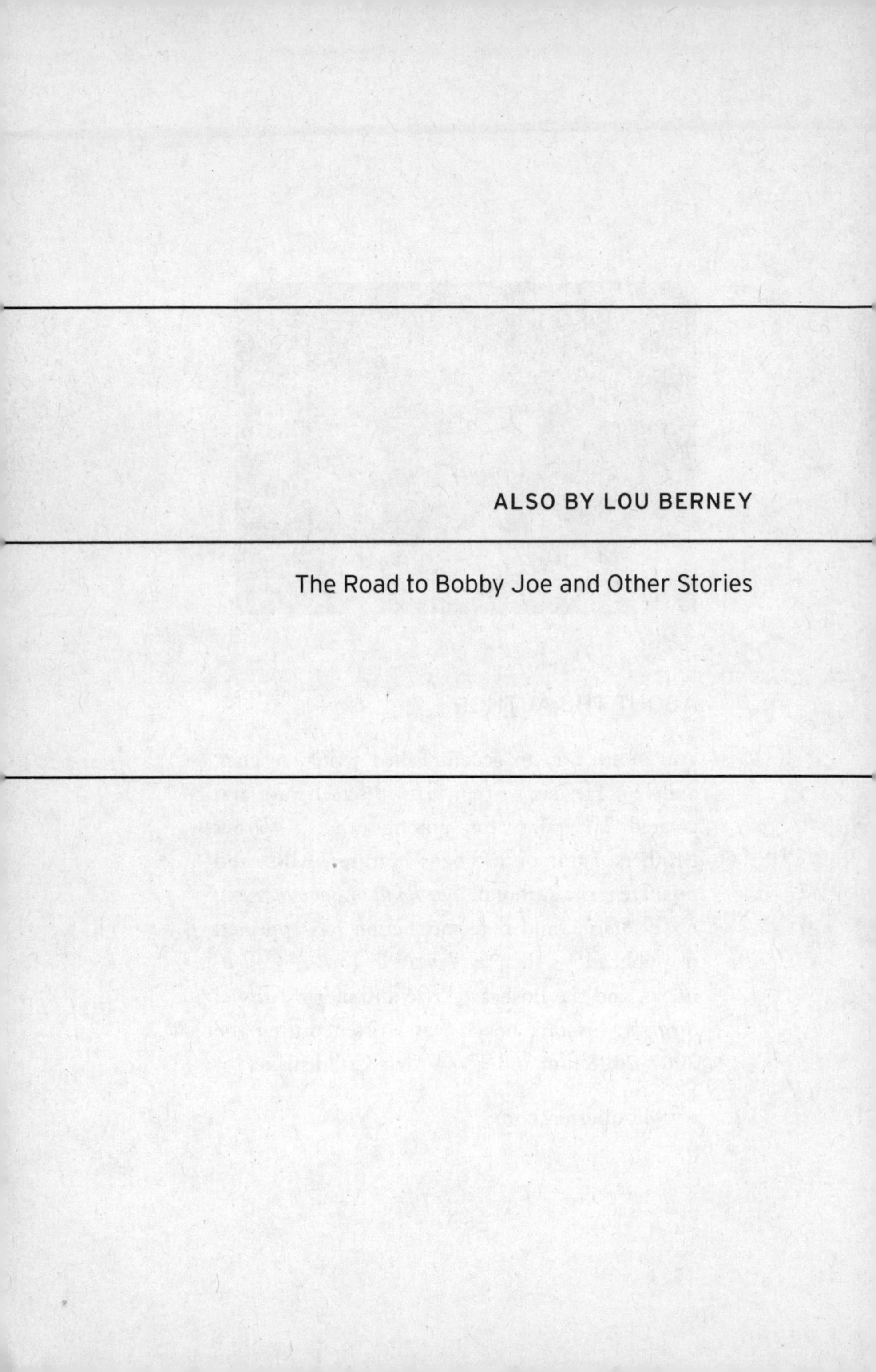

ALSO BY LOU BERNEY

The Road to Bobby Joe and Other Stories

GUTSHOT STRAIGHT

Lou Berney

HARPER

NEW YORK . LONDON . TORONTO . SYDNEY

HARPER

This book is a work of fiction. References to real people, events, establishments, organizations, or locales are intended only to provide a sense of authenticity, and are used fictitiously. All other characters, and all incidents and dialogue, are drawn from the author's imagination and are not to be construed as real.

A hardcover edition of this book was published in 2010 by William Morrow, an imprint of HarperCollins Publishers.

FIRST HARPER PAPERBACK PUBLISHED 2011.

The Library of Congress has catalogued the hardcover edition as follows:

Berney, Louis.
Gutshot straight / Lou Berney. — 1st ed.
p. cm.
ISBN 978-0-06-176604-6
1. Ex-convicts—Fiction. 2. Crime—Fiction. I. Title.
PS3552.E73125G88 2010
813'.54—dc22 2009025215

ISBN 978-06-176634-3 (pbk.)

11 12 13 14 15 OV/BVG 10 9 8 7 6 5 4 3 2 1

For Christine

Chapter 1

Charles Samuel Bouchon—"Shake" for short, ever since his first fall for grand theft auto when he was nineteen—took another look at his hole cards.

He tended to fold with a bullet showing and his opponent betting big, but Shake was sitting on a pair of hearts, and he was pretty sure the beast across the table from him wouldn't recognize a flush if it jumped into his lap and kissed him on the mouth.

The beast was Vader Wallace, a mean young black con from Block C who was one long rope of muscle, braided around and around and around until it was a wonder he could walk. He was doing a dozen years behind a first-degree-manslaughter charge, aggravated. Extremely aggravated, according to the rumors.

Shake, on the other hand, was just a rangy white guy up on another GTA, forty-two years old and feeling every minute of it. But he'd survived the last fifteen months here at Mule Creek and wasn't going to roll over just because some pumped-up, puffed-up con glared at him.

He called Vader's bet. "I'll pay to see that last card," he said, and gave Vader a friendly smile.

Missouri Bob, the dealer, took his time with the river. Missouri Bob's hand was tooled with crude blue tattoos—roses and rose stems and thorns.

Finally, dramatically, he showed them the last card.

Queen of hearts.

"Tramp of hearts," Missouri Bob said. "Lovely but dangerous. Beware."

Shake waited till he was sure Vader was watching him and then he frowned.

Vader saw the frown and smirked. Shake felt a little sad, how easy this was.

"Bet it all," Vader said. He pushed his entire bankroll of Top Ramen noodles into the center of the table.

"The bad-tempered brother wrongly convicted of manslaughter bets it all," Missouri Bob said.

"I heard what the bad-tempered brother said," Shake said.

"Small-change white bread stalls for time."

"I don't know how we'd manage without your commentary, Bob." Shake gave the queen of hearts another frown, just to see Vader smirk again. He noted that Vader's head was too small in relation to all the muscle it was perched atop. His mouth, by contrast, was too large in relation to the head.

The fourth person at the table, a tweaked-out kid with one eye focused, the other swimming, tried to get a peek at Shake's cards.

"That right, Shake?" he asked. "You're small change?"

"Walks outta here a free man in seventy-two hours," Missouri Bob said.

"Sixty-eight," Shake said. "Not that I'm counting."

"Call or fold, motherfucker," Vader said.

Shake pushed his call in. "Show me yours, I'll show you mine."

"Three aces."

Vader started to rake in the pot. Shake dropped his flush.

Missouri Bob clapped a hand to his bald head and woo-heed. Vader stared at the cards with affront and confusion, like a dog that'd just banged its head against a glass door it didn't know was there.

"Say what?"

"Five hearts," Shake explained, tapping them one by one. "Young and in love."

Vader turned to Missouri Bob. His expression was both plaintive and murderous. "Don't beat three aces, do they?"

Missouri Bob shook his head sympathetically. "Like a rented mule."

Vader slammed his forearms against the table. The impact bounced the queen of hearts to the concrete floor. "Motherfucker!"

He stood up. His expression was just murderous now. Not plaintive. The tweaked-out kid's good eye went wide, and Missouri Bob began edging discreetly away.

"Motherfucker cheated," Vader said.

Shake gathered up his winnings. It wasn't smart to start a beef with sixty-eight hours left on your ticket. He hadn't cheated, though, and resented the accusation. Plus, he had a hunch, glancing up at Vader, that this beef had started without him; it was just a question, now, of how it ended.

There was a CO across the room, watching some *cholos* play checkers, but Shake knew that the guards weren't paid enough to intervene in Vader's business, not until it had been safely resolved.

"Said the motherfucker cheated!"

"No, Vader," Shake said, "you just weren't paying attention. Odds tell you I'm playing hearts in the hole."

"Fuck the odds, motherfucker."

Shake shrugged and bent to pick the queen of hearts off the floor. From beneath the table, he saw Vader shift his weight to his back leg, preparing to strike.

"You can run, motherfucker, but—"

Shake kicked hard and drove his heel into Vader's kneecap. Vader's back leg snapped with a soft, damp crack, and he dropped like he'd been chopped in half.

"Woo-hee!" Missouri Bob said, and then he beelined for the door as fast as his legs would carry him. Shake followed close behind, trying to think of a good parting shot, while Vader thrashed around with pain and rage.

"You a dead man!" Vader bellowed. "You ain't leaving here but in a motherfucking bag!"

"I think I'll just walk," Shake finally came up with, but not until he was already out of the room, halfway across the yard.

AT LUNCH, SHAKE CARRIED HIS TRAY across the room and found Tatum. Tatum was considered the best go-to guy in the California state system. Even the blacks and Mexicans, who had their own fixers, used him for important acquisitions. Tatum was wired top to bottom, inside and out, and could score just about anything, for a price that was generally fair.

"I need something," Shake said, sliding in next to him. "Chop-chop."

"Like what?" Tatum said. "A coffin?" He cracked himself up.

Shake waited patiently for him to finish laughing. "Word travels fast, doesn't it?"

"You gonna need a bazooka take Vader out."

Shake passed him a piece of paper.

Tatum read it once, then twice. "A say-what?"

"By tomorrow afternoon."

"Why—"

"Can you get it? That exact one?"

Tatum shrugged. "Course I can get it."

THE LINE FOR THE WORKING pay phone was long. Shake approached the guy at the head of the line, a Fresno Bulldog he knew from laundry detail. He slipped the Bulldog a pack of Crest White Strips he'd won last week playing Omaha, and the Bulldog surrendered his place in line to Shake. Just in time, because a minute later Vader came limping along.

Shake picked up the phone and listened to the dial tone. When he could feel Vader right behind him, sour and sweaty, he shook his head.

"No, I said Tuesday," Shake said into the phone. "If you don't hear from me by Tuesday, I want you to do it. Understand?"

He hung up before Vader heard the dial tone and realized there was no one on the other end of the line. Shake turned and pretended to notice him for the first time.

"Vader! What's happening?"

Vader glared at him. The cords in his neck were as thick and rigid as rebar. "Motherfucker."

The CO at the door sensed the sudden spike in electricity. He moved a thumb to the panic button on his radio.

"Buddy of mine on the outside," Shake explained, tapping his knuckle against the phone. "Nice to have friends, you know?"

"Ain't no friend of yours gonna hear from you by Tuesday," Vader said. "Guarantee that shit, motherfucker."

Vader let the threat sink in. Shake assumed an expression of appropriate gravity.

"Is that right?" he asked.

"That's right." Vader nodded—once up, slowly; once down, slowly. Then he pushed past, smacking Shake hard with his shoulder.

Shake watched Vader limp off, then checked the clock on the wall.

A QUIET SUNDAY, AFTER CHOW. A couple of boom boxes were dueling. 50 Cent on tier two, Metallica just above. Most of the cons were still in the yard, though, scheming and dreaming and dying slowly from boredom.

Shake stretched out on his bunk, hands behind his head, and worked on the menu for the restaurant he planned to open once he was a free man.

Pan-fried chicken, maybe, lightly floured and lots of spice. Mashed potatoes and cream gravy. A few gumbos, of course, with a roux like Shake's grandmother used to make.

Grilled fish of some sort, whatever was fresh and good. W

grenoblaise sauce, maybe, though that might be too fancy for the effect he was after.

Shake let his mind wander. The only thing, in here, that could. He remembered something he'd heard about death row up at San Quentin. A condemned man, so he'd heard, could request anything he wanted for his last meal—lobster and crème brûlée, barbecued shrimp, you name it. Apparently, though, orders were filled in-house, with whatever the prison mess had on hand, so the poor doomed bastard who ordered filet mignon and strawberry ice cream usually ended up with chopped hamburger steak and a cherry Popsicle.

That was pretty shitty, Shake thought, to get a guy's hopes up like that, even if he was more than likely a baby-killing sadist. But that was the California Department of Corrections for you—experts at making your life pretty shitty.

He heard the squeak of rubber wheels. Tatum, rolling a meal cart for the keep-locks. He stopped outside Shake's cell.

"Got it?" Shake said.

Tatum checked the tier for a nosy CO, then handed Shake a package wrapped in brown butcher's paper. It was the size and shape of a phone book.

"You sure you don't want to tell me what you need it for?"

Shake slid the package under his bunk. "Sure am."

VADER DIDN'T COME ALONE. Shake hadn't expected him to. Just before lockdown, Vader showed up with another black con, leading him on a leather leash attached to a rhinestone-trimmed dog collar. Both of which, Shake guessed, had been procured by Tatum.

Shake, sitting on the edge of his bunk, gave Vader and his boy a polite nod. "Help you fellas?"

"This here my top punk," Vader said. "Mad Ty."

Shake considered. "Mad as in angry, mad as in crazy, or mad in the hip-hop sense meaning excellent?"

Mad Ty lunged on the leash and snarled. He was cranked up, or hopped up, or both.

"He gonna shut that smart-ass mouth of yours once and for all," Vader said.

"Think he can handle the assignment?"

Vader grinned. "Either way," he said. "You get lucky and jack Mad Ty, you go straight to the hole, stay right here at the Creek and don't walk."

"And you stay clean."

"That's right."

"Not a bad plan," Shake admitted. He reached under his bunk.

"Go on. Get out your shiv."

"I don't have a shiv, Vader. I believe in the power of the printed word."

Shake produced what had been in the brown paper package the size and shape of a phone book:

A phone book. Clark County, Nevada, white pages, 2007–2008.

Vader was momentarily perplexed. "The fuck is that?"

Shake didn't answer. He assumed that the question was rhetorical, though with Vader you could never be sure.

Vader finally gave a derisive snort. "You gonna hit him with that?"

Shake hefted the heavy book in his hands. Not the worst idea in the world, come to think of it. But instead he dropped the book to the floor. It landed with a boom.

"Two-eighty-one Manzanita Ranch Court," Shake recited from memory. "Henderson, Nevada."

Mad Ty lunged again. "Lemme kill that peckerwood! Kill!"

Vader yanked Mad Ty back. "Hold the fuck on, motherfucker."

"Your brother and sister-in-law live at that address, right?" Shake asked pleasantly. "Couple of nieces?"

He waited for Vader to remember the conversation at the pay phone. Then he gave Vader a little help, just to speed things along.

"'If you don't hear from me by Tuesday, I want you to do it.' What I told my buddy on the outside, remember?"

"Kill! Gonna tear off that peckerwood's head and stick my—"

"Shut the fuck up."

Vader gave Mad Ty another yank, even harder, and the rhinestone collar bit into his throat. Mad Ty made an *ack-ack* sound, like he needed to cough up a fur ball, and shut the fuck up.

"You mentioned one time you had family in Henderson," Shake said, "so I looked it up. Sure enough."

"The fuck you think you playing at?"

"You see, V," Shake said, "I was just paying attention. What I've been telling you."

Vader's braided muscles vibrated helpless rage. He started to open the mouth that was too big for his head that was too small for his body. Shake had to smile.

"Motherfucker," Shake said. "Yeah, I know."

SHAKE WOULD HAVE PREFERRED a giant iron gate rattling open, sunlight pouring down and making him squint, the wide horizon stretched out limitless before him, a swell of violins, all that. That's how you were supposed to leave prison a free man, wasn't it?

Instead a CO walked him out a side door, through a couple of chain-link gates, and left him in a gravel parking lot across the highway from a bus stop.

Shake didn't complain.

Chapter 2

Shake rode a city bus into town. The next bus to L.A. didn't leave for a few hours, so he ate lunch at a fast-food place. Where—Jesus—the scope and variety of choices on the brightly lit plastic menu board left him a little dazed. Salads, pita wraps, burritos. Saver size, supersize, brown-bag combo. He had to step away from the counter for a minute and regroup before he ordered.

He carried his tray to a table by the window. He had a little more than four hundred dollars in cash on him. He had the clothes he was wearing when he was busted and was wearing now—a pair of Levi's 501 jeans; a striped, pale green button-down shirt; a pair of comfortable brown leather shoes he'd bought on sale at Nordstrom; a brown leather belt. He had a key to a storage unit in Inglewood, by the airport. In the storage unit were a few more clothes, his books, his tools, and another grand or so. The storage unit would be his first stop when he got back to L.A.

And then?

That was the question.

Shake decided not to tackle it till after lunch. Right now he'd just enjoy his grilled chicken pita wrap and appreciate the view of dusty green strawberry fields, no barbed wire or gun towers in sight. He'd ignore both future and past and live in the present, live in the moment, just as he'd been advised to do by one of the COs—a reformed crack dealer and self-styled Buddhist—the first week of his first fall, all those years ago back in Louisiana, Shake just a kid and scared out of his gourd. Live in the moment. Shake, even now, couldn't decide if that was the best advice you give a man doing time, or the very worst.

"You all done with this?" asked an empty-eyed girl in a bright orange uniform.

Shake looked down at his tray, at the balled-up wrappers and flattened ketchup packets. He realized he must have been waiting for the whistle, tell him chow was over.

ON THE BUS TO L.A., he sat next to a tiny bird of a woman who seemed impossibly old, a hundred years at least. She was already asleep, snoring softly, when he took his seat.

Ten minutes into the trip, the sun set without fanfare. The world bled out suddenly and left behind nothing but the bright bubble of the bus, rocketing along through the darkness. With the flare, every minute or so, of the green mile markers when the bus headlights hit them.

Shake tried to figure out who he'd call when he got to L.A. He knew a couple of women who had nice places, and if they were still single, he was pretty sure they'd put him up for a few nights. But if they were still single, that meant those few nights would be complicated. It was probably better, he decided, to find a cheap motel, maybe one near the beach, stay there while he lined up his next job.

His next job. After he got settled, he'd drop in on Frank. Frank was certain to have something for him, or know someone who did. Shake didn't consider himself the best driver in the business—only assholes and beginners thought in those terms—but he knew that a lot of people on the West Coast would be eager to hire him, now that he was in play again.

That thought should have made him feel good, had in the past, but right now it had the opposite effect. Here he was, forty-two years old, and what did he have to show for it?

Four hundred bucks, the clothes on his back, a key to a storage unit in Inglewood, and a path ahead, if he wasn't careful, that looked a lot like the path behind.

He wondered where exactly in his life his shit had gone sideways, and why. It was hard to say. It hadn't been a couple of momentous decisions that had determined the course of his life. No volcanic eruptions that altered and fixed his personal topography. Instead what had happened were all the little decisions along the way, most of which he didn't even realize at the time were decisions, the bits of coincidence and circumstance, good luck and bad, the steady, slow accretion of rock and soil and sediment.

He needed a volcanic eruption. He needed to make a move. If he didn't want to find himself back here on this bus again, ten years from now, ten years older, thinking these very same thoughts. Or dead. Or worse.

He had good ideas for the restaurant he wanted to open, and he knew he had the chops to make it work in the kitchen. But the business end, the money, permits, partners, the ridiculous odds against staying above water—Shake tensed up even thinking about it.

You had to be young, he supposed, to enjoy a volcanic eruption. Young or dumb or convinced of your own miraculous ability to beat the odds. Shake was none of those, unfortunately.

The old lady in the seat next to him stirred and woke. She clutched her purse in her lap with small, veiny hands and examined Shake with the clearest blue eyes he'd ever seen.

"I suppose you just got out of prison," she said.

"Yes, ma'am," he said.

She nodded, satisfied, then proceeded to chatter cheerfully on for the next two hundred miles. She told Shake she visited her sister in Riverside every month. She told Shake she'd once been courted by Walt

Disney. Which, in case Shake couldn't figure it out, meant she'd had a fling with him. She told Shake she'd married a marine the day after VJ Day. They'd had four children, none of whom had turned out to be worth a damn. Those four children, however, had given her a dozen grandchildren, all of whom, surprisingly, *had* turned out to be worth a damn. One was the mayor of a small city in Arizona. Her husband had passed years and years ago, when LBJ was still president. She learned to be independent, something her own mother had never been.

"I suppose you expect me to give you some wise advice or such," she said.

"I wish you would," Shake said. "I could use it."

"I don't have any advice to give. You pick out the kind of person you want to be, then you try your best to be that person."

"I think that's pretty good advice."

She scoffed, as if she thought he was humoring her. Which he wasn't.

When they finally reached L.A., well after dark, he helped her down off the bus and carried her suitcase to a waiting cab.

She gave Shake's forearm a surprisingly strong squeeze and looked at him with her clear blue eyes. "You're on parole?"

"No, ma'am, I'm free and clear."

"Get a haircut. You're a good-looking fellow. You've got good-natured eyes and a nice nose. But you look like you got your hair cut in prison."

He smiled. "That I did."

"You have a girl?"

"No, ma'am."

"Had one?"

He thought he knew what she meant. "I'm not sure."

She scoffed. "You'd be sure."

"Yes, ma'am," he said.

"Stay that way."

"Free and clear?"

"Bingo."

He watched the cab drive off with her. When he turned away, he discovered that a long black limo had eased silently up to the curb next to him.

No one knew where he was, no one knew he was even out of prison. Why, then, was Shake not surprised when the tinted back passenger window melted slowly into the door frame and he saw Alexandra Ilandryan smiling out at him.

"Hello, Shake," she said.

"Hello, Lexy."

"You are surprised to see me?"

Shake shook his head.

"You are happy to see me?"

That one was more complicated. He gave her a wink.

"Depends," he said as she popped the door open for him.

Chapter 3

Shake settled himself in the limo across from Alexandra and took a nice long look at her. She hadn't changed a bit since they'd last met—the languid gray eyes, the cheekbones, the lips parted slightly with a hint of amusement.

"You just seem to get younger and younger," he told her. He felt the limo pick up speed as it merged onto the highway. "If I didn't know better, I'd suspect you made a deal with the devil."

She brushed off the thought with an elegant, pale hand.

"The devil," she said dismissively.

Alexandra Ilandryan was probably the most beautiful woman Shake had ever known. She was also—not probably, but certainly—the most formidable. Shake didn't know all the details, but enough of them. Married off at age sixteen to a brutish, midlevel warlord in the mountains just across the Armenian border from Turkey, Alexandra had by the age of twenty dispatched the husband, taken over his operation, driven all local competitors out of business. A few years later, she immigrated to America. Within a decade she'd used her charm, her smarts, and a bottomless reservoir of sheer ruthless will to assume control of the entire Armenian mob in L.A. She was the boss, the *pakhan.* The devil came to Alexandra Ilandryan for favors, not vice versa.

She dropped an ice cube into a glass. She was wearing a silk blouse the same smoky color of her eyes, tailored slacks, and simple black sandals that Shake knew must have cost a fortune.

"Maker's Mark?" she asked. "Rocks?"

"Good memory," Shake said.

"You are impossible man to forget, Shake."

"I'll take that as a compliment."

She poured his drink. Her smile revealed nothing. It never did.

"You spend fifteen months in a hard place," she mused. "I wonder why do you not make plea bargain?"

Shake shrugged. "Dime out the most dangerous lady on the West Coast? And possibly the best kisser?"

"Possibly?" She arched an eyebrow and studied him. He wondered why he was here. Some kind of business, no doubt, but there might be more to it than that. He and Alexandra had enjoyed a brief but intense relationship several months before the job that sent him to Mule Creek. Shake still wasn't exactly sure why the relationship had petered out, or which of them exactly had been responsible for the petering.

"I appreciate your loyalty," she said finally. "Now I return favor. I have little something for you, put some money in your pocket."

He shook his head. "I don't know, Lexy. The timing."

"You're at this time in your life, the middle of things." She smiled at him. "You want a fresh start. Et cetera."

He didn't say anything. He didn't have to. She reached across and touched his shoulder.

"Just listen first before you decide," she said. "Yes? What can this hurt?"

Shake sipped his drink and watched the city lights flow past.

What could it hurt?

"It's your car," he said. "I'm just along for the ride."

SHE TOOK HIM TO DINNER at a time-capsule steakhouse in Hollywood—framed head shots from the forties and fifties, red leatherette booths, grouchy old Iron Curtain waiters in tuxedos and starched aprons.

He ordered the New York strip, hot and rosy in the center, and the creamed spinach. Both were excellent. Alexandra let Shake savor the meal and an after-dinner brandy before she brought up business. It was a simple job, she said after she explained what was involved. Then she corrected herself.

"No. 'Job' I think is too . . . grand a word."

"Errand?" he suggested.

"Yes."

"I drive a car to Vegas. I meet a guy and give him the car."

"Could not be simpler, no?"

"The guy gives me a briefcase. I fly back to L.A. and give the briefcase to you."

"A small errand."

"And you give me twenty thousand dollars. Because . . ."

"Because I am fond of you, Shake. Because you have paid debt to society and deserve fresh start in life."

"What's in the trunk of the car?" he asked.

"Is not your worry."

"What's in the briefcase?" he asked.

She laughed musically, a run of sweet notes climbing the scale. Her gray eyes twinkled.

"I miss you, Shake. Your sense of humor."

"How about the guy I meet in Vegas?"

"He works for a man," Alexandra said. "Dick Moby."

"The Whale?"

"You are familiar?"

Shake was familiar. You didn't do time west of the Mississippi without meeting someone who'd worked for, borrowed money from, or narrowly escaped being murdered by Dick Moby. Often all three. The Whale owned a strip club in Vegas, but his real business was drugs, shylocking, extortion, immigrant sex slaves.

"So," she said.

Shake tried to think of the name of the actor in the head shot above Alexandra's head. He'd been in *The Killers* with Burt Lancaster, a character actor who often played a guy you thought was good but turned out bad. Or vice versa. Shake couldn't remember.

It never worked that way in real life, those sudden character twists, but it made for good movies, he guessed.

"I'm serious, Lexy," Shake said.

"I know you are."

"I'm forty-two years old."

"Yes."

He explained to her that if, *if* he took this job, it would be his last one. And he'd only be taking the job so he could put the twenty grand toward the restaurant he planned to open. Twenty grand wouldn't be nearly enough, of course, but it was a beginning. And he was resolved to make a new beginning.

She listened politely. He knew she didn't believe him. He knew she didn't believe he believed it himself.

Their waiter, a dead ringer for Nikita Khrushchev, stomped over and glared at Shake's empty brandy snifter.

"Another?" he grunted.

Alexandra looked at Shake.

He hesitated. He did believe it himself. At the same time, though, he couldn't deny how relieved he'd felt when Lexy's limo had rolled up. When he realized he could just give himself up to the current, one last time, and let life take him where it wanted.

He'd go to work on that new beginning tomorrow.

He shook his head at the waiter. "I've got a long drive to make tonight."

Chapter 4

Alexandra took out her cell phone and made a call from the table, a few curt words in Armenian. When they exited the restaurant, a black Lincoln Town Car was parked next to the limo. Parked next to the Town Car was Alexandra's personal bodyguard and number-one hatchet man, Dikran Ghazarian, a prehistoric thug with a shaved head shaped like a bullet that hadn't been fired yet. His squashed blob of a face, however, looked like a bullet that *had* been fired, then dug out of a concrete wall.

"Shake," Alexandra said. "You remember Dikran?"

She knew he did, of course. Not only was Dikran possibly the ugliest man on the face of the planet, he was a stupid, sadistic bully who'd once tried, stupidly, to bully Shake. Shake, stupidly, had refused to back down. This was years ago, on Shake's first job for Alexandra. She'd intervened to impose a truce. Dikran—denied what he considered his

God-given right to tear the spine from Shake's body and strangle him with it—had resented Shake ever since.

"Still waiting for evolution to come back for you, Dikran?" Shake asked pleasantly. He knew that Dikran would never dare come after him while he was under Alexandra's explicit protection. Shake also knew that if for some reason she ever withdrew that protection, nothing in this world or the next would stop Dikran from killing him. Either way, Shake's fate was decided, so he always tried to see how far he could goad the big ugly lizard before Dikran burst a blood vessel. "Still waiting for those higher motor functions?"

Dikran took a menacing step toward him and spit onto the asphalt between Shake's feet. Dikran was wearing a short-sleeved madras shirt and black satin parachute pants that were too short for him. Dress shoes with no socks.

"Fuck you," Dikran said. "Still fuck you mother?"

"Boys," Alexandra said. She snapped her fingers. Dikran, still glaring at Shake, handed her an envelope, a set of car keys, and a cell phone. During the transaction Shake noticed a cloth patch stuck to Dikran's bare bicep.

"What's that?" he asked Dikran. "Get a tattoo of your phone number so you won't forget it?"

"The doctor tells Dikran his cholesterol is too high," Alexandra said. Her expression was solemn, but Shake could tell she was enjoying this. "He says Dikran has testosterone too low."

Dikran made a sound like a strangled cough, and the skin beneath his eyes darkened.

"A testosterone patch?" Shake said, amused. "Any side effects?"

"Fuck your mother," Dikran said, which was pretty much the extent of his repertoire. He turned his squashed face toward Alexandra. "Why you give ass-lick this job?"

"Headaches?" Shake wondered aloud. "Nausea? Persistent erections?"

Alexandra put a hand on Dikran's shoulder.

"Because I am the *pakhan,*" she told him. Her voice was mild but deadly. "Yes?"

Dikran held the pose for a second, then stalked over to the limo, got in, slammed the door shut behind him.

"This patch," she explained to Shake. "It make him crankier than usual. Hard to believe, I know."

"Where's the meet?"

"Motel on Las Vegas Strip. Seven A.M. tomorrow. Address is in envelope." She handed over the envelope, the car keys, and the cell phone. "And three thousand dollars cash to start. You say thank you now."

"Thank you, Lexy."

Shake opened the door to the Town Car and climbed in. Alexandra leaned close. One last thing.

"Shake?"

"Yes?"

"This Dick Moby, in Las Vegas. He is not one to fuck with."

"I know."

"Shake?"

That inscrutable smile of hers.

"Neither am I."

He nodded, smiled back. "I know."

HE LEFT LOS ANGELES AROUND one-thirty in the morning. By three he'd left the ugly sprawl of suburbs behind—West Covina, Ontario, Rancho Cucamonga—and was deep into the dark, empty desert, soaring along just a hair below the legal limit of seventy. Windows rolled down, a sweet-scented springlike wind whipping through the car.

The wind was chilly, but he didn't mind. Fifteen months locked up at Mule Creek and this was what Shake had dreamed about most. More than a good meal, more even than a woman. This—driving, just driving, a wheel in his hands and the low-throated thrum of a 240-horsepower, 4.6-liter V-8 making every molecule in his body vibrate. Shake couldn't recall his first kiss, but he did remember precisely the first time he'd driven a car, which also happened to be the first time he'd stolen one. Eighth grade, age thirteen, New Orleans, Louisiana. He wasn't a bad kid, just a little wild, fallen in with some older kids who were even wilder. The car was a 1974 Ford Maverick, white with a tan hardtop, and the owner had left the keys in the ignition while he popped into a K&B convenience store. His mistake. Shake and his two friends, Whelan and Chunks, tooled around town for a couple of hours, inventing (so they thought) the bootlegger slide in the deserted parking lot of a defunct supermarket. They ditched the Mav down by the levee, and then Shake walked home euphoric, exhausted. That night he slept like the dead and didn't wake till three o'clock the next day. Shake smiled at the memory.

Whelan would die a few years later when a jack failed and the boosted Corvette he was working on crushed him. Chunks was a dentist, last Shake had heard, living somewhere in Florida.

A sign flashed by that said LAS VEGAS, 100 MILES. Shake flipped through FM frequencies until he found a station with a clear pulse. It was playing slow jazz, unfortunately, not the sound track you wanted when blasting down the highway, so he kept flipping. Rap, rap, country. Finally, at the far left end of the digital dial, he found an old Springsteen B-side, "Be True." The Big Man's sax growled, Bruce sang in a refreshingly grown-up way about the provisional nature of love and trust, and for three beautiful minutes everything in Shake's world was just about perfect.

Shake drummed along on the wheel as Mighty Max's tom-toms built to a thunderous crescendo. He'd just about convinced himself he hadn't made the wrong decision, taking this job. He'd just about convinced himself it *had* been a decision, and he wasn't falling back into the old lazy habits again.

The song faded abruptly into a fuzz of static. Shake heard, behind him, a soft *whump, whump, whump.*

Flat tire. He tapped the brakes and steered the Town Car onto the shoulder. Odd thing, the wheel didn't tug like it should have, but Shake didn't give it much thought. He cut the engine and opened his door. If the spare was full and the bolts forgiving, he'd be out and back in under ten minutes.

Except that when he walked around to the rear of the car, he discovered that neither tire was flat. Not a scratch on either.

"What the hell," he had time to murmur aloud once, before the *whump-whump-whump*-ing started again, and he realized it was coming from inside the truck.

Get back in the car, Shake told himself. *Do not open the trunk. Get back in the car and drive to Vegas. Deliver the car, fly back to L.A., collect the rest of the money from Alexandra. Take the money, and figure out a way to start a restaurant, and never, ever, take a job like this again.*

Do not open the trunk.

He opened the trunk.

Inside was a young woman in her twenties, gagged with electrical tape and handcuffed. She stared up at Shake with wet, scared eyes.

The wind had died down, and the night felt suddenly too warm, too still, as if the desert were a big sweaty palm, the fingers closing slowly over him.

The girl started struggling again, kicking the wheel well—that was the sound he'd thought was a flat tire. Shake saw that the cord used to bind her legs had come loose.

A second later, headlights splashed him, and he turned to see a Nevada state trooper rolling up twenty feet behind him. The girl kicked again, and the boom sounded to him like a bomb going off in the dark night.

"Shit," he said. But he didn't panic. Never panic. That was the first and only rule. He reached into the trunk and pulled the cord tight around the girl's legs, tied it off with a knot he hoped would hold. He slammed the lid of the trunk shut just as the state trooper slammed his car door.

Shake strolled back toward the trooper and met him halfway between the two cars.

"Almost hit a coyote," Shake explained. "Thought I blew a tire, but I'm okay."

The trooper moved his chin in a way that maybe was a nod, maybe not. He was a long-timer with small eyes crowded together in the center of a big, thick face. His belly strained the buttons of his uniform shirt.

"Where you headed?"

"Where else?" Shake said.

"Play them slots?"

"Little brother's getting married. Bachelor party tomorrow night at the Flamingo."

The state trooper waited, like there'd be more.

"Stripper or two," Shake went on. "Beer and pretzels. Nothing fancy."

"Thought they tore that one down coupla years ago," the trooper said.

"What?"

"The Flamingo."

Shake laughed, tried to make it sound easy.

"Sure hope not," he said, "or I'm in trouble." That was the first true thing he'd told the trooper.

The trooper tugged thoughtfully at the skin beneath his chin. A lone semi thundered past, east to west. Shake wished he was in it.

"Might be the Sahara I'm thinking of," the trooper said finally. "Hell if I know. I can't keep 'em all straight anymore."

"Could be."

"Stay away from them slots. The house always wins, even when you think you got you a system."

"You got that right." Shake suspected that the trooper spoke from experience. Either way, the point was a sound one.

"All right, then. Have a safe trip."

The trooper walked back to his cruiser. Shake watched him drive off. When the burn of taillights finally disappeared in the distance, Shake slowly released the breath he'd been holding for what seemed like the last ten minutes or so. A second later the trunk of the Town Car started *whump-whump-whump*-ing again.

"Shit," Shake said.

Chapter 5

Just before sunrise Shake reached the southern edge of Vegas. He turned onto the Strip as a thin, bloodred crack appeared on the horizon. Pyramids, Empire State Building, Eiffel Tower. Shake wondered how long before they opened a *Vegas*-themed hotel and casino that was an exact scale replica of the city around it, including a replica of the Vegas-themed hotel itself, and so on down to microscopic infinity.

He shook his head and took a deep breath of cold air. He was getting a little loopy. He'd been awake for—how long? He asked for nothing more right now than a soft bed and a few hours of sleep. And no girl bound and gagged in the trunk of the car he was driving. Yeah, that, too, don't forget.

He didn't know what he was going to do about the girl. He supposed this was his punishment. For not listening to the old lady on the bus who told him to stay clean and free. For taking this job because it was the easy thing to do.

Live in the moment, Shake advised himself. He checked the dashboard clock. He still had an hour before the meet with Dick Moby's bagman. He'd find the motel, get a room, try to sort things out.

Traffic was light, so Shake guessed he'd missed the casino shift change. He followed the Strip north until it lost its enthusiasm and turned seedy—big new hotels giving way to big old hotels, big old hotels giving way to small old hotels, small old hotels giving way finally to liquor stores, adult bookstores, crackhead apartment complexes, and skanky by-the-hour motels.

The Apache Motor Inn was on the corner of West Utah and South Las Vegas Boulevard, across from a strip club called the Jungle. It wasn't the skankiest motel on this stretch of the Strip, but close enough. Shake turned in beneath a sign shaped like a wigwam and parked in back, next to an empty pool half filled with rust-streaked toilets and bathroom sinks.

The clerk at the desk gave him a room key. The key was attached to a hard red rubber bulb scored with teeth marks. Adult teeth, unmistakably. Shake didn't want to imagine the circumstances. He unlocked the room and propped the door open with a chair, then returned to the parking lot, which was empty except for the Town Car.

He crouched next to a back tire, as if he were inspecting it for tread damage.

"Can you hear me?" he said.

No answer.

"Kick once," he said.

Whump.

"I'm gonna let you out of the trunk. But I need you to stay quiet. Okay?"

Whump.

Shake glanced around to make sure the parking lot was still empty, then unlocked the trunk. The girl's face, the part not covered with electrical tape, was pale and dirty, streaked with the paler, less dirty tracks of dried tears.

"I'm not gonna hurt you," Shake said. He unwound the cord from around her legs. She was wearing jeans, a sweatshirt, no shoes. Her hands were cuffed in front of her, so he looped her arms around his neck, grabbed her waist, and lifted her out of the trunk. Her legs cramped up the second her bare feet touched the ground, and they both stumbled to the asphalt. Shake untangled himself and tried to help her stand, but it was like she was paralyzed from the waist down. Finally he just picked her up again. Her blond hair, pressed against his nose, smelled strongly like tire rubber and faintly like peaches.

He carried the girl into the room, kicked the door shut behind them, and lowered her to the bed. He knelt in front of her.

"Thirsty? You want some water?"

She nodded.

He found a plastic cup in the bathroom and filled it with cold water. Then he turned the tap to warm and soaked a washcloth.

He looked at the reflection in the mirror above the sink.

"Any bright ideas?" he asked it.

The reflection shook its head sadly. Nope.

Shake returned to the room with the cup of water and the washcloth. The first thing he noticed was the door: open. The second thing he noticed was the bed: empty.

The girl was gone.

He dropped the cup and the washcloth and sprinted outside. His heart started beating again when he saw that she hadn't hobbled far—barely halfway across the empty parking lot. Even before Shake reached her, she'd crumpled to the ground. She began crying when he lifted her to her feet.

"Come on," he said quietly, and led her back into the room.

He put her in a chair and tied off her ankles with pillowcases.

"This is gonna hurt," he said, "but it'll probably hurt less if I just do it all at once."

He found an edge that had come free and pulled the electrical tape off her mouth. The girl didn't make a peep. She just closed her eyes and bit her bottom lip.

It was a nice lip, Shake noticed. Plump and rosy. He realized for the first time how pretty the girl was, dirty face and all. Eyes that seemed brown until you looked closer and saw the underwater green. Perfect cheekbones and an imperfect nose, a strong-minded nose, with a dusting of freckles across the bridge. The nose, the eyes, wholesome but not dull—the girl reminded Shake of a girl who could have been homecoming queen but had better things to do with her time.

Shake guessed she was a little younger than he'd first thought, probably around twenty-three or twenty-four.

So how did a girl like this end up in the trunk of a car, express delivery to a bad dude like Dick Moby? Shake tried not to consider the possibilities.

She moistened her lips with her tongue.

"If you start to yell," he warned her, "I'll have to put the tape back on."

She nodded and said something he couldn't hear. He bent closer. Her voice was soft, hoarse.

"Water."

He brought her a fresh cup of water. Her cuffed hands trembled as she lifted it to her mouth and drank. He found the warm washcloth and gently wiped some of the grime from her face.

"What's your name?" he asked.

Her big eyes couldn't seem to make up their mind, if they were brown or green.

"Gina," she said.

"Gina," Shake said. "Tell me why you were in the trunk of that car."

"Please, you have to help me."

"I want to help you. But first—"

"I don't know! I'm just a . . . I'm a mom! I have two little boys."

She made a sound that was part cough, part sob. Shake brought her another cup of water, which she gulped down.

"Where am I?" she asked.

"Las Vegas."

Surprised. "I live here!" she said.

"But you were in L.A.?"

"On vacation. With my husband. We left the boys with my mom, and . . . we were supposed to go to Catalina Island? To have a picnic? But then Ronnie went out to buy a paper and didn't come back." The words tumbling out faster and faster, one over the other. "And the next day this man broke in the door and—"

"Slow down."

"Can I— I have to take this off." She pointed her chin down at the baggy UNLV sweatshirt. "I'm burning up. Please."

Shake hesitated, then pulled the sweatshirt up over her head. Underneath she was wearing a thin white T-shirt, damp with sweat, no bra, her boobs small and perfect. Shake blinked like a man who'd just stepped out of a dark movie theater into the sunshine. Then he looked quickly away and concentrated on getting the sweatshirt over the cuffs. In the end, because he couldn't find anything sharp, he had to bite the seam and tear the fabric in half.

"Thank you," she said.

He sat down on the bed across from her and tried to fit the pieces of the puzzle together.

"Your husband. Ronnie? He went out and didn't come back?"

"It was like he was saying good-bye, when he said good-bye."

She started crying again, softly. A fat teardrop rolled down her cheek and caught for a second, trembling and translucent, in the corner of her mouth.

"I think he left me," she said. "I don't know why he left me."

"Gina," Shake said. "Think hard, Gina."

"There's nothing, really. I just—"

Suddenly she looked up at him.

"What?"

"He liked to gamble."

"Ronnie did," Shake said.

"Everyone at our church tried to help him stop. We're Mormon? But he just kept borrowing money, and I don't know . . . I don't know why I—"

"Gina. Stay cool for me, okay?"

She took a deep breath. Shake glanced over at the clock radio on the table between the beds. A quarter to seven. *Tick. Tock.*

"Did he ever mention anyone by name? Who he borrowed money from?"

"No," she said. "Maybe one time. Dick something, or something Dick? I don't remember, but Ronnie was—"

Shake began to understand what had happened. He felt his stomach do something unpleasant, like a dog turning a circle before it flopped to the ground.

"Dick Moby? The Whale?"

"The . . . what? Maybe. Yes. Dick Moby."

She watched him closely.

"What is it?" she asked, and Shake knew that his poker face had failed him this time.

"I think your husband split because he owed money he couldn't pay back."

"But why—"

"Dick Moby couldn't find your husband. So he put the word out. The person I work for found you."

"Me? What does he— Dick Moby? What does he want with me? I don't have any money. Ronnie always kept all the . . ."

The girl's voice trailed off. Shake watched as her eyes went slack. She was a smart girl. Shake had been right about that.

"He's going to kill me," she said finally, softly, "unless I tell him where Ronnie is."

Shake stood and walked to the window. He spread the blinds with a finger and squinted out into the hard, dazzling light, where the black Town Car was still the only car in the lot.

"Could be he just wants to scare you. Maybe he just—"

"And I don't know where Ronnie is."

Her voice was calm and flat. Either she wasn't buying his bullshit or she hadn't heard it.

Shake turned back from the window. The girl looked a little dazed, but she was holding it together. He doubted that most people in her situation would have been able to do the same.

Shake had a pretty good idea what Moby would do to her and wished, more than he'd wished anything in a long time, that he could help her. He wished, to the same degree, that he just had a choice in the matter.

A former associate had once told Shake he was too nice for this business but not nice enough for any other.

"Gina," he said. "I'm sorry. If I let you go? It'll be *me* in the trunk of that car."

He expected her to look away, but she held his gaze.

"I understand," she said.

Shake could tell she meant it, which made him feel even worse than he already did.

A single sharp knock on the door made the girl flinch. Shake looked at the clock radio. Seven on the dot.

The girl lifted her chin and straightened her shoulders.

"I had a really happy life," she said. "My mom loves my boys, and she'll take great care of them. She has a big, nice house and a pool and—"

Another bang on the door. Shake reached for the strip of electrical tape he'd set aside on top of the TV.

"Will it be over fast?" Gina asked.

Shake hesitated, then smoothed the tape back over her mouth.

"I'm sorry," he said again. It came out softer than he intended, sand in his throat, and he didn't know if the girl heard him or not. She'd closed her eyes and was taking slow, even breaths.

Shake opened the door to the motel room. The Whale's guy was a big one, with the bottom-heavy construction of an offensive tackle. Round face, sleepy eyes, mocha-colored skin.

He looked Shake over in a mellow but alert way.

"Hey," he said.

"You the Whale's guy?" Shake asked.

"He don't like to be called that." The statement was more conversational than threatening.

"I'm Shake."

"Jasper."

He looked past Shake, into the room, and saw Gina sitting on the edge of the bed.

"She suppose to be in the car," Jasper said after a few seconds, in the same conversational tone.

"Come on in," Shake said.

Jasper entered the room. He placed the leather briefcase he was carrying on the dresser, then popped the locks and opened the lid. He took a polite step backward so Shake could inspect what was inside.

Inside, set into a custom-cut foam bed designed to protect it from jolts and jounces, was another case. It was the size of a large manila envelope, not much thicker than one, and made entirely of glass. Pressed inside the glass were dozens and dozens of square, thumbnail-size pieces of what looked like dried, yellowed parchment. Shake counted: ten rows across, ten rows down.

"A hundred," Jasper said. "They all there."

"Postage stamps?" Shake asked.

Jasper shrugged. Who knows?

Shake picked up the glass case, which was surprisingly heavy, to take a closer look. There was no writing or marking on any of the pieces of parchment, though each one was slightly, subtly different from the next—smooth, textured, flecked with brown, bleached white at a corner.

Shake placed the glass case back in its foam bed.

"I didn't even know what I'm supposed to take back," Shake admitted.

"This is it," Jasper said. He closed the lid of the briefcase and pressed the snaps into place. "We all set here?"

Shake nodded. *Don't look over at the girl,* he warned himself, just before he looked over at the girl. Her eyes were still closed. Her expression was . . . peaceful, almost. Cheeks flushed, a curved slice of blond hair falling across her face.

An image flashed through Shake's mind, startling in its clarity: Gina, standing on the porch of a nice house, watching two little boys play on the lawn.

Then the Gina in the image glanced up and smiled—right at Shake.

"Wait a second," Shake said as Jasper took a step toward her.

Jasper paused. "What?"

Shake couldn't believe what he was about to do. It was such an unbelievable thing, he had to shake his head and chuckle. Then he pulled a deep breath in through his nostrils.

"I'm gonna keep the girl," he said. "If that's okay."

Jasper eyeballed him for a long time, absorbing this. Shake wondered if the big guy was a little slow, a little stoned, or just very, very calm. Hard to say. Finally—

"You gonna keep the girl?" Jasper said mildly.

"You can keep the . . . whatever they are. The briefcase. Take it back to your boss. Tell him the deal's off, but everything's cool."

A small smile flickered across Jasper's big, moon-shaped face, like he'd just figured out the punch line to a joke.

"I'm suppose to tell Mr. Moby deal's off and everything's cool?"

"There you go," Shake said with a shrug, to indicate how simple the equation was. He crossed to the nightstand next to Gina and picked up the phone book sitting there. "You happen to know, Jasper, where I can get some good Texas-style barbecue around here? Last fifteen months straight, I've been craving it. Hill Country brisket, I'm talking about, not East Texas ribs with all the sauce."

Jasper took another long, leisurely look at Shake—wondering, measuring, sorting his options.

"Let's go," he said finally, to Gina.

Shake considered, one last time, the consequences of what he was about to do. Then, as Jasper stepped past him toward Gina, Shake squeezed the phone book tight, swung hard, and hammered Jasper in the back of the head with it.

Jasper staggered forward. Shake hit him again. Jasper banged into the wall, rebounded drunkenly, and crashed backward into the nightstand. It splintered beneath him, and he hit the carpet hard, lamp tumbling down on top, one arm tangled in the cord.

Shake, his hands stinging, dropped the phone book and grabbed Gina's arm. He pulled her toward the door, not looking back. *Stay calm.* Behind him he could hear Jasper grunting, already stirring in the wreckage.

Shake dragged Gina out into the parking lot. Jasper's SUV was parked next to the Town Car. He hadn't thought to block them in, luckily—it was just supposed to be a routine handoff, and why would Dick Moby's bagman anticipate anything different? Shake would have liked to yank the SUV's distributor cap, but there was no time.

"We have to run," he told Gina, and they did, across the hot, spongy asphalt. Gina stumbled once but quickly regained her balance. When they reached the Town Car, Shake dug in his pocket for the keys and looked over his shoulder. The doorway to the motel room was still empty, and Jasper wasn't on their tail, not yet. He turned back to the Town Car, noticed that Gina was holding, in her cuffed hands, the leather briefcase.

"What are you doing with that?" he asked.

She shrugged. "I just thought, I don't know, I thought it would be a good idea."

There was no time to discuss.

"In," Shake told her.

He pushed Gina into the car, then slid in after her. The last he saw of the Apache Motor Inn, as he gunned the Town Car onto South Las Vegas Boulevard, was Jasper in the rearview mirror, staggering out of the motel room with a .45 automatic in one hand and an unhappy expression on his moon-shaped face.

Chapter 6

Traffic on the Strip had turned heavy. Shake was glad for it. He buzzed lane to lane between annoyed tourists in their rented PT Cruisers until he was certain that Jasper wasn't tailing them. Then he shook his head at the sheer audacity and suicidal stupidity of what he'd just done.

"Holy shit," he said. "Wow."

"Thank you, mister," Gina said. "Thank you so much. I don't know what— I just . . ."

He checked the cup holders and glove compartment, then slid open the ashtray. There it was.

"Here." He handed Gina a small silver key. She tried to unlock the cuffs herself, but her hands were shaking, and she almost dropped the key. At the next red light, Shake turned in his seat and did it for her. He dropped the cuffs on the floor next to the briefcase and showed her how to massage the feeling back into her raw, red wrists.

"It's Shake," he said. "My name."

"Oh, God. They were gonna kill me."

Not right away, he started to say, then didn't. Instead he glanced up ahead at the big casinos lining each side of the Strip and told her they needed to get the Town Car off the street.

"Are you hungry?" he asked.

"Starving," she said. "Yes."

THE IRON CANNON BOOMED. Flames burst from the deck of the ship. A female pirate with boobs swelling out of her lace-up corset fell from the crow's nest, turned one slow somersault in midair, sliced the water with a perfect dive.

The crowd packed onto the wooden dock applauded.

Shake leaned close to the window and waited for the diving pirate to surface. She didn't. Probably they had a scuba tank waiting for her underwater, or there was a hidden air lock that all the dead pirates passed through on their way back to the dressing room. Whatever the case, it was a neat trick—a snap of the fingers, then vanished forever. Shake wished he had something like that up his own sleeve.

"Good morning, mateys!" the waitress said. "Avast ye!" She wore a ruffled shirt, a bandanna, and an eye patch. Her shoes, though, Shake noticed, were New Balance cross-trainers. "Can I get you something to drink?"

"Are you gonna think less of me," Shake said, "if I order bourbon with my breakfast?"

The waitress broke character for a second to smile and roll her eyes. "This is Las Vegas, dude."

"Right," Shake said. "Then a double on the rocks. Maker's Mark if you have it, Jack if you don't." He glanced over at Gina. Her adrenaline rush was subsiding, he guessed, and full-blown post-traumatic stress syndrome was setting in. She stared down at her menu like it was written in Swahili. "You want something?"

"What?" she said.

"Do you want a drink?"

"Lemonade?"

"A Mormon," Shake said. "I forgot."

"It's not what you think," she said, a little annoyed. "Not all Mormons— It's not like you see on TV. We're just normal people."

Then she seemed to remember where she was, what had happened to her.

"Oh, my God," she murmured, closing her eyes and shaking her head. The waitress eyed her with curiosity.

"We'll both have the bacon and eggs," Shake said quickly.

"Over easy?" the waitress said.

"Scrambled soft, with shallots and a little crème fraîche."

"Aye-aye." The waitress wrote down the order and padded off across the dining room in her cross-trainers, her pantaloons rustling. Gina opened her eyes and looked at Shake.

"Are we . . . are we safe here?"

She meant the coffee shop at Treasure Island, right now. But even if she'd meant planet Earth, for the rest of their lives, Shake's answer to the question would have been the same.

He waited till the waitress returned with his bourbon. He swallowed half with one long pull, then sighed. He wondered who the more immediate threat was: Dick Moby or Lexy. Long-term, it was no question.

"No," he said. "But we'll probably be okay for the time being."

"I can go to the police. I can—"

"You can't."

"But—"

"No police." Shake had no doubt that Dick Moby had a whole chess set of the city's finest in his pocket—beat cops, detectives, maybe even a captain or two. "Don't go home. Don't call any friends or family. Just get on a plane and leave. As far away from Dick Moby as you possibly can."

"I don't have any money," Gina said. "And my boys—"

"Get on a plane and leave."

He watched her struggle to absorb all this, the sudden vertigo of a life flipped sharply and irrevocably, in the course of a single heartbeat, upside down.

"I feel," she said, "a little, a little . . ."

"Sick?"

She nodded. He pushed the glass of lemonade closer to her. She lifted it to her lips, then lowered it without drinking. She smiled faintly.

"Oh, my God. Last week I was worried would we have enough gumdrops for all the kids in third grade to do the craft project? You know?"

"I know." He did.

She seemed to have a short conversation with herself in her head, then nodded once and reached across the table. She picked up Shake's glass and took a sip of his bourbon. Her nose wrinkled, and she gave the glass back.

"I think I better stick to lemonade."

"I'll give you money for a plane ticket," he said.

"I can't . . . I can't even begin to thank you. Shake."

He shrugged. The waitress returned with their food, and they ate. Some color started to creep back into Gina's cheeks. Shake, too, began to feel slightly more serene, if not exactly hopeful, thanks to the food in his stomach and the bourbon circulating in his bloodstream.

"What are you going to do?" Gina asked when they'd finished eating.

"I've got the briefcase at least, thanks to you, which might appease the lady I work for."

And it might not. It all depended on how badly Lexy wanted those stamps—or whatever they were. How much she valued her business association with Dick Moby. How forgiving she felt toward an old lover who never dimed her out and did fifteen months because of it.

Shake would make sure to remind her of that.

"You're in a lot of trouble?" Gina asked.

Shake couldn't help but smile. "I got out of the joint less than twenty-four hours ago. This must set some sort of new world record." He finished off his bourbon. "I probably should be on that plane with you."

He'd meant it as a joke, but the way she looked at him—eyes surprised but pleased—made him realize that maybe he hadn't meant it as a joke after all.

He glanced away, embarrassed, and quickly changed the subject. "Go ahead. Ask."

"It's none of my business."

"I was in for grand theft auto. I did the full fifteen months because I wouldn't play ball with the D.A."

"You steal cars?"

"Well . . ." Shake hesitated. Then figured, after what they'd been through together, there was no reason to be coy. "I drive them. I'm a wheelman. Getaway driver?"

"Wow," Gina said. "That must be so exciting."

"Not really. Mainly it's just making sure you drive the speed limit and don't get pulled over. Check the oil beforehand, the tire pressure, brake lights."

The waitress came by and asked Shake if he wanted another bourbon. He did—he wanted to keep drinking until his brain was so filled with soft, sweet, cotton-candy fuzz that there was no room in it for Dick Moby or Alexandra Ilandryan, for electrical tape and .45 automatics—but he knew better. His wits were all he had, and he knew he'd have to keep them about him. He refused the drink. The waitress said she'd bring the check and left.

"How old are your kids?" he asked Gina.

"Will's four, Jeff's two. Do you—"

"No."

They sat for a moment in silence. Someone, far away on the casino floor, hit a slot jackpot and started cursing with delight.

"Oh, I get it now," Gina said. "You steal it first. The getaway car?"

"So they can't ID it. Some people just steal a set of plates. If you're in a hurry, that's better than nothing."

"How do you do it?"

"Do it?"

"Steal a car. Where do you steal them from?"

"I like to use long-term parking at the airport. Boost a car, do the job, get it back before anything's even reported stolen."

She looked up over the lip of her lemonade glass and gave him a crooked smile. "So why'd you get caught, if you're so smart?"

The teasing took him by surprise. A side to her he hadn't expected. "Who said I'm so smart?"

He smiled back, and for a second it was like that instant when you crossed two bare ignition wires and felt it in your fingertips, the plugs sparking and the engine stirring.

Then the waitress returned with the check. Shake and Gina looked away from each other at the same time.

"Take a cab to the airport," Shake said. "The Town Car is too risky."

Gina frowned. "Is there any way— Do you think I have time to get a room here? Just for a shower?"

Shake thought about it, then nodded.

"Why not?"

Chapter 7

Those long, suffocating nights in the joint, hours inching past—these were some of the things he'd dreamed about: A real mattress. A real pillow. And silence, more than anything else. Just the hum of the air conditioner cranked to high and the soothing hiss of the shower from the bathroom.

Shake stretched out on the bed, put his hands behind his head, and lay perfectly still. He wished he could close his eyes and just sleep for a week. Then wake up back in time, back walking out that gate at Mule Creek, still a stranger to Gina and Jasper and all the shit he was swimming in now.

"That's not your real name?" Gina called from the bathroom. "Shake?"

Except, to be honest, Shake wasn't entirely sure he wanted to be a stranger to Gina. He stared up at the ceiling and realized, to his surprise, that maybe he wouldn't want to go back in time after all. Crazy as that sounded.

"Nickname," he called back.

He heard the shower faucet squeak off. The curtain rattled.

"Because you like milk shakes?"

"Because I'm white like a milk shake. Some of the black guys started calling me that my first time I went down. Vanilla Shake. It just stuck."

"How old were you, your first fall?"

Shake remembered climbing off the county bus that first time, belly chain clanking, sweat gathering in the small of his back. A tower guard with an M16 slung over his shoulder was eating a candy bar. The sky was pale blue and cloudless. Shake remembered thinking, *This is wild; this is unreal, man.*

"Nineteen," he said.

"Maybe they thought you were cool like a milk shake."

"I doubt that."

The door to the bathroom opened and Gina stepped out, wearing only a towel. Her hair was damp, and her bare shoulders were lined with glittering beads of moisture. When she smiled at him, it was a smile he hadn't seen from her before, lazy and sly, a smile that seemed to belong to a different person entirely—a beautiful girl who looked a lot like Gina but didn't have much else in common with her.

"*I* think you're cool," she said.

Shake stood. As Gina crossed the room and put her arms around his neck, he felt the same strange detachment he'd experienced that first time off the county bus. *This is wild; this is unreal.*

Her face was so close to his that he could taste the wintergreen toothpaste on her breath. Her face was too close; he couldn't keep it in focus.

"You're making me dizzy," he said.

"I've been known to have that effect."

He blinked and looked away. The whole room was going blurry now, not just Gina's face. The walls bent at impossible angles, and Shake felt himself bending with them. Gina's arms around his neck were cool and smooth.

"How did you know it's called that?" he asked. "When you go to prison? A fall?"

"Shhhhh," Gina whispered. She withdrew her cool, smooth arms, and the floor began to roll, very slowly, out from under his feet. Shake staggered, then managed to take a few steps toward the bathroom, where there was cold water he could splash on his face. He'd almost made it to the sink when the floor finished sliding away and he toppled heavily backward, onto his ass.

From the bathroom Shake watched Gina toss her towel aside and start putting her clothes on. He tried to climb up off the tile, but his arms and legs were pudding. The light dimmed, as if a cloud had passed across the sun. His tongue felt thick.

He knew it wasn't love that was happening to him. It wasn't bourbon.

"Okay," he said, trying hard to concentrate. "Hey. What . . . ?"

Gina sat on the edge of the bed as she pulled on her jeans.

"Gamma hydroxybutyrate, sweetie," she said.

Shake's brain translated sluggishly. "You roofed me."

"I always keep one in my pocket, in my Burt's Bees lip balm tin, in case of emergencies." She zipped up her jeans. "I know what you're thinking."

Shake doubted that. He wasn't even sure himself what he was thinking.

"I didn't have a chance to use it earlier," she explained, apologetic. "They grabbed me too fast, put me in that stupid trunk."

She entered the bathroom with the handcuffs he'd found her in. She snapped one cuff on Shake's wrist, the other to the pipe beneath the sink. Then she bent down and brushed a quick kiss across his lips.

"I really do think you're cool," she said.

"Oh, man," Shake said.

She grabbed the briefcase, then paused at the door to give Shake a wink.

"I owe you one, okay?" she said.

Shake managed a wry smile even as total darkness descended on him.

"You're not a Mormon housewife, are you?"

"Not exactly," she said.

Chapter 8

Four days, thirteen hours, and nine minutes earlier, approximately 150 feet across Las Vegas Boulevard from the Apache Motor Inn, Gina had lit the last Marlboro in her pack, tipped her head back, and blown a lazy plume of smoke toward the ceiling, where the spangles of light off the disco ball danced and shimmied. She'd downed the shot of tequila the bartender had poured her and beamed.

"Zowee!" she'd said.

"No," the bartender had said, before she could say anything else.

"The other girls get mad at you when you give me free drinks, don't they?"

"Yes, they do."

"But I'm not like the other girls, am I?"

He sighed, shook his head, and poured her another one, just like she knew he would.

"No," he agreed, "you're not."

Gina gave him a wink and turned on her bar stool so she could see the booth. The new DJ was a metal freak with no ear for rhythm. When he glanced up from his turntables, she made a pistol with her thumb and forefinger and pointed it at him. He tried any of that head-thrasher crap during her set, she'd personally kick his ass.

He thrashed his head and grinned like a retard at her. The shrieking guitars of the last song faded out. The girl on the main stage—cute in pigtails and a plaid Catholic-school skirt—used the toe of one Mary Jane to scrape together the crumpled dollar bills scattered like carnations along the edge of the stage.

"Gentlemen," the DJ breathed into the mike, "The Jungle is proud now to present, on stage number one, the sexy, the sizzling . . ."

Slowly, languidly, Gina moved through the packed house. She was wearing one of her favorite outfits—black leather thigh-high boots, red leather boy shorts, and a tiny cutoff T-shirt that said DUH—and in her platforms she was a head taller than most of the dopes staring slack-jawed up at her.

She felt great. She felt sleek and fluid. She felt like a silk curtain drifting in a breeze.

Gina giggled. Or something like that.

Tonight was the night.

"Gentlemen, put your hands together for . . . the queen of the jungle."

She climbed the steps to the main stage, and the first funky riff of Prince's "Kiss" kicked in. Gina blew the DJ a smooch—good song, good boy—as guys from every dark corner of the club oozed toward the stage, crowded the rail, and the sky rained money.

TWO SONGS LATER—RILO KILEY'S "Smoke Detector" and "Turn It On" by the Flaming Lips—Gina was down to her thong, her boots, a light sheen of perspiration, and nothing else. Normally the top girls bought their way out of the stage rotation—the real money was on the floor, in the VIP rooms—but tonight Gina needed the elevated perspective. And sure enough . . .

Right on time she spotted the Whale as he rumbled into the club. Fat and scowling, so pale he glowed like a grubworm under the Jungle's black lights. Gina spotted him during her final stroll along the rail and felt a little chill of fear and excitement.

The Whale gave the room a quick, bored glance, then turned to ream out the doorman about something. Lucy was with the Whale, and so was Jasper, his varsity-team muscle, and also some ferrety dude Gina didn't recognize. The Whale had one hand on poor Lucy's ass and the other deep in his front pocket, gently jiggling loose change and, probably, his own wiener.

All the silly stories Gina had heard about the Whale before she took the gig at the Jungle, she now—after five months working for the foul-tempered, foul-smelling creep—believed most were probably true. Didja hear about . . .

How one time a dancer smarted off to the Whale and he slapped her so hard he broke her jaw?

How one time the Whale set a guy's car on fire, with the guy inside it, then went to dinner downtown at the Golden Nugget afterward and ordered the porterhouse special?

How he used his titty clubs to launder money from his drug operation and didn't bother with a safe for all his cash, because who the fuck was stupid enough to rip off the Whale?

Gina smiled and plucked a ten from the teeth of a gray-haired guy with his chin propped on the rail. She hoped that last story at least was true. She was counting on it.

The song ended. Gina sat on the stage steps to pull her T and shorts back on. She watched the Whale, his hand still on Lucy's ass, make his way toward the door across the room marked NO ADMITTANCE.

"Hey, cookie," the gray-haired guy from the rail said. He squatted next to her and breathed cheap, watered-down gin into her face. "What say you and I go back to my hotel for a private dance? I'll make it worth your while."

Gina stood up, hands on her hips, and gazed evenly down at him. She was a hundred feet tall, and he was a sad gray mouse.

"You really think you can handle me in private?" she asked.

A second passed before he blinked.

"No," he admitted weakly.

She gave his cheek a friendly pinch and followed the Whale through the crowd.

LUCY KNEW THAT HER HANDS gave her away when she was nervous, so to keep them busy she opened her purse and fumbled for a Tic Tac. The Whale gave her an annoyed scowl, then leaned across his desk.

"What'd you say?" he asked O.T.

Lucy took a deep breath, disguised as a yawn. She glanced at her watch. She felt like she was going to hornk up her lunch, she was so scared. She started saying a rosary in her head, in Spanish, and that helped some.

O.T. shifted around in his metal folding chair and tried to smile. I said, "Mr. M, I'm a little short again this week, but it's because—"

"Do I give a fuck?" the Whale said. He flipped through the stack of hundred-dollar bills on the desk in front of him. Bored. "Jasper?"

"Mmmm?" Jasper was standing directly behind O.T., against the door.

"Do I give a fuck?"

"Nuh-uh."

"Didn't think so."

The Whale slid open the cabinet door behind him, the one with the fake wood paneling, and tossed in the stack of hundreds. Lucy got a quick peek before he slid the door shut: shelves loaded with stacks and stacks of bills.

Dios te salve, María, llena eres de gracia. . . .

"You need to get you a safe, Mr. M," O.T. said. He laughed nervously and looked around like maybe he hoped someone else in the room was laughing, too.

The Whale laid his arms on the desk. Big, pale, pimply slabs, like they should have been hanging from hooks and attracting flies in an outdoor village market. He stared at O.T. "Why is that?"

O.T. stopped laughing. "What? I just meant—"

"Why do I need a safe?" the Whale asked. "Who the fuck is stupid enough to steal from me?"

Lucy caught Jasper looking at her, but not in the creepy way most guys—the Whale especially—looked at her. Jasper looked at her like she was a human being, somebody's daughter and sister, which she was, not just a pair of admittedly rockin' 36Ds in a too-tight spandex mini-dress and three-inch spikes.

Jasper was the only gentleman in this place. He always made sure, if he was around, that one of the bouncers walked her out after a shift. He did the same thing for the other girls, too, not just her, which made Lucy like him even more.

The Whale called Jasper a dumb shine, sometimes right to his face. Lucy didn't think Jasper was dumb. His round face was intelligent, just in a quiet, a sleepy, a shy way; she wished she'd had a big brother, growing up, exactly like Jasper.

Jasper's skin was a pretty color. A bit dark, a bit creamy, like expensive wood. His sleepy eyes were darker and less creamy, but a pretty color, too.

She gave him a friendly half-a-smile. Jasper glanced quickly away.

"I asked, 'Who the fuck is stupid enough to steal from me?' "

"Mr. . . . Mr. M," O.T. was stammering, "I didn't mean—"

"Except you," the Whale said. He stood up.

Jasper cleared his throat. The Whale scowled at him.

"What?"

Jasper nodded at Lucy. "You want me to take her outside? Lucy?"

"I know her fucking name. No." The Whale had moved behind O.T., who wasn't sure if he should turn around or keep looking straight ahead. "She's a big girl. She'll survive."

"Mr. M," Jasper started to say, but then the Whale suddenly hooked a fat, pale, pimply arm around O.T.'s neck and jerked him out of his chair.

Lucy stared in horror as O.T. gagged and kicked. The Whale squeezed harder. O.T. twisted, flailed. His eyes had too much white in them, an awful wet white, like they were going to plop out of their sockets.

Lucy would have kept staring, frozen, but Jasper moved across the room toward her. He lifted a big hand and gently covered her eyes with it.

"Be all right," he murmured.

JASPER DRAGGED O.T.'S BODY DOWN the hallway toward the back exit. The Whale locked his office door.

Lucy felt blank, light-headed. The narrow, dimly lit corridor was thick with the smell of cigarette smoke and watermelon-scented body spray. The Whale's voice came to her from the end of a long, long tunnel.

"Let's go eat a steak."

He started walking, then turned back when he realized she wasn't following him. "What?"

"I gotta use the ladies' room," she said.

"Hurry the fuck up. I'll be in the car."

GINA FINISHED CHANGING INTO HER street clothes—a pair of Dark Baja True Religions that fit her like a glove and a Runnin' Rebels sweatshirt—then touched up her lip liner. She put her hair up in a ponytail, then tried it down. Up? Down? She decided it looked better up. Half past midnight. A minute later, Lucy pushed open the door to the undressing room and stepped inside.

She looked like hell, her face bloodless and eyes empty. She went to the sink and ran some cold water, then just stared in a daze at herself in the mirror. Gina gave her a second, but they couldn't afford much more than that. She reached over and turned off the faucet.

"Lucy?"

Lucy continued to stare at her reflection.

"You sure you want to do this?" Lucy said finally, her voice shaking.

Gina put two fingers under Lucy's chin and turned her face away from the mirror. Kissed her on the lips. Kissed her again. Took Lucy's upper lip between both of hers and tugged gently.

"Don't wig on me now, Loosey Change, okay?"

Lucy drew in a deep breath and held it. "You really mean it?" she whispered. "You love me?"

She gazed up at Gina with those black Spanish eyes of hers. Gina felt a faint familiar ache of sweet melancholy, fading almost as soon as it started, like a breath of wind not quite strong enough to rattle the leaves in a tree.

She took Lucy's hand and pressed the warm palm to her sternum. "You have the key to my heart, sweetie."

"Three A.M.," Lucy said.

"Three A.M."

"The volcano."

"You know I'll be there," Gina said.

Lucy nodded and hurried out of the room.

Gina smiled and picked up the key Lucy had left on the edge of the sink.

THE WHALE'S PRIVATE OFFICE WAS at the far end of the hall on the left, between the undressing room and the fire exit. Foot traffic was bad for a few minutes, girls on crystal breaks clattering on high heels to the bathroom and back. But then Gina heard the next song start pounding through the walls—seriously: more of that stupid hair metal?—and the hallway cleared.

She slid the key into the lock and heard the velvety snap of the dead bolt. She slipped inside Dick Moby's office and shut the door behind her. Flicked the lights on. The cabinet was behind the desk, beneath the mini-fridge, right where Lucy had said it would be.

The air in the room was hot, stale, heavy with Whale funk. Gina knelt on the carpet and pulled open the cabinet doors. She almost giggled out loud when she saw all the money stacked on the shelves inside—bricks of hundred-dollar bills, ten grand per. Thirty bricks, thirty-five, forty. Shit! She cupped a hand to her mouth and did, then, giggle out loud.

She helped herself to one of the Whale's Kools from the pack on the desk and tucked it behind her ear for later. She figured he wouldn't miss one little cigarette, a thought that almost started her giggling again. Instead she assumed her most serious, all-business frowny-face, yanked down the zipper of her gym bag, and started stuffing in the money.

DICK MOBY HONKED TO HURRY the dumb cooze across the parking lot, but—as always—Lucy took her good, sweet time. Your average jig had nothing on a Mexican girl when it came to sheer laziness—Mexican or Costa Rican, whatever the hell she said she was. Lucky for Lucy she had a blow-your-mind bod. Long, long legs, riding up to a perfect round ass. Put her in those shorts where the bottom half of her brown ass hung out and it was like looking at a painting in a museum. Big tits, real ones, just the right amount of give and jiggle. Probably in a few years the whole package would sag and wrinkle beyond rescue, what always happened with the Mexicans. The Indian blood in them. By then, though, who'd give a fuck? Not Dick Moby. He'd have long since plucked another fresh peach from the tree and let the juices dribble down his chin.

He tapped the horn again, but lightly because he was in an indulgent mood after the fun with O.T. Besides, waiting for Lucy to cross the Jungle parking lot gave him time to remember he'd left his cigarettes in the office.

Lucy climbed into the Caddy. Dick Moby cut the engine.

"What's wrong?" she said, a flinch of fear in her voice that both annoyed him and pleased him.

"Forgot my smokes," he said.

"In the office?"

"Where else but the fucking office?"

He popped the door and heaved himself out of the Caddy. At the door he shoved through a pack of drunk conventioneers waiting to pay their cover. The longhair working the door, the one thought he was a rock star, spotted him and looked nervous.

"Uh, Mr. M, I thought—"

"Hurry up and move these assholes inside," Dick Moby said. "Like a fucking bus station out here."

"Hey!" one of the conventioneers slurred cheerfully. "Who the hell you calling asshole?"

Dick Moby ignored him. Time was you could beat a drunken asshole to a pulp in the parking lot and a crowd of off-duty cops would cheer you on. Nowadays, though, every other beatnik faggot was a VP for some big company that made fiber-optic Internet microchips or some shit, and you so much as raised your voice, they'd have lawyers crawling up your butthole till the end of time. Dick Moby didn't need the aggravation. Besides, he was so hungry for a porterhouse he could taste it.

Out of habit he paused to check the main floor. The four stages were occupied, most of the wall booths, no girls were lounging around the bar playing video poker. Satisfied, he pushed open the door marked NO ADMITTANCE.

One of the newer girls, Gina, came walking down the hallway toward him. Already dressed out, a gym bag slung over her shoulder. She gave him a calm, indifferent glance.

Dick Moby grabbed her arm as she passed and stopped her.

"What?" she said, annoyed.

He studied her, eyes slitted. Something was off, he could feel it—the nerve ends at the base of his skull tingled—but he wasn't sure what. A mob guy he once worked for back in Dallas used to tell him he had reptile radar. Dick Moby had taken that as a compliment.

"Thought you were on till four," he said. She was one of his top earners, though he himself didn't pretend to understand it. Fix that nose, stick a couple of real tits on her, teach her how to smile more like a whore and less like she could be teaching Sunday school—then she'd bring in even more dough.

"Was." She shrugged. "But I started my period about an hour ago, so unless you want it to look like a slasher flick out there every time I give a lap dance, get your paws off me."

Dick Moby had to smile, a little, at the girl's balls. Maybe that's why she made so much money; maybe that's why some guys liked her. He dropped her arm.

"I don't trust you," he told her. "I got my fucking eye on you."

She shrugged again. "Yeah, whatever."

He watched her saunter calmly down the hall and out the door behind him.

"I got my fucking eye on you," he growled again, then turned and rumbled down to his office. He swiped the pack of Kools off the desk, then paused. That weird reptile radar of his again. He walked his eyeballs slowly around the office once, then twice: the desk, the desk chair, the cabinet behind the desk, the TV on the cabinet, the door, the chair, the cardboard file boxes filled with the dancers' sheriff cards, the meat-colored carpet, the liquor license in the frame with the cracked glass, the desk, the desk chair, the—

The cabinet behind the desk.

He squatted, with effort, and peered at the dented metal door of the cabinet. Closed tightly and carefully.

Too tightly, too carefully.

Dick Moby suddenly felt half a century of undigested animal fat in his body, the weight of it, porterhouses and prime ribs, dialing down the aperture of his arteries until they were just pinpricks, squeezing off the blood to his heart and making him dizzy. A faint concentric throb spread out from the center of his chest, like ripples on a pond.

He slid open the door to the cabinet. Inside, the briefcase was still there, but the shelves were empty and all the cash was gone.

"Bitch," he hissed.

Dick Moby gripped the cabinet door with both hands and wrenched it off the rails, flung it pinwheeling so violently across the office that it stabbed through a cardboard file box and stuck there. He stormed back through the club, shoving aside convention geeks and dancers, into the parking lot. But the cab stand was empty, and the bitch—Gina—was gone.

LUCY SAT ON A BENCH beneath the volcano and watched it erupt—smoke boiling, red lights flashing, a few tourists gaping—for maybe the fifth time since she'd arrived. She looked at her watch. Four A.M. Gina was an hour late. A cab pulled up, but it was two men in business suits who climbed out.

Maybe Gina was just running late?

Maybe Gina had gotten caught in traffic?

Maybe Gina had stopped off to buy a bottle of champagne so she and Lucy could celebrate?

Maybe Gina had meant to say four o'clock instead of three?

Maybe Gina . . . ?

The businessmen from the cab went into the casino. The tourists watching the volcano erupt moved on. The Strip outside the Mirage was almost deserted. Lucy told herself not to look at her watch again. She told herself not to cry.

Four-oh-nine A.M.

The volcano was quiet now, just the scent of sulfur and chlorine drifting slowly over Lucy, choking her.

GINA TOOK A CAB STRAIGHT to the airport. That's where the Whale would expect her to go, and she wanted a few eyewitness accounts to throw him off track when his goons sniffed around.

She instructed her cabdriver to pull up outside the international terminal, then asked him was this where you caught Air France? He said yes. Air France, you're sure, to Paris? Yes. She tipped the cabdriver a C-note so he'd be sure to remember the conversation.

Once inside, she made her way across to the domestic terminal and down to baggage claim. All the rental-car places at McCarran were open twenty-four hours. Gina ignored the booths staffed by twenty-something boys and picked the one occupied by a hard-eyed gal in her forties, ex-hooker or ex-dancer or both. Bleached-blond hair, sun-cured skin, perfect manicure. Either the woman would hate Gina on sight or else she'd recognize the ghost of her young self materialized right before her and feel a pang of motherly tenderness. Gina was counting on that second one.

"Hi," Gina said, "I need to rent a car, but I don't have a credit card? Just cash?"

"You have to be qualified for a cash rental."

"Okay," Gina said. "Great. I'll do that."

The woman looked her over. Gina thought she saw the woman's expression soften a little.

"Takes three to four weeks, sugar."

"Oh."

"I'm sorry."

Gina leaned forward. She made her voice tremble, but not too much. "Please, it's really important. If I don't— I have to— Is there any way at all you can, you know . . ."

A long moment of silence passed. Gina felt the woman wavering, sensed her filling in the blanks from her own experience. Maybe a drugged-up boyfriend years ago, who used to beat her. Maybe a drugged-up boyfriend years ago, she shot in a fit of rage because he used to beat her, then had to get out of town pronto.

"Sugar." The woman finally sighed. "I—"

Gina slid a packet of hundred-dollar bills across the counter. Ten grand.

"And you never saw me," Gina said. "You don't remember a thing about me."

The woman eyed her for a second, then turned away and started punching numbers into the computer. Gina looked down and saw that the ten grand had already disappeared off the counter, just like magic. She smiled.

"Full-size all right with you, miss?" the woman asked.

THE CAR WAS A BUTTER-COLORED Ford Crown Victoria, big and luxurious, with butter-colored leather seats and a primo sound system. Gina set the cruise control to eighty-five—why dawdle, right?—and blew through the deserted desert night. She stopped briefly in Barstow for coffee, then hit the outskirts of L.A. just as the sky behind her turned pink and pearly.

She swung off the 10 and wound through Beverly Flats to Wilshire. The valet at the Peninsula took her keys with a polite smile and didn't give her a second glance. In her jeans and sweatshirt, sunglasses and baseball cap, she was just another movie star on the down low, for all he knew.

She crashed out and slept till early afternoon, then ordered room-service pancakes and champagne. After that she strolled over to Rodeo Drive and hit the shops. She bought a black cocktail dress with a hint of flapper sass at Gianfranco Ferré, heels to match at René Caovilla, some panties so expensive she had to laugh, a pair of teardrop pearl earrings. She had a latte at an outdoor café, then bought some more shoes, a bag, a necklace. She bought five hundred dollars worth of makeup. Another dress, another bag, a couple of cute James Perse tops, some high-end denim.

"I could get used to this," she confided to an Arab woman in a burka who was standing next to her at the corner, waiting for the light to change. The woman's eyes darted over to Gina, then darted quickly away. Gina thought she saw a smile crease the dark cloth.

Gina did get used to it. For the next couple of days, she lived like a fairy-tale princess, or at least the kind of princess in the kind of fairy tale *she'd* write. She hit Melrose for funky casual, a handmade leather bag from Argentina and more bling, Montana Avenue for beachwear and high-end lotions, oils, and exotic ungents (and more bling), the Grove for an iPod and a supply of trashy magazines. In between the heavy shopping, she went total spa jihad—Thai massage, seaweed wrap, facial, hot stone something or other. Back at the hotel the afternoon of her third day in L.A., she spread out all her purchases on the bed. Not bad for fifty-some grand and a few days' work. At some point she'd want to figure out how to retrieve her stuff from Vegas, where it was safe for the time being. If doing that proved impossible, though, no big wiggie. There was nothing she owned, Gina knew, that money couldn't replace—more of and even better.

She soaked for an hour in the tub, then put on the black Gianfranco Ferré and the pearl earrings. She went downstairs to the hotel bar. She ordered a martini and checked the crowd for movie stars. The only guy she recognized was a guy from TV, one of the lesser networks, a roly-poly sitcom dad who also did fried-chicken commercials. He gave her the eye from across the bar, but Gina could see neither the fun nor the profit in it, so she picked up her martini and carried it out into the lobby.

Two beefy black guys in suits aroused her attention. They stood motionless across from the concierge desk, flanking a big wooden door. Curious, Gina made her way over. Before she even had a chance to select which of her many smiles to lay on them, the beefier of the two guys stepped aside and opened the door for her. She glimpsed glittering chandeliers inside, heard the plaintive coo of a string quartet.

"Miss," the beefy guy said.

Gina nodded, not missing a beat, and entered a ballroom almost as vast as the hotel lobby. Even posher, if possible. Marble pillars, walls draped with Asian silk tapestries, a polished parquet dance floor around which men in tuxedos gracefully guided their bejeweled partners.

Now *this,* Gina noted with approval, was a party. She crossed to a bar set up opposite the string quartet and exchanged her empty martini glass for a crystal flute of champagne. She took a sip and looked out over the crowd, tried to gauge the cumulative net worth. Most of the men were in their fifties and sixties, silver-haired and pink-cheeked, while the women averaged a good ten years younger. Clearly a gala for wives, not girlfriends. There were only a few twentyish girls like Gina, who made it a point to ignore her.

"Hello, there," said a voice behind her. Gina felt a hand on her elbow, gentle but proprietary. She turned to find a rich old coot grinning at her. He'd just come off the dance floor, and there was a faint dew on his pink cheeks and forehead, along the edge of a hairline too perfectly uneven to be real. He smelled musty, but expensively so. "My wife went to call the sitter, so I thought I'd come flirt with the most beguiling girl at the party."

"How sweet," Gina said. How creepy, she thought, that an old coot like this had kids young enough to need a sitter.

"Bernard Craig," he said. He paused, still grinning, as if he expected her to know the name and be impressed. Gina was bored already.

"Caroline Graham," she said.

"Let me guess," Bernard Craig said. "You're a curator at the Getty. Early impressionists."

Gina smiled and reached for another glass of champagne. She noticed a striking woman standing by herself at the end of the bar. The woman was probably late thirties but looked a decade younger, with glossy black hair cut in bangs and eyes the color of pale gray frost. She wore a *très* tasty silk dress the same shade as her eyes.

"Vice president of acquisitions at Sotheby's in New York," Gina said. "My area is Near Eastern antiquities, though I also have an interest in jade."

"Aha," Bernard Craig said, pleased with himself. "Not far off, was I?"

"Quite close," Gina said. By now she'd idly ascertained, by the way the fabric shifted when he moved, that Bernard Craig's wallet was in the inside pocket of his jacket. "And I do enjoy the early impressionists."

Bernard Craig started to say something he clearly anticipated to be witty but then glanced over her shoulder and stiffened. Gina figured he'd spotted his wife. She took the opportunity to stand, lean close, and strum her fingers lightly but suggestively across the pleats of his tuxedo shirt.

"Caroline Graham," she whispered. She let her lips brush against his ear. "Our Beverly Hills office has my number, if you'd like to give me a call."

Then she was off, without a glance back. She passed the two beefy guards at the door and made her way to the lobby ladies' room.

In the ladies' room, she plucked Bernard Craig's wallet from her bag and held it to her nose, inhaled the rich scent of calfskin. She played the game she always played with herself and guessed, let's see, eight hundred dollars inside? A black American Express?

Before she could open the wallet and check, though, she heard the outer door to the ladies' room swing open. Gina had just enough time to drop the wallet back into her bag and turn to the mirror. The striking woman with the black bangs and gray eyes entered. She joined Gina at the mirror. Gina pretended to check her hair, then realized after a second that the woman was gazing at Gina's reflection, not her own.

"You look familiar to me," the woman said. Her voice was as silky as the dress, with an accent Gina didn't recognize—Russian, maybe.

"Do I?" Gina asked.

"Are you a movie star, perhaps?"

Gina smiled and turned to the woman. She'd been in more of a boy mood when the night began, but she always made it a point to keep an open mind.

"Are you hitting on me, perhaps?" Gina asked.

The woman smiled back at her.

"I know now," she said. "A business acquaintance of mine in Las Vegas. He faxed me photo this morning."

Gina turned back to the mirror. She took out her lipstick.

"Vegas?" she said. "Never been, but I hear it's fun."

"This girl in photo? She could be your twin, I think."

"They say we all have one somewhere."

"And here you are!" the woman said, still smiling. "Life is funny, yes?"

"Sure is." Gina popped her lips, snapped the lipstick shut, then gave the woman one last smile. Coolly, calmly, in no particular rush, she exited the ladies' room. Coolly, calmly, she sauntered across the lobby to the elevators. When the doors opened on her floor, she pushed a bellhop out of the way and sprinted down the hall to her room, high heels in hand. She stripped off the cocktail dress and threw on her True Religions and a sweatshirt, then dragged the gym bag full of cash out from under the bed. Sixty seconds later she was pounding down twelve flights of bare cement service-emergency stairs. She hit the crash bar running and burst through the fire door into an alley. She stopped for a second to get her bearings—Wilshire was . . . left, then left—then took off again. She was almost out of the alley when a car screeched to a stop and cut her off. Her momentum carried her hard into the side of the car. She pinballed off and tumbled to the asphalt, ripping a hole in her jeans and scraping her knee.

Big hands grabbed her shoulders and jerked her to her feet. A giant, bald, unbelievably ugly guy grinned down at her. Gina tried to fight free, but he slapped her so hard she saw sparklers.

"Let me go," Gina said quietly, reasonably.

The bald guy just kept grinning, then said something she didn't understand in a foreign language she didn't recognize.

"Fuck you," Gina said, which she guessed was pretty universal. He slapped her again, and for a quick second, Gina thought she was back onstage at the Jungle, watching the disco balls scatter broken shards of bright light across the ceiling. She licked the corner of her mouth and tasted blood.

"Ah," someone said.

Gina turned to see the woman with the pale gray eyes and the silky accent.

"Hi," Gina said. She blew a strand of hair out of her face and smiled cheerfully. "Think we can make a deal?"

The woman lifted a hand and gently stroked Gina's cheek. She smiled, not unsympathetically, then shook her head.

Chapter 9

Jasper's head felt stepped on. Inside and out. Ached like a son of a bitch.

From a phone book—who would have thought that?

Jasper had been hit in the head by a lot of things in his life—elbows, fists, fists holding a roll of quarters, other heads, chairs, butt of a gun, fiberglass spoiler ripped off the back of a Ford Contour—but none of them, at least as far as he could recall, had resulted in such a lingering, stepped-on ache. He considered for a long moment the bottle of extra-strength Tylenol he'd picked off the shelf, then decided it wasn't up to the task at hand. He needed something with a little more fight in it.

He moved to the end of the aisle, past a pyramid of soda-pop bottles—this was the Walgreens on the south Strip, across from what used to be the Aladdin and was now (Jasper had to think for a second) the

Planet Hollywood—and got in line at the pharmacy counter. There was a white lady tourist in line ahead of him. Thirty years old, give or take, expensive-looking eyeglasses, blue jeans with some interesting stitching on the back pockets, but no butt to speak of.

The pharmacist looked at the piece of paper the lady tourist gave him and smirked at it. Then he smirked at the lady. Then he smirked at Jasper.

"The honeymooner's affliction," the pharmacist told the lady. "We get a lot of that in Vegas." Then he smirked again at Jasper.

Jasper didn't like that. He felt sorry for the lady, the back of her freckled neck blushing with embarrassment. Jasper knew from the girls at the club that a bladder infection wasn't anything to joke about. He stared the smirk right off the pharmacist's face.

"Why don't you hurry on up and go get the lady something for her headache," he told the pharmacist.

The pharmacist did that. He handed the lady a white paper sack. She gave Jasper a whiff of a thank-you smile before she hurried off. Jasper didn't smile back, because his head hurt when he moved his skin at all. He'd discovered this when he told the pharmacist to hurry up.

"Can I help you?"

"Need something for a headache."

The pharmacist looked up at Jasper, a little confused.

"You got a bladder infection?" he whispered.

"I got a headache," Jasper said, impatient. "Bad one."

"Do you have a prescription?"

Jasper sighed.

Jasper could tell that the pharmacist didn't like the way his day was starting. He glanced at Jasper's hands resting half curled on the counter. Jasper had always had big hands, ever since he was a child.

"Listen," the pharmacist said, but then he didn't seem to have anything for Jasper to listen to.

Jasper waited. Finally the pharmacist went to the back and returned with a little white sack.

"Appreciate it," Jasper said. He dropped a hundred-dollar bill on the counter and left.

JASPER FIRED UP THE EXPEDITION so he could run the air conditioner, swallowed three of the little white capsules, and reclined the leather seat a bit so he could think better.

It was a little after nine. Jasper did not look forward to calling Mr. Moby with the bad news. The good news was that Jasper didn't have to do that yet. Mr. Moby always stayed up late and slept late and didn't even turn his cell phone on till noon at the earliest. And he wasn't expecting to hear from Jasper about the exchange until later tonight. Which gave Jasper plenty of time to hunt down the girl, the briefcase, and the guy who'd belted him with that damn phone book. If he could find them, or even (Jasper took a second to work this out) just the girl, then he would not have to call Mr. Moby with the bad news. There would be no bad news.

That was good news.

Jasper could feel the white capsules starting to do their thing. He didn't like to think about what Mr. Moby stayed up all night inflicting on poor Lucy. He felt bad for her. He felt bad for many of the girls, the kinds of lives they led. Full of drugs and asshole customers and evil boyfriends and bladder infections and not very much of what you would call a spiritual dimension. But Jasper felt a special kind of bad for Lucy, and not just because Mr. Moby was a special kind of evil boyfriend, which most certainly he was.

Jasper had read a newspaper article once about a river in the jungle that flooded, and how the tops of the trees drooped heavy and black with tarantulas.

That had made him—he didn't know why—think of Mr. Moby.

There was a sweetness about Lucy. A spiritual dimension, or at least maybe the potential for one. She saw the human in you.

Jasper wondered if he might be in love with Lucy. Not that it mattered one way or another. It mattered about as much as whether or not the food in Pakistan or Siberia would agree with him.

But when he thought of that poor girl with Mr. Moby all night . . .

Shut it down, boy, he told himself, *shut it off.* Jasper was good at that:

keeping the focus. Like when he played football. Watch the line. Find the hole. Go.

That was another thing he'd been hit in the head with. A head in a football helmet.

Focus.

Jasper rearranged himself in the Expedition's leather seat. He walked himself back in time till he was once again outside that motel room this morning, knocking on the door. Jasper knew he wasn't the quickest thinker in the world, but he had near-perfect recall, and when he had time to work things through at his own pace . . . well, then there wasn't hardly a knot he couldn't solve.

He closed his eyes and pictured the door to the motel room opening. The girl sitting on the bed. Holding a plastic cup of water. There was another plastic cup sideways on the carpet. The guy—Shake was his name—had a prison haircut and looked tired.

Jasper could see it all, spread out before him in vivid, luxuriant detail. He turned the air conditioner up another notch and, eyes still closed, started searching for clues.

Chapter 10

Gina waited till she was sure Shake was out cold, tested the handcuffs, then left the room. She shut the door behind her and slid the do not disturb card into the slot. She felt bouncy with energy, with optimism, with beatific goodwill toward her fellow man. Never underestimate, she confided to herself, the restorative power of a hearty breakfast, a hot shower, and a narrow escape from murder and dismemberment and God knows what else the Whale had planned for her. Now all she needed was a cigarette and she'd be perfectly golden.

Those had not been a good couple of days, back in L.A., after she'd been thrown into the trunk of the Town Car. The bald, ugly giant drove her to some abandoned place on the water and locked her in a cargo container with no light, no air, no smoking, and a smell she'd never forget as long as she lived. Which, at the time, had not seemed like it was going to be very long at all—just however long it took for the lady with the pale gray eyes to work out her price with Dick Moby.

But all that was history, ancient. Gina held the briefcase in one hand and put her other hand on her hip like she was standing on top of a mountain. Took a big, long breath of fresh mountain air.

"Ah!" she said.

Gina suspected she might be feeling just a teensy bit guilty about what she'd done to Shake, but she wasn't sure. That was the tricky thing about guilt. It always landed on her so lightly—barely a soft, butterfly-wing breath—that she never knew if it was really there. Gina promised to consider the issue more thoroughly at a later, more convenient date. If, at a later date, of course, it was still an issue, which in her experience it rarely was.

She just needed some clothes now. Or at least a top. She couldn't walk around Vegas in the grimy, sheer, practically see-through tank she was wearing, not if she didn't want to attract more attention than usual.

At the far end of the long hallway, a housekeeping cart was positioned outside the open door of a room.

Gina did a rumba around the cart and breezed into the room.

"I forgot my camera!" she called into the bathroom.

A maid poked her head out. She gave Gina a skeptical and vaguely unfriendly look, then went back to picking pubes or whatever off the toilet seat.

Gina marched straight to the suitcase that was propped open on the suitcase caddy. Pink: jackpot. The jeans in the suitcase were designer knockoffs of questionable taste, but Gina found one top she liked, just about her size: a long-sleeved, waffle-knit henley with a flattering cut and some funked-up Chinese characters silk-screened across the front. She peeled off her grimy tank and tossed it in the trash can. She pulled on the henley, then rummaged around in the suitcase.

What she could really use now . . .

Shazam, and there it was: a long-billed J.Crew baseball cap.

But no Marlboros. Apparently there was a limit to Gina's superpowers.

In the bathroom the maid flushed. Gina pulled her hair into a ponytail and screwed the cap on low. Borrowed a pair of DG shades and slid those on. She checked herself out in the mirror, then remembered to go back and grab the briefcase she'd set on the dresser and almost forgotten.

That would have sucked.

"Gracias!" she called to the maid on her way out.

AFTER SHE BOUGHT A PACK of cigarettes in the hotel gift shop, Gina drove out to Summerlin. She couldn't go back to her apartment, of course, so she was grateful she'd thought to keep her passport stashed in a box at a Mail Boxes Etc. At the airport she cut past the rental-car booths to get to the escalators. She thought she glimpsed the hard-eyed gal at Avis, and it spooked her out a little. This was where—just less than a week ago, hard to believe—she'd taken the first step down the path that eventually led her straight, and handcuffed, into the trunk of a Lincoln Town Car.

That had been a shitty path. Gina wasn't going anywhere near that path again. She was going to be smart this time and blow this Popsicle stand, the Popsicle stand being in this case the entire North American continent, thank you very much.

At the Delta Airlines ticket counter, she produced the wad of bills she'd taken from an envelope in Shake's pocket after he blacked out.

"Where can I go in Asia, first class, one way, right now, for . . ." She paused to count the money. It was less than she'd been hoping, about what she'd expected. She subtracted enough for a hotel once she got to wherever in Asia she ended up. ". . . for, say, a couple of grandish."

"Are you serious?" the gay guy behind the counter said.

"Do I look serious? Or Dubai, maybe."

He lifted one eyebrow, then *tap-tap-tap*ped on his keyboard.

"First class is out of your price range," he said, "but a coach seat to—"

"Ugh. Please."

"Ugh yourself."

"What about Europe?"

Tap-tap-tap.

"London is four thousand."

"How much is coach?" Gina said, then, "Fuck it. Never mind."

She scooped the cash back up, wheeled around, and found a seat in the waiting area that was shielded, mostly, from the rest of the concourse by a bank of slots.

She was going to have to give this situation some serious analysis. A couple of grandish, plus enough for a week in a decent hotel, was not the kind of stake money that got you off on the right foot; it was definitely not sufficient right-foot kind of stake money.

So.

She nibbled a thumbnail. A guy walking past gave her a glance. Nothing hinky about it, though it was hard to tell for sure. Gina knew she was radioactive in Vegas. The Whale's network ran wide, and the kite on her had been up for almost a week. By now every sketchy character in town, and every boyfriend/girlfriend/lover/bartender/cabdriver of every sketchy character in town—and who did that leave, exactly?—had an eyeball peeled for Gina and the big coin she'd pay out if they rung her up.

Gina remembered the way the pirate waitress at Treasure Island this morning had kept looking at her, wondering, trying to place where was it she'd seen Gina before.

She nibbled her other thumbnail and shivered. She didn't like thinking about eyeballs getting peeled; she didn't like the way this train of thought was dragging down her hearty-breakfast, hot-shower, plucked-from-the-jaws-of-the-Whale, good-vibe bounciness.

She snapped open the briefcase and looked inside. Just like she'd heard them discussing back at the motel: a hundred antique postage stamps, yellowed with age, lined up neatly ten by ten beneath the glass of a second case. All of them were blank: no numbers, no writing, no pictures. Was that what made them so valuable? Or was it because they were old? They looked crazy old, some of the paper so thin, so fragile it was almost translucent.

Just *how* valuable?

Gina could guess how badly the Whale wanted to get his hands on her. Really, really badly. Which meant the price he'd been willing to pay—the stamps—must be really, really high.

So.

So . . . what if a girl, into whose hands fate had delivered these stamps, what if this girl managed to sniff out someone—just saying—willing to take them off her hands at a win-win sort of price? Even at fifty cents on the dollar of what they were really worth, those stamps would definitely get her off on the right foot. Much more than a couple grandish would, that's for sure.

Staying in Vegas for another day or two—was it worth the risk?

Gina thought of that hard-eyed gal downstairs at the Avis counter and felt spooked all over again. If that woman had recognized in Gina the ghost of her young self materialized before her, didn't that mean, when you flipped it around, that Gina had been looking straight into the hard, tired, bitter, broken-down eyes of her own future self?

Had that woman been, twenty years ago, where Gina was now? Sitting in a plastic mother-of-pearl chair in an airport terminal, trying to decide if a risk was worth taking?

Spooky.

Gina shifted uncomfortably in her plastic mother-of-pearl chair. *No way,* she assured herself, *am I that woman. No way, in twenty years, will I end up hard, tired, bitter, and broken down, working a rental-car counter at the airport.*

Which, okay, is probably exactly what that woman twenty years ago had assured herself, too.

Gina had every intention of remaining young and hot forever, but she also admitted the improbability of that outcome. Not the hot part—she took really excellent care of her skin and stayed out of the sun as much as possible—but the young part, the part where the currency of her looks would never be stronger against the dollar, the euro, the yen. That part was a bubble just waiting, like all bubbles, to pop.

Gina was ready for it. She knew she had better be ready for it.

SHE TOOK THE SHUTTLE BACK to long-term parking and—cautious—instructed the driver to drop her off a couple of rows from the Town Car. After he drove away, she used a dime to unscrew the Town Car's license plate and switched it out with one from a nearby Escalade. The Escalade was sparkly clean, like it hadn't been sitting out here in the desert dust for days and days, getting blasted with jet exhaust from above. Like it had just been dropped off and the owner wouldn't be back for a while.

She smiled and figured Shake would be proud of her for thinking of that.

She was still thinking about that guy. Which was unusual, but not unpleasant.

He was late thirties, she guessed, maybe a little older. Fit, a face with some mileage, but the more interesting for it. Eyes that had thrown her when he first opened the trunk. His eyes weren't the eyes of a guy who should have been driving that car, doing a job like that. Thank God.

She drove back to the Strip. She slipped through the lobby of the Venetian in her cap and sunglasses. Without, she hoped, being spotted. She laid out a couple of bills for a room, went upstairs, then came back down to complain about the smell of puke in the room. The room didn't really smell like puke, but it was such a plausible lie that the desk clerk didn't blink. He switched her information in the computer and gave her a key card for a new room two floors up.

Gina had no intention of using the new room. She hurried back to the old room, where she'd left the door propped open with the brass security claw.

If someone *had* spotted her, or if the desk clerk ratted, Gina didn't intend to make it easy for them.

She raided the minibar for a Luna protein cookie and a miniature bottle of vodka. She dragged the yellow pages out from beneath the nightstand and flopped them open on the bed.

She leafed to the S's.

"Stamps and Coins, Rare—Dealers."

That was easy. Gina finished the vodka and Luna cookie and realized how sleepy she was. She couldn't remember the last time she'd slept, not counting maybe an hour or two in the suffocating trunk of the Town Car that left her more tired than when she started.

She tore the page out of the phone book and decided to take a nap.

Reward for a mission accomplished more quickly than expected. Even a go-go-go girl like herself had to stop occasionally and recharge.

It was still early. Lots of daylight left. She'd have plenty of time, when she woke up, to find a buyer for those antique stamps.

Gina stripped down to her undies, curled up at the end of the bed, dragged the comforter over her.

What was the harm in a nap, just a little one?

Chapter 11

When Shake woke up, he had no idea, for one unnerving moment, where he was. The room he was in was dark, quiet, cool. Prison was none of those, so at least he knew he wasn't back there. His right wrist hurt like hell—he wasn't sure why—and his mouth tasted as if something rank and furry had crawled inside, dragging with it something even ranker and furrier.

He tried to turn onto his side, but a stab of pain in his wrist put him back down fast. Then he remembered the handcuffs, the rusted U-bend pipe under the sink, the hotel room with the faux-vintage pirate treasure map framed above the bed.

He remembered Gina.

"Shit," he said.

Very slowly he sat up, careful not to torque his aching wrist. He reached up and moved his free hand around the bathroom counter until he found the wall-mounted hair dryer and, just beneath, the light switch. He flicked the switch, and the flare of brilliant white light, bouncing mirror to mirror, was like a hammer hitting his little glass eyeballs.

He didn't know what time it was. He pushed open the bathroom door with his foot. He didn't have an angle on the hotel room's window, but along the wall he could see alternating pickets of light and shadow. It was still light out at least, though not for much longer.

That meant it was probably . . . what? Five o'clock?

"Shit," he said again.

He tested the cuff around his wrist. There was a little play, not much. He reached up and moved his free hand around the counter again until this time he found a trio of small plastic bottles. Shampoo, conditioner, body lotion. He deliberated, then selected the shampoo for its gelatinous quality. He opened the cap with his teeth, then squeezed the goo—it smelled like lavender—over his hand, his wrist, lubed it up under the cuff and all around. Then, careful not to pause to consider how much this was going to hurt, Shake yanked hard.

SHAKE SAT ON THE EDGE of the bed, gently massaging his hand, the cordless room telephone cradled between his ear and shoulder. According to the clock radio on the nightstand, it was almost 5:30 P.M. Even later than he'd thought.

He listened to the phone ringing.

Don't answer, he thought. *We can do this some other time.*

She answered.

"Yes?" Alexandra said.

"It's me."

"It is done? No problem?"

Shake considered. "Small problem."

"Ah."

"The girl got away," Shake said. "With the briefcase."

There was a pause.

"Just curious, Shake," Alexandra said lightly. "What in this situation would you call 'big' problem?"

Shake winced and went into the bathroom to run cold water over his hand.

"I'll get the girl back. Or the briefcase. Both."

"You just a need a little time," Alexandra said.

"Yes."

"Fine."

Fine. Shake winced again. Not because of his hand this time. Because this was going even more badly than he'd expected, and he'd expected it to go pretty badly. He waited for her to ask the question.

"Where are you staying, by the way?" Alexandra said. "In case I need to reach you?"

Shake pictured the hotel across the street: gondolas, Doge's Palace.

"I'm at the Venetian Hotel," Shake said. "Room 1512."

"I call you tomorrow," Alexandra said. "Get some rest, then find the girl and the briefcase. Both. Yes?"

"Yes. Both."

Shake clicked off the phone, turned off the cold water, and noticed the soap dish for the first time. He dried his aching wrist and sighed. In the perfect center of the soap dish, alongside a chocolate turndown mint wrapped in foil, Gina had left the small silver handcuff key for him.

Chapter 12

Alexandra hung up the phone and took a sip of tea. She did not indulge the desire—fleeting, but powerful—to sigh.

There was no place for melancholy in the heart of a *pakhan.* The heart of a *pakhan* was a small, smooth, round stone. If this stone occasionally appeared to glisten as though wet from the rains or the river, that was merely a trick of light and perspective, a testament to the beauty of the stone, and nothing more.

Alexandra took another sip of tea and sighed, okay, a small sigh, sure. Did it not make her an even more formidable *pakhan,* that she could feel and yet still see the world with clear eyes? That she could act without hesitation or doubt on what she saw and ignore what she felt? A wet stone was still a stone, after all.

She had affection still for Shake, yes, but it was no more than that. She had given him this little errand because he had always been loyal. Because he had always been reliable. It was just good business.

Was it just good business, she asked herself, that she went personally to send Shake on this little errand? When she just as easily could have sent Dikran or someone else?

Shut up, please, she told herself back.

The deputy attorney general came padding out of the bathroom in a robe, smiling shyly, stupidly.

Alexandra looked at him, then looked away and thought, *Oh, Shake, Shake, Shake, Shake. Why do you put me in such a position? Why do you force me to turn my heart to stone and make such an unhappy decision?*

Then she picked the phone back up. It was suddenly heavy, this small object, as if it—or she—had been enchanted by a witch in a fairy tale. Alexandra needed all her strength, all her will, just to raise the phone to her ear. But she did.

DIKRAN TOLD THE HOUSE MOTHER to bring him another bitch—not a Chinese this time.

"She Thai."

"Do I care?"

"You want a Ukrainian?"

"Yes. Bring a Ukrainian. Now!"

Dikran found the remote under the pillow and turned on the TV. The Chinese bitch on the bed next to him snored. Chinese were too small. No stamina. Ukrainian girls were sturdier.

The Little Soldier in his lap lay heavy on his thigh. Purple, sticky, and sore, but already starting to stiffen again. Dikran wished only to watch ESPN and go to sleep. But the Little Soldier taunted him.

Dikran glared angrily at the testosterone patch on his arm. He did not blame the Little Soldier for these troubles of his. He blamed this stupid patch and the stupid fucking doctor who said wear it or maybe your heart collapse *floosh* like a smashed football.

An irony was that Dikran much preferred Chinese girls. Their secret eyes and white smiles. But with the testosterone patch, Chinese girls were not sturdy enough for the Little Soldier. Had not the stamina.

On TV on the field sideline was babbling a girl with orange hair and tits spilling out. The Little Soldier stirred. Like the taut string of a violin plucked by a finger. Twang, twang. Fuck! What business, Dikran thought angrily, had a woman on ESPN on the sideline with tits spilling out every which way? Dikran wanted to sleep, but he was too angry.

"Where the fuck the Ukrainian bitch!" he hollered through the wall. He pounded the wall to punctuate each word, twice for the exclamation point.

Stupid fucking doctor. Dikran thought he would like to kill that fucker. Roll a testosterone patch very, very tight, it could be done, and stick it up his—

The phone rang. Dikran answered.

"Okay," she said.

"Where is the ass-lick?"

"He said he was at the Venetian. Room 1512."

"Good. I will go there."

She clucked impatiently at him. "He's not at the Venetian, Dikran."

"I will check anyway. I will find him."

"Make it quick. You understand? I don't want a big mess."

Dikran realized he was grinning, the first time in a long time—he was feeling anger, but the joy sort.

"Don't worry," he said. "I put down plastic and clean up afterward."

Chapter 13

Shake took a quick shower, then ate a can of almonds from the minibar. When he opened the door to the hotel room and stepped into the hallway, he glanced down and saw that Gina had left the PLEASE DO NOT DISTURB/POR FAVOR, NO MOLESTAR card inserted in the key slot. Shake removed it and smiled. Then he heard the *click* of a hammer cocked back.

A .45 automatic, if he was not mistaken.

Cold metal touched the nape of his neck.

"Back inside," the voice behind him said.

Shake stepped back inside. Dick Moby's bagman eased the door shut behind them.

"That was fast," Shake said.

"On the bed."

"Jasper, right?"

"That's right. Sit."

Shake obeyed. "How'd you find me?"

A shrug. "What I do."

"No, really," Shake said. "That fast? C'mon, I'm curious."

Shake saw an embarrassed smile flicker across Jasper's round, sleepy-eyed face.

"Got lucky," he said. "The waitress at the restaurant downstairs."

Shake thought for a second. The pirate waitress. "She recognized the girl."

Jasper nodded. "She knew that Mr. Moby was looking for her. He put the word out last week. So she gave me a call."

"For the record, you remember, Jasper," Shake said, "I really didn't want to have to coldcock you with that phone book, back at the motel."

"I remember."

"The girl's long gone."

"Figured that," Jasper said.

"With the briefcase. You know her?"

"Oh, yeah."

"She roofed me. My head feels like a piñata. After the party."

Jasper thought for a second, then reached into his pocket and tossed Shake a pill bottle. Vicodin. Shake opened the bottle and swallowed a couple.

"Thanks."

"She a serious piece of work," Jasper said.

"Cute, though, don't you think?"

"That what you want to talk about right now?"

"Is her real name Gina?" Shake asked.

"Gina Clement," Jasper said.

"What is she? A stripper?"

"Yeah. She ripped off Mr. Moby."

"She told me she was a Mormon housewife."

Jasper smiled again. "You believe her?"

"I think I probably would have helped her out either way," Shake said, "tell you the truth."

Jasper didn't have anything to say about that. He stood between Shake and the door, far enough away that Shake couldn't make a grab for the gun, close enough to blow a hole in him, sleepy eyes closed, if Shake tried.

"You gonna pop me?" Shake asked.

"After you tell me where she is."

Shake had to appreciate the guy's candor, but it didn't make him feel any better about the situation he was in.

"You think I know?"

"Not really."

Shake thought he recognized something familiar about Jasper's accent. He took a stab.

"Jasper, you're from New Orleans?"

"That's right."

"Whereabouts?"

"Lower Ninth. Before it went underwater."

"Gentilly," Shake said. "I heard it got hit hard, too, though not like the Ninth."

"Fats Domino."

"Right. His house was three blocks from mine. I used to get my hair cut at a little place in the Ninth. You remember the baseball player Will Clark, played for the Giants, who was from New Orleans?"

Jasper nodded. "Barber had a picture of him right above the sink."

"Small world," Shake said.

"Seem that way sometimes," Jasper said, "but really it ain't."

Shake sensed that Jasper's capacity for patience was impressive but not limitless.

"Let me ask you something, Jasper."

"Go ahead."

"Are you under orders to pop me, or is that your own initiative?"

"My . . . what?"

"The Whale doesn't know anything's gone sideways yet, does he?"

Jasper didn't answer. Apparently there was a limit to his capacity for candor, too.

"That's why you have to find the girl and the briefcase with those stamps fast," Shake went on. "Before he finds out." Shake gathered himself for the closing argument. "So that makes the two of us, doesn't it, just two guys punching the clock and taking home a paycheck. We're in the same boat here."

Jasper looked down at the .45 in his hand.

"You've got the gun, I realize," Shake said.

"Different boat," Jasper agreed.

"Yeah. But I know you don't want to pop me. It's a pain in the ass for you, all the way around."

"Nothing personal."

"We could work together to find her. You help me, I help you."

"How you gonna help me?" Jasper asked mildly.

Shake worked that one around for a second. He had a few answers. None plausible. None persuasive.

"You don't know where she is?" Jasper said.

"No."

"Stand up," Jasper said.

"Jasper," Shake said, "if you just—"

There was a knock on the door. Shake and Jasper turned.

"Housekeeping!" a woman's voice called.

Shake heard the *snick* of a key card.

"Get it," Jasper told him. The door started to open, and Jasper slipped behind it, surprisingly nimble for a guy his size. Shake caught the door and stopped it halfway, decided Jasper must have been a defensive end, not an offensive tackle.

The Latina housekeeper peered around the blocked door and up at him.

"We're all set here," Shake said.

She seemed dubious and mildly disgusted. "You no want some towels?"

"No thanks. Everything's just *bueno.*"

She shook her head and wheeled her cart away. Shake started to close the door, then slammed it back wide, fully open, nailing Jasper in the face. The .45 tumbled to the carpet. Shake grabbed it and closed the door.

Jasper crouched, dazed, and held his bloody nose.

"Damn," he said.

Shake checked to make sure a round was chambered, then pointed the .45 at Jasper. He motioned toward the bathroom.

"In there," he said.

JASPER SAT ON THE FLOOR by the sink, and Shake handcuffed him to the U-bend pipe beneath it. Then he handed Jasper a towel for his nose and the bottle of Vicodin.

"Better watch out," Jasper said.

"Don't hold a grudge, Jasper. Like you said, nothing personal."

Jasper shook his head. "Not me you better watch out for."

"The Whale?" Shake asked.

"The girl," Jasper said.

Chapter 14

A valet whistled at Shake when he stepped out of the hotel.

"Taxi?"

Shake showed him the crumpled twenty Gina had left him—or, more precisely, had neglected to find when she went through his pockets.

"Will this get me out to the suburbs?"

"Not back," the valet said.

"Not a problem," Shake said.

THE CAB CREPT DOWN THE STREET until the driver spotted 281. The house was a small but attractive Spanish-style three-bedroom, designed to look larger than it really was, with a red tile roof and an improbably lush green lawn. It was more or less identical to every other house in the development, but Shake wasn't a snob about that kind of thing.

He rang the doorbell. He heard, inside, a soft booming chime. A second later a little black girl, call her eight years old, flung open the door with gusto.

"Hi," Shake said.

"Hi."

"What's your name?"

"Nancy," the little girl said. "With two *e*'s."

Shake had to think about that for a second. Nancee.

"That's a pretty name."

"It's French," Nancee said. "My sister is Amy with two *e*'s."

Aimee.

"I like names like that," Shake said. "That are unique but without working too hard at it."

The little girl studied Shake, then shut the door.

A few seconds later, the door opened again. Standing there now was a black woman in her thirties. She was sharp-angled and regal.

"Hello, there, Aimee," Shake said. "I was just talking to your sister."

He thought the woman might smile at that. She didn't.

"Uh-huh," she said.

"Artemis Wallace?" Shake asked.

"We're getting ready to eat dinner," she said, "if you're here to sell me something."

"You're Vader Wallace's sister?"

The woman's eyes narrowed. "Sister-*in-law.*"

"My name's Shake. I'm a friend of Vader's from—"

Shake stopped himself. He noticed Nancee peering at him from behind her mother.

"—from the office," he said. "He told me to come by if I was ever in town. On a business trip."

"What office, Mama?" Nancee asked.

"This man was in prison with your Uncle V," Artemis told her.

Nancee's eyes went wide. "Uncle V has a *white* friend?"

The mother, Artemis, took a long look at Shake. She was asking herself, Shake figured, the same question.

SHAKE SAT AT THE KITCHEN TABLE, sipping a Coke and watching Artemis Wallace prepare dinner. Nancee and Aimee, a year or so younger than her sister, sat across the table, watching him.

"So you just stopped by to say hello," Artemis said without looking at him. It was less of a question than a general musing.

"Well," Shake told her, "Vader always said, actually, I ever needed anything, when I got out, you-all might be able to help."

"He said that."

"We were pretty tight. He watched my back, I watched his."

Shake thought he heard a soft chuckle, but Artemis had her own back to him and he couldn't be sure.

"*You* watched *V's* back?"

"Prison can be a complicated place," he said. That much at least was true.

"What's prison?" Aimee asked.

"He means the office. Where Uncle V works," Nancee explained to her younger sister.

"Right," Shake said. Then, "Excuse me," he told Artemis, "you don't want to do that."

Artemis finally turned to look at him. Without an overabundance of fondness. "Don't do what?"

"Crush your garlic. It's always better if you slice it."

"You're a chef?"

"No, but I'm a pretty good cook. And I know better cooks than me who'd have a stroke if they saw what you were doing right now."

She looked at him for a long time, then turned back away. She put down the garlic press and drew a butcher's knife out of the wooden block. Started slicing.

"What did you say your name was again?"

"Shake."

"Shake."

"I'm hoping to open a restaurant someday. But it's a hard business."

Artemis glanced up at something behind Shake and to his left. "Hi, baby," she said.

Shake swiveled around. Standing in the doorway to the kitchen, frowning in a business suit, one long rope of dark braided muscle and malice, was Vader Wallace.

Shake held on to his smile for dear life.

"Vader," he managed to say, "my man."

Vader shook his head. "I'm Darth," he said.

"They're twins!" the two little girls chirped.

Shake's relief was expansive: It spread to the horizons then dropped off and enveloped the entire globe in a big bear hug.

"He never— That's right," Shake said. "Of course. When he said identical, I didn't really think—"

"Daddy has a mole," Nancee said.

"Be still now," Darth told her affectionately. He gave both little girls a kiss, then turned to Artemis. "Who's this?" he asked about Shake, not unfriendly.

Artemis considered. Shake knew she was too smart to believe a word he'd said about his warm, close, personal relationship with Vader. But he also sensed she didn't exactly feel the love for her jailbird brother-in-law. And just maybe, what the hell, she'd appreciated Shake's performance.

"This is Shake," she said finally. "He's a good friend of Vader's."

AFTER DINNER DARTH TOOK SHAKE out to the garage. He dug out a cardboard box marked in Sharpie with a giant *V.*

Shake started going through the box while Darth checked stock quotes on his iPhone.

"We were never anything alike," he said. "That's the funny thing. I had my comic books, my X-Men collectible figures. You know? Stayed indoors and out of trouble."

"The yin," Shake said. He came across Vader's Rolex. Probably a fake, but he slipped it in his pocket anyway. "Or is it the yang? I can never remember."

"The nerd is what I was. But it worked out. Junior high, a teacher turned me on to the music of numbers, best thing that ever happened to me."

Shake paused to wonder for a second what he'd consider the best thing that ever happened to him.

"Except for my three ladies in there, of course," Darth said quickly.

"Those have to be the two cutest little girls on the face of the planet," Shake said, and meant it. "You've done well for yourself."

Darth sighed. "What I tell my brother. You have to work hard and make an investment in your own self-worth; it all comes back to you manifold. You ever read *The Purpose Driven Life*?"

"Can't say I have." Shake dug a pair of Jordans out of the box. A couple of sizes too big. He started to toss them back, then stopped to think. He stuck his hand deep into one of the shoes and came out with a roll of bills.

"It's like any book, need to take a lot of it with a grain of salt, but there's some truth in there. Or something close enough to the truth to be useful, you know what I mean?"

"I remember that book," Shake said. "The guy killed that judge in Atlanta and escaped from the courthouse. Killed a deputy and another person, too."

"That's right," Darth said. "Took a lady hostage in her apartment, but she talked to him. Told him about this book she had. How God had a plan for him. They stayed up all night, talking about the book. He didn't kill her, and she made him pancakes in the morning."

"Convinced him to turn himself in."

"Funny thing? Came out later she'd had a stash of methamphetamine. They snorted that all up first. That's how she got him to untie her. They didn't put that part in the papers when it happened."

"If God's got a plan for me," Shake said, "I'm not sure I want to know what it is."

Darth put away his iPhone and turned to Shake, who flinched a little despite himself. It was uncanny how much he looked like his brother.

"You want to see V's ride?"

"His ride?" Shake said.

Darth led him across the garage, past the Honda Pilot, and pulled the dust cover off the other car. A candy-apple red, mint-condition 1969 Plymouth Road Runner.

Shake gazed at the car with the admiration he usually reserved for a bowl of homemade gumbo.

"Boy howdy," he said.

"He tell you about this?"

Shake heard a phone begin to ring back in the house.

"He told me," Shake said, "that if I put so much as a scratch on it, I'd be going home in a motherfucking bag."

"That's V." Darth chuckled.

The phone in the house stopped ringing.

"Who is it?" Darth called to Artemis.

"Nobody," she called back.

Darth nodded at the Road Runner. "Go on," he told Shake. "Keys are in it."

Chapter 15

"Who you calling nobody?" Vader said into the phone. Stuck-up high-yellow bitch. He had to admit she was a good mother, though. He loved those little girls. "Just told you it was me."

"A friend of yours just left," Artemis said.

Vader sniffed the plastic mouthpiece. It smelled bad, like pickles gone off. He caught a CO watching him sniff the phone. The CO looked away *real* quick. Yes he did.

"What you talking about?" he said. Bitch. "Put my brother on. What friend?"

"You know. Shake."

All the sound in the yard dropped away like a door slammed shut.

"Shake," Vader said.

"He borrowed your car, like you told him he could."

Vader hung up the phone. Then he picked the receiver back up and pounded it against the cinder-block wall until the plastic burst into pieces and spun away. Then he ripped the rest of the phone off the wall and pounded that to pieces. Then he pounded his fist against the wall until it looked like raw meat and the cinder block was streaked red, and two, then three, COs came flying out of nowhere to drag him bellowing down to the floor.

Chapter 16

Gina dreamed that Lucy was driving a cab in New York City. It was raining, but Lucy wouldn't stop for her. Gina in the dream felt annoyed, aggrieved. Like, c'mon, how long can one person hold a grudge? Shake might have been in the back of the cab. It zoomed by too fast for Gina to tell for sure.

She woke up and looked at the clock by the bed. It was almost four o'clock in the afternoon. She'd been asleep for—oh, shit, her heart busted a little hip-hop move in her chest—three hours.

She sat up fast. Three hours. If one of Moby's guys had spotted her at the airport, or in the hotel lobby, he would've had plenty of time to check out the decoy room, go talk to the desk clerk, figure out what had happened, and—

The door to the room beeped. A key card in the lock.

Gina leaped off the bed. She'd bolted the door, hadn't she? She looked around for something to use as a weapon, but the door was already clicking open. She hadn't bolted the door.

A guy in his early thirties entered the room, wrestling two roll-on suitcases behind him. When he saw Gina standing there topless in her undies, he stopped.

"Oh," he said.

"I'm here for the threesome your wife arranged," Gina said.

The guy blinked.

Gina looked at her watch. "Am I early? Fuck. Sorry."

She hurried her clothes on, grabbed her shoes, the briefcase.

Coming down the hallway toward Gina was the guy's wife. She was walking slowly and using both thumbs to type rapidly on her BlackBerry. At the same time talking into a Bluetooth headset.

"That's ridiculous," the wife was saying, exasperated. She barely glanced at Gina.

"Back in an hour!" Gina called over her shoulder as she blew past and ducked into the elevator.

GINA PULLED IN TO THE PARKING LOT. The strip mall was on the sketchy side, even as strip malls went. A Laundromat, an Asian-foods grocery store, a place (disturbingly adjacent to the Asian-foods grocery store) with a sign that said SNAKES, ETC.

The place she was looking for, next to the Laundromat, was on the sketchy side, too. Grimy windows and a big rip flapping through the plastic canopy above the front door. Across the canopy, beneath the rip, was printed MARVIN OATES FINE JEWELRY AND PAWN.

On the door, painted in smaller letters, it said PURVEYOR OF RARE COINS, STAMPS, AND OTHER FINE COLLECTIBLES.

Sketchy.

This was disappointing. Gina had been expecting . . . oh, she didn't know, maybe a cozy book-lined shop with comfy leather chairs and a Dickensian vibe. A kindly old proprietor with pince-nez and a sweet-smelling pipe.

On the other hand, though, she admitted, the sketchiness of Marvin

Oates Fine Jewelry and Pawn was also promising. At least when it came to the kind of quick, cash, no-questions-asked buyer she wanted Marvin Oates to hook her up with. Gina told herself not to jinx things by thinking of a number. Good luck with that. She hoped, fingers crossed, the stamps in the briefcase might bring fifty grand. That seemed reasonable, didn't it?

Dubai, here I come. Dubai or wherever.

She took the briefcase and locked the car behind her. On the street in front of the strip mall, a few cars whizzed by without slowing; no one, she was sure, had followed her here.

The shop door was locked, but next to it was a red button that looked sticky. Gina pushed it with her elbow. After a second, a buzzer buzzed and the door clunked open a crack.

Gina stepped inside and squeezed past a pair of dusty glass cases filled with coins, watches, rings, what looked like a couple of old bullets. At the back of the shop, sitting behind another dusty glass case, was a chubby, bug-eyed guy in his fifties who looked sour with indigestion.

"We're closed," he said.

"Then why'd you buzz me in?" Gina said.

"I thought mistakenly you might be a serious collector."

"Who's to say I'm not a serious collector?"

He grunted and picked up the book he'd been reading. A fat paperback with a dragon on the cover, and a girl in a metal bra, a tiny guy with a huge sword.

Gina wasn't being mean, just factual—the guy's resemblance to a bug was astounding. His big, bulging eyes were so far apart on his head that it was like they were this close to dangling on stalks.

Other than that he looked fairly normal, if you called wearing a plum-colored sweater vest and khaki shorts normal.

"Are you Marvin Oates?" Gina said. "This is your place?"

"Yes," he said. "Now go away."

She sneezed. All the dust. She put the briefcase on the counter in front of him.

"How's about you take one quick peek at what I've got in here," she said, "and I'll blow you afterward?"

He looked up from his book, startled.

"Really?" he said.

"No," Gina said, "but I'll give you permission to imagine it after I leave."

She smiled sweetly at him. He scowled at her, but then snapped open the case and looked inside.

"Tell me how much these stamps are worth," Gina said. "Don't lie to me, 'cause I'll know it."

He didn't answer. He sucked in his breath and stared down at the stamps. Gina waited for him to exhale, but he didn't. Curious, she watched as the top of his bald head started to splotch with a pinkish archipelago.

"You okay?" she said. It would be just her luck if the guy had a cardiac event before she could find a buyer for the stamps.

He exhaled finally, then looked up at her again. His bug eyes seemed like they wanted to bulge with excitement, but they were already at maximum bulge and had nowhere to go.

"These aren't stamps," he whispered.

GINA FOLLOWED MARVIN OATES to the back of the shop, which was even dustier than the front and cluttered with books, boxes, bags. And a NordicTrack treadmill in the corner that, Gina guessed, hadn't seen much action.

Marvin Oates put the briefcase on a table and bent over it with a jeweler's loupe.

"Perfect condition," he muttered. "Astounding. I'd read about relics like this, rumors and vague conjectures and whatnot, but of course—"

"A relic?"

"A historical object of great religious significance," he said. He gave Gina a testy glance, then quickly turned his attention back to the . . . whatever it was under glass in the briefcase. "Collected, preserved, venerated. The remains of a saint, a nail from the true cross, cloth from a burial shroud."

"Like *The Da Vinci Code*?"

He didn't even bother with a testy glance this time. He just rolled his bug eyes, which was something to see once and then never, Gina hoped, again.

"Relics were important to the early Christians," he said. "But then, during the Middle Ages, with the crusades, the acquisition and exhibition of relics turned into an all-out frenzy. They were the ultimate status symbol for the church's elite, the bishops and cardinals and whatnot. Whose cathedral had the oldest relics? Which collection represented the most important religious figures? Who had the most fabulously bejeweled philatories?"

"Philatories?"

"A transparent reliquary."

Gina sighed. She really didn't have time for this. "So, excellent, they're relics."

She peered over his shoulder at the small squares of parchment lined up in ten neat rows of ten each. She guessed maybe they were pieces of paper torn from an old Bible or scroll. Or possibly some kind of ancient dried-out fabric sample. Whatevers. Gina's interest in the question was close to total nada. The real question . . .

"What are the little fuckers worth?" she asked.

"Don't you want to know what they are?"

She looked up from the briefcase to find Marvin Oates grinning at her.

Fine. If it would move things along.

"Okay." She sighed again. "What are they?"

"Guess."

She lifted her fist to punch him. He squeaked, cringed, and covered his face with his pudgy forearms.

"They're foreskins!" he said.

Gina was too surprised to lower her fist. She must not have heard him correctly.

"Did you just say—"

"One hundred foreskins. Yes."

"As in—"

"Have a look." He angled the case toward her and handed her the loupe.

Gina debated. Mild curiosity triumphed over mild disgust. She took the loupe, wiped off any potential bug-eye juice, and pressed it to the top of the glass case.

Now that you mentioned it, the little stamp-size squares *did* kind of look like skin. Like the skin you peeled off your nose when you had a sunburn?

"Foreskins from babies?" she asked. "Like from a circumcision?"

"Oh, ho, ho, ho, no," Marvin said. He seemed to be having the best time he'd had in a long time. "These foreskins are from full-grown men."

"But—" she started to say.

"People were smaller back then," Marvin said. "In every respect, if you know what I mean."

Then he snickered. "I'm just kidding. I mean, people *were* smaller back then, yes, but these specimens are small of course because they're only a *part* of the foreskin. You didn't need to keep the entire thing, just enough for a trophy."

"A trophy?" Gina didn't like where this was going, but—intrigued despite herself—she reached out to unlatch the glass case and get a closer look.

"Don't open that!" Marvin squawked. He batted at her hand until she withdrew it.

"Okay. Sheesh."

"Do you have any idea how fragile these things are? They're probably a thousand freaking years old! They should be in a museum!"

He paused to narrow his eyes at her. Which, in the case of bug eyes, was relative.

"Where did you get these?" he asked.

She thought about constructing an elaborately delightful and convincing lie, then decided that this guy wasn't worth the effort. So she just narrowed her eyes back at him and lit a cigarette. Marvin went into a big, fake coughing fit.

"You mind? I have asthma."

"Deal with it."

He started to say something, but she held up a finger.

"Shush," she said, and listened hard.

There it was again, out back: a sound like a tire crunching very slowly, very gently through gravel, as if the car was tiptoeing.

"Do you hear that?" she asked.

"I just hear my chest constricting because of your smoking, my lungs shriveling and turning black with—"

She blew smoke in his direction, then crossed to the back of the back room and cracked the emergency exit door just a hair.

She peered out. The sun had gone down, and the deserted alley behind the shop was dark. Just a little weak, watery light from a single street lamp. The crunching-gravel sound had stopped.

An odd feeling crept over Gina. Like, maybe, the alley wasn't really deserted after all.

"So these museum-quality foreskins," Gina said. She peered out into the alley and wondered what was the point of a streetlight if it didn't provide any light? "Just how much are they worth, exactly?"

"Five million," Marvin said. "That's what I'd guess."

She glanced over her shoulder, saw that he had the loupe to his eye again.

"Five million?"

"Bad news is, you'll never find a buyer for them."

"Five million *dollars*?"

Gina's skin prickled. She took a deep, calming drag from her Marlboro Red and hugged herself against the chill of the evening breeze blowing in off the desert. She wanted to go give Marvin a big kiss on the top of his pink, splotchy head. Theoretically, at least.

Five. Million. Dollars.

"Oh, I'll find a buyer," Gina said. Bet your ass she would.

"No reputable collector will touch these," Marvin said, "no matter how bad they might want them."

"So we just rustle up one lacking a little repute."

"With five million to burn? Ha."

He was quiet for a second.

"What?"

"There is one guy. The obvious candidate, of course. I hear he's in Panama now."

"Panama? What's his name?"

Marvin didn't answer for a long time.

"Nobody," he said abruptly. "Nothing. Never mind. Forget it. Just a rumor. I doubt these are genuine anyway. Worthless, probably."

Gina flicked her cigarette out into the alley. Orange sparks scattered on the asphalt, and she thought she saw something move by the Dumpster.

She tensed again. Probably just a shadow. Probably she was just being paranoid. Right?

Marvin let rip a big, explosive cough behind her, and Gina almost jumped out of her skin.

"Sheesh!"

She peered back into the alley. Still nothing. She quickly pulled the door shut and made sure it was locked. Marvin coughed again.

"You better not get your cooties all over my ancient foreskins," she told Marvin.

He snapped the briefcase closed and brought it to her.

"This conversation is over. I want absolutely nothing to do with the contents of this briefcase, which I do not acknowledge having opened or examined."

"You pussy."

"I suggest you seek the counsel of an attorney or contact your local law-enforcement authorities."

"How am I supposed to find a buyer?" she asked.

"Why don't you ask the people you stole it from? Who were *they* planning to sell it to?" He took a hit from his asthma inhaler and snickered. "Might be awkward, I realize."

Gina, pissed, yanked the briefcase away from him.

"Thanks for nada," she said. "And that imaginary blow job I offered you? Forget about it."

Chapter 17

Vader's Road Runner could definitely do just that—run roads, and with panache. Shake couldn't resist taking an extra lap around downtown, the perfectly tuned 426 Hemi growling sweet nothings back to him every time he goosed the gas. Around 10:00 P.M. he pulled up to the Clark County Bureau of Records. He parked, paused to admire the Road Runner from a couple of different angles, then went inside.

The lobby was crowded with applicants for marriage licenses. Several of the men wore cheap tuxedos, and many of the women were in full, flowing, white-trash bridal regalia. Acres of white polyester lace, rhinestone tiaras, six-foot trains the brides-to-be had to keep bunched under their arms so they wouldn't get stepped on. Just about everyone looked drunk.

Shake got in line behind a cheap tuxedo and a rhinestone tiara. When the female clerk informed the couple that the Nevada legislature had recently instituted a proof-of-identity requirement for marriage licenses, they didn't take the news well.

"That ain't right!" the man said.

"Is bullshit!" the woman said. She held her bunched-up train in one hand and a yard-long plastic tube filled with beer in the other. She was drunker than her fiancé, though not by much.

"I wish it wasn't the case," the clerk behind the window said, sighing. She was cute—why he'd picked her window—but had the glazed look of a long-stretch CO.

"Whose bullshit is this?" the man demanded.

"The Nevada legislature," the clerk said.

"Is bullshit!"

Shake took a step forward. "Excuse me," he said to the man. "But there's no proof-of-identity requirement in Reno."

The man wheeled around, too far, wheeled part of the way back to face Shake.

"Serious?"

"Serious."

"Reno." He processed this new information while his bride-to-be slammed back half a foot of her beer. "How far?"

"Reno? Half an hour, maybe. Straight up Highway 95. Can't miss it."

A cagey look spread across the groom-to-be's face. He wheeled back to the clerk, smacked the counter with his palm, gave her a triumphant glare.

"Ha!" he said.

He marched toward the exit. His bride-to-be hurried after him, swishing (the train) and sloshing (the beer).

Shake stepped up to the counter. The clerk smiled at him.

"There's a proof-of-identity requirement in Reno, too, you know."

"Is there?"

"And it's a lot more than half an hour from here."

"Live and learn," Shake said.

"Thank you for that," she said.

She had an interesting tattoo on the inside of her forearm, a frog. Shake imagined that every guy who hit on her said how much he liked that tattoo. So instead he said, "I'll bet getting that tattoo on your arm was the worst mistake of your life."

"What?" The clerk laughed. She'd liked him before, but now—more important—she was also intrigued. "Why do you say that?"

"Because I bet every guy who hits on you tells you how much he likes that tattoo."

She watched him. Tried to figure out his angle. Discovered it was more fun trying to figure out his angle than it was dealing with drunk people demanding marriage licenses.

"So you don't like my tattoo?" she asked. "Or do you?"

"I'll answer that question when we've concluded our official business. I don't want our personal relationship to compromise your professional judgment. Deal?"

She laughed again. "Deal."

"Exotic dancers in Las Vegas," he said. "They need a sheriff's card to work, right?"

"That's right."

"And you have a record of the information on those cards?"

"Yes, but—"

"You're not allowed to give out the information."

"I'm sorry."

"She's my little sister. She called last night, crying, and now she's not answering her cell phone."

"I really can't."

"She has this new boyfriend who likes to slap her around. I drove down from San Francisco, and now I don't know what to do."

The clerk hesitated. Shake felt bad. He was a pretty good liar, but he didn't like lying to nice people and tried to avoid it unless absolutely necessary. He'd felt relieved when Vader's sister-in-law had seen right through his bullshit.

No, he revised with a slight smile, he really wasn't even a pretty good liar, not compared to Gina.

"Never mind," Shake said. "I shouldn't have even asked."

"You're her brother?" the clerk said. "You're not some kind of a stalker customer from the club where she works?"

"I am most definitely not anything like that. I promise."

She studied him. She seemed to sense that was the truth, which it was. "What's your sister's name?"

"Gina Clement."

The clerk went to the back. After a minute she returned with a slip of paper. She handed it to Shake.

"If I'm still in town tomorrow night," Shake told her, "I'm gonna come back here and ask you to dinner."

That was the truth, too.

"Oh, yeah?" she said, smiling. Then, as he turned and headed toward the door, "Hey."

"What?"

"You never told me if you liked my tattoo or not."

"Probably not as much as I'm gonna like your other one."

She blushed. Shake winked and pushed out through the door.

THE APARTMENT COMPLEX WAS A SERIES of featureless faux-adobe concrete boxes painted the shade of Pepto-Bismol. The sign said MOUNTAIN PALMS, but there were no palms in sight and the closest mountains weren't close.

Shake climbed the metal stairs to the second floor of Building B and knocked on the door to 201.

The peephole blinked light to dark. Then, after a long moment, back to light. A Latina babe in a bathrobe opened the door, chain length, and peered out at Shake.

"Hi," she said. She flashed ferocious dark eyes at him and rattled an aerosol can at him. "Do you want me to pepper-spray you now or wait till after you tell me what the *fuck* you want knocking on my door at eleven o'clock at night?"

"After," Shake said. "Definitely."

"Let's hear it."

"I'm looking for a friend of mine. Gina Clement."

The fierceness in the Latina babe's dark eyes wavered.

"She gave you this address?"

"Sort of."

The Latina babe shut the door. Shake heard the chain slide back. The door opened again, all the way this time. The Latina babe looked like she might be about to cry.

"I can't believe she gave you this address."

"My name's Shake."

"Lucy."

"It was on her work card. She doesn't live here?"

The fierceness in her dark eyes flared again. "*No,* she doesn't live here. *No,* I haven't seen her. *Yes,* I'm gonna kill her if I see her, so if that's why you're here, get in line."

"You want to take it easy with that pepper spray, Lucy?"

"Oh." She slipped the can, which she'd been waving around without much regard to safety, into the pocket of her bathrobe.

"Any idea where she might be?"

"On the moon? I don't know. She blew town, like, a week ago."

"She's back," Shake said.

"I doubt that." Lucy looked Shake over. "So are you her latest?"

"Depends on what you mean by 'latest.' "

Lucy snorted. She seemed to understand what he meant.

"There is this one place she used to go," Lucy said. "A guy she knows has a houseboat there."

"Lake Mead?"

"I don't know the guy's name. Dobney something. Or maybe that's his last name. Did she ever happen to mention me?"

"Mention you?"

"Just in passing or, you know—"

"I think so," Shake said, to be kind. "I'm pretty sure."

"Lake Mead, yeah, but don't waste your time." Suddenly Lucy looked again as if she might cry. "I've already been up there to look for her, like, a hundred times."

SHAKE CROSSED THE PARKING LOT of the Mountain Palms. To his left were the lights of the Strip, a few miles away, smoldering on the horizon. To his right the sky was darker, deeper, richer, and you could even make out a few stars.

Lake Mead.

He shook his head, slid behind the wheel of Vader's Road Runner, and fired it up.

Chapter 18

Lucy watched the guy walk away. She shut her door, bolted it, reattached the chain.

"He's kind of a hottie, isn't he?" Gina asked. She was sprawled on the couch, eating an apple, her bare feet resting on the coffee table. On the third toe of her right foot, she still wore a silver ring Lucy had given her. The weekend trip to the beach, a few weeks after they met. Lucy had found it on the boardwalk in Venice and knew right away it was the perfect gift.

Take it off, please, she wanted to tell Gina but didn't.

"Who is he?" Lucy said.

"Oh, just a guy who gave me a ride back from L.A.," Gina said.

"I'll bet."

"Hey, now, Loosey Screw. Don't be jealous."

"I'm not jealous," Lucy said. It was true. She was just stupid and pathetic. "I'm just stupid and pathetic."

Gina stood up and bounded over and wrapped Lucy up in a big hug.

"Don't say that! You're not. You're loyal and loving, which are excellent qualities in a person."

"In a golden retriever."

But Lucy didn't pull away from the hug, and Gina kept squeezing. Like she could make Lucy believe anything, do anything, be anything, just through the sheer force of herself.

Which of course, Lucy knew, she could.

Gina had been only the second girl Lucy had ever slept with. Until Gina, Lucy had rarely even *thought* of other girls in that way.

Lucy closed her eyes and breathed Gina in—peach and smoke and shimmering vitality. When Lucy opened her eyes, Gina was looking over her shoulder.

Of course.

"We should make sure he's gone," Gina said.

Lucy sighed and went to the window. She peeked through the blinds. Down in the parking lot, the guy, Shake, was unlocking his car door. He *was,* Lucy had to admit, kind of a hottie. She watched him kick gravel at whatever predicament, thanks to Gina, he'd found himself in. Lucy knew the feeling and shook her head without realizing it. He climbed into his car and drove off.

"He's gone." Lucy turned away from the window. Gina already had the wig on. A jet-black number with long braids that Lucy sometimes wore when she danced, part of her Harajuku getup.

"Ah-so," Gina said.

"You're crazy, you know," Lucy said. "You're gonna get us murdered, Gina."

Gina just smiled and examined herself in the living-room mirror. She plucked the cigarette from behind her ear and looked around for her lighter, even though Lucy had asked her a million times to "please smoke on the balcony if you're gonna smoke."

This was not a healthy relationship. Lucy tried to imagine how liberated she might feel if, right now—right this very instant, without a second of hesitation—she snuck her cell phone into the bathroom and sent a secret text message to Jasper. Told him the person he was looking for was sitting on the couch right here in Lucy's apartment.

One little text message and Lucy would be finished with Gina forever.

"I've got to pee," Lucy said. She felt a thrill of guilt and fear and joy and horror, even though she knew she'd never go through with it.

"Okay."

"I'm gonna take my phone in there. Maybe I'll send a text or two."

"Go ahead, Loosey Cannon."

Instead Lucy sighed and flopped down on the couch.

"I thought you had to pee," Gina said.

"I wish you'd smoke on the balcony, if you're gonna smoke."

"This Shake guy is pretty good," Gina mused. She seemed pleased. "He might actually find me someday."

Chapter 19

Jasper put one foot against the wall to the left of the pipe and one foot against the wall to the right of it. He wrapped his hands around the pipe and pulled. The pipe didn't want to come loose, but after a spell it had no choice. Water sprayed everywhere, which gave Jasper an excuse to go home and change clothes before he went to see Mr. Moby.

The handcuffs were still locked tight to his wrist, too, which gave him another excuse, to stop by the trailer of a friend who wasn't a locksmith but had all the tools.

Jasper got to the club around eight. The young bouncer with long, greasy hair in his eyes, the one all the girls thought looked like some rock star or another, was on tonight. He was always friendly and deferential, but Jasper disliked him anyway. Maybe because he was *too* friendly, *too* deferential. Jasper wasn't sure. Maybe it was because Rock Star thought he was pretty when by any sane standard of measurement he wasn't. Maybe it was because one time Rock Star had said to Jasper that he bet Lucy would know how to throw a party, wouldn't she, did Jasper know what he meant, hee-hee? Jasper had just nodded. There was no sense letting someone like Rock Star know your true mind.

"Hey, Jasper!" he said, flipping his long, greasy hair around so it ended up even more in his eyes than it had started. "What's going on, my man? How you been?"

Maybe, above all else, Jasper disliked the boy because he made Jasper picture in his imagination what Mr. Moby might have been like when he was twenty-two, when he was still whip thin and eager to get started on all the evil he'd do in his life.

Not that this pretty-boy Rock Star was ever going to be near as smart as Mr. Moby. Not many people were. Jasper supposed every living one of God's creatures should thank Him for that.

They should probably thank Him that there weren't more people like Jasper, too. Jasper didn't dispute it.

"What happened to your nose, dude?"

"It ain't broke," Jasper said. His friend who wasn't a locksmith also wasn't a doctor but had all the tools for that as well. He'd looked over Jasper's nose and pronounced it fit. "Where's Mr. M?"

"He called and said he'd be in around midnight. He wants you to wait for him. Sounds like he's in a bitch of a mood."

Jasper touched his nose and swallowed two more of the white capsules. He considered how his day had started bad and then—improbably—turned even worse. And now, instead of finally reaching the apex of worseness, the day was going to drag him on behind it like roadkill caught under a car for another four long hours.

"You want a drink while you wait?" Rock Star asked him.

MR. MOBY CURSED HIM BACKWARD and forward, upside and down, spittle flying off him and his teeth glistening with it.

Jasper weathered it impassively, his eyes fixed on a spot just to the left of Mr. Moby's ear. He didn't know if this sort of reaction mitigated or further enflamed Mr. Moby's fury. Jasper was impassive by nature, though, and didn't know how else to act. Plus, he couldn't deny he deserved to be cursed, not after what he'd let happen.

"You know what I should do to you, you dumb fucking shine?"

Jasper didn't want to think about what Mr. Moby would do to him. Or what Mr. Moby would hire men from Los Angeles or Chicago to do to him. These men came in on a plane and left the same day, usually.

Jasper had been one of those men originally. That's how he'd ended up with this job.

"How the Jesus *fuck* do you let some half-wit ex-con errand boy just *walk off* with the fucking girl I've been looking for day and night for a fucking week? And the fucking briefcase, too? Why didn't you give the cocksucker the keys to your car and your fucking *kidney,* too, while you were at it, you dumb motherfucking retard? Do you know how fucking humiliating this is for someone in my position, in the eyes of my business associates?"

Mr. Moby had talked to the Armenians in L.A. before Jasper'd had the chance to fill him in, which had not helped Jasper's position at all.

Mr. Moby took a deep breath because he was out of it, then burped. He was a fat, fat man, but not the jolly kind. And not the weak kind, the ones looked like they might have a heart attack any second. You thought a man like Mr. Moby would ever let a heart attack sneak up and kill him, you were a fool.

"Jesus fucking Christ, Jasper," he said, not quite so loudly and without so much spittle, "I fucking *count* on you!"

That hurt Jasper more than all the rest.

"I'll find them."

"You better fucking believe you'll find them!"

Then suddenly, just like that, Mr. Moby plopped back in his desk chair and chuckled.

"This does remind me of the old days, I gotta admit."

Jasper knew better than to ask.

Mr. Moby sat there for a minute, rocking in his desk chair, savoring what seemed to be a pleasant memory.

"I ever tell you about Laos? Back in the sixties?"

Jasper knew better than to answer.

"Maybe I needed something like this to get my juices flowing again," Mr. Moby said. "I was getting too soft." He savored for another minute his pleasant memory of a less soft time in his life, then noticed Jasper and started cursing him all over again.

Chapter 20

Gina parked the Town Car on the far side of the lot, made sure she had a clear angle on the front entrance of the Jungle, killed the lights. Lucy, in the passenger seat, was trying again to talk her out of the plan, but Gina was only half listening. Or maybe just a quarter. She was busy instead:

- Scoping the front entrance.
- Calculating the odds that the Harajuku disguise would work.
- Trying to ignore the Van Halen song "Panama" that had been going through her head ever since Marvin Oates had told her where he thought the buyer for the foreskins was.
- Picturing Shake baking his brains out in the sun tomorrow at Lake Mead, looking for her and finding zipkus.
- Thinking about the many and varied uses she could make of $5 million.

She knew she wanted to start her own business. She knew she didn't want to blow the money like some idiot, on clothes and jewelry and expensive cars that cost a fortune just to insure. Well, she'd blow some of the money, of course, but then she'd get busy. She had tons of ideas, and not the sort of kooky, half-baked shit your typical stripper came up with in the slow early-evening hours before the club filled up and the world seemed full of hope and possibility. Lucy, for example, bless her heart, had wanted to use her end from the Moby score to build a Disneyland for dogs. Gina tried to talk her out of it, but Lucy held firm. She had been convinced, by Oprah or somebody else on TV, that if you just followed your passion, you'd make millions.

Gina knew that wasn't true. It was one of those things that made you feel warm and gooey inside but had no basis in reality.

Most rich people, Gina knew, got rich in boring but smart ways. By doing boring but smart things. By having a passion for making millions, whatever that took.

One of Gina's ideas: a chain of high-end dry cleaners. These would be places with wood floors and lots of light, comfy chairs and no dry-cleaning smell. Where you could drop off your clothes on the way to the office and pick up a premium nonfat vanilla latte at the same time.

Get it? You take a chore most women dread and you make it not so dreadful. And you give the busy businesswoman a chance to knock off two errands (dry cleaning, latte) with one stop. Like killing two birds with one stone.

Gina wondered if that would make a good name for her company: Two Birds, One Stone. Now, *that* was a philosophy she could get behind.

One thing for sure: As much fun as schemes could be, she wasn't going to spend the rest of her life running them; a little voice told her that the older you got, the less fun the schemes became.

"You know?" Lucy said.

"I know," Gina said. She hadn't been paying any attention and had no idea what Lucy was asking. "I do."

She squeezed Lucy's hand, which she was holding in her lap. Lucy squeezed back, and Gina wondered if they had time to fool around a little, before the shit jumped off.

If only Shake had been here in the car with them, too, Gina considered, wow, that would have been fun for the whole family.

She traced a fingertip along one of Lucy's legs—Lucy had the world's most luscious gams—but then, nope, too late, the doors to the Jungle swung wide. Light spilled into the parking lot, and out stomped the Whale. To say he looked angry would have been a colossal understatement. To say Jasper, following behind, looked unhappy would have been an even bigger one.

"Looks like somebody just got some bad news," Gina said.

Moby and Jasper crossed to the Whale's car, got in, drove off.

"Gina—" Lucy started to try one more time.

Gina pressed her finger to Lucy's lips. "Shhh," she said.

FOO FIGHTER AT THE DOOR didn't recognize Gina in the wig and the makeup.

Lucy, bless her heart, played it perfectly cool.

"Fresh meat for the graveyard shift," she told him, and pushed Gina along with her into the club.

THE KEY TO THE WHALE'S office was right where Gina had ditched it last week when she'd spotted the Whale rumbling down the hallway toward her—on the carpet, against the wall, next to the base of a potted fake fern. Good karma for sure, though not a good reflection on the Jungle's crack team of crackhead Dominican janitors.

Gina knelt and pretended to fix the strap on Lucy's glitter-crusted stacked-heel peep-toe. When the hallway was empty, she slipped the key into the lock.

"Grrr," she said. "Aargh."

"What?" Lucy asked.

"The dipstick changed his locks."

"I thought he did. I told you. And he bought a safe finally."

"I don't need to get into the safe this time."

"Let's please, Gina, just forget this and—"

"Don't worry. I know how to pick a lock."

Not really. But Gina had seen it done on occasion, heard it explained by a former customer, figured how hard could it be, right?

"What if he comes back? Sometimes he comes back."

Gina had come prepared with a lock-pick set she'd borrowed from that former customer a few weeks ago. In anticipation of a moment just like this one.

She slid one pick into the lock and felt around with it. Felt a thingy she could press down. Then she slid the other pick in and sort of turned them both like she'd been instructed.

She was more startled than Lucy by the sharp *click.*

"Hey!" she said. "How'd I do that?"

She hustled Lucy into the Whale's office and shut the door behind them.

"Go unplug the phone and computer cords," she told Lucy, just to keep the girl busy and not flipping out.

Gina shuffled through Moby's Rolodex. It was massive, unfortunately, probably three or four hundred index cards. But she couldn't rush; this was her one shot, and she knew it.

Lucy finished disconnecting the phone and computer cords. She stood by the door with her eyes closed and appeared to have entered the catatonic phase of flipping out, which under the circumstances suited Gina fine. Just as long as she stayed quiet.

But, seriously, *damn*. This was taking forever.

"Just grab the whole fucking thing!" Lucy blurted, her voice rough and panicked.

Gina kept shuffling methodically through the Rolodex and didn't look up.

"He can't notice anything's missing," Gina said. "That's the whole point." She tapped her bean. "You see? Always thinking."

And then, finally, almost to the very last card—there it was. Had to be.

ROLAND ZIEGLER.
PANAMA.

No address, but a phone number.

"Let's go!" Lucy said.

Gina copied Roland Ziegler's phone number onto the inside of her wrist with a ballpoint pen, then put the card back where it belonged.

"Gotcha," Gina said with a smile, as Eddie Van Halen's opening riff started ringing all over again in her head.

Panama . . . ah . . . ah.

BACK IN THE PARKING LOT, Gina took Lucy's hands in both of hers.

"I really appreciate everything you've done for me, Loosey Ends."

"Let me come with you."

"Too risky. I'll call you the minute I cash out. Then we'll hook up on Maui."

"No you won't. We won't."

"I promise! I will!"

Lucy usually wasn't very complicated, but Gina was surprised by the smile Lucy gave her now—resigned and amused and pissed. Heartbroken, but also relieved.

"You promise," she said.

"I do!" Gina protested. But before she could go on, Lucy gave her a quick kiss to shut her up.

"Take care of yourself, okay?" Lucy said. Then she turned and walked away and hailed one of the cabs that lurked along the east side of the Jungle.

How, Gina wondered, did Lucy know she was lying about Maui, when Gina herself hadn't even realized it until a second ago?

That question, and Lucy's walking away without a smile or a wave back at her, made Gina feel a little melancholy.

She climbed into the Town Car and fired it up, then rolled down her window, because this time of night, three in the morning, the breeze in the desert was never cooler, never sweeter.

Before she could shift into drive, though, a bright red muscle car rolled up in front of her, cutting her off.

She felt a little trill of excitement—fight! flight!

Shake!

He strolled over, rested his forearms on her open window, smiled.

She smiled back.

Chapter 21

Mr. Vanilla Milk Shake," she said.

"What's a nice girl like you doing in a place like this?" he said.

Shake supposed he should be mad at her for everything she'd done to him, and he was. But more than mad, he was relieved, especially when he spotted the briefcase she'd stolen lying in the backseat behind her.

And, oddly, more than relieved, he was just happy to see her again.

Eyes a pale green in this light. Crooked smile. Dusting of freckles across the bridge of her interesting nose. Shake had liked Gina's face the first time he saw it, but he found it even more appealing now that he'd had a glimpse of what was really behind it.

"I just knew it," she said. "I had a feeling."

"Did you?"

"That you were following us."

"Your sexy friend doesn't lie nearly as well as you do."

"She's got a heart of gold," Gina confided.

"What's your heart made of?"

She scoffed. "Who needs a heart these days?"

She was looking in the rearview mirror. Shake decided to provide assistance.

"There's a car parked behind you. I'm parked in front of you. You're not going anywhere."

"Why would I want to go anywhere?" she asked with surprise that seemed so genuine that Shake had to think, or hope, at least part of it might be.

Then, "Sexier than me?"

"I'd lose the Pocahontas wig," Shake said. "It doesn't really suit you."

She seemed suddenly to remember the black wig with braids and peeled it off.

"Are you gonna answer the question?" she asked.

"Sexy is subjective," he said. "It's in the eye of the beholder."

"Does that approach really work on some girls?" she said, amused. "Where you pretend you're not that interested? Throw them off and make them wonder?"

"You're sexier than your friend with the heart of gold and the great legs," he admitted. "Yes."

"Was that so hard?"

Shake smiled, though, because he could see that Gina couldn't help wondering how her own legs stacked up. But the hell if she was gonna let *him* know that.

"I was thinking earlier," she said. "It's like *Snow White.* You know? The evil queen sends her huntsman to kill Snow White. He takes her into the woods, but then he feels sorry for her and lets her go."

"Funny. I don't remember Snow White drugging the huntsman, cuffing him to a bathroom sink, and robbing him blind."

"I'm pretty sure it's in there. You should rent the DVD."

And with that she grinned, jerked into reverse, cut the wheel hard to the right, punched the gas. The Town Car's nose whipped left, almost knocking Shake on his ass. The back bumper clipped the Honda Civic parked behind. The Civic, much lighter than the Town Car, lurched sideways, and Gina, cranking her wheel, careened backward through the gap.

"Shit," Shake said. He hopped back into Vader's Road Runner and took off after her. He gunned toward the parking-lot exit to cut her off, but she anticipated that and—still in reverse—jumped the curb behind him. By the time he made it onto the Strip, she was at least several blocks ahead of him.

Good luck with that, he thought. No Lincoln Town Car in the world was going to win a race with a 1969 Plymouth Road Runner that could do the quarter mile in thirteen seconds. Even discounting, Shake thought modestly, the professional wheelman who was making that run.

He ate up the distance between them in about a heartbeat.

Gina slalomed between two cabs and stomped it on the straightaway.

"Huh," Shake mused to the miniature travel gnome hanging by a miniature noose from the rearview, "all that and the girl can drive, too."

He slalomed around the same two cabs. Gina glanced in her mirror at him. Shake lifted a finger off the wheel to wave.

"Better watch the road," he counseled her as they neared the south end of the Strip, where traffic was heavier, even at three in the morning. Up ahead, across from the Venetian, a fender bender had locked up most of the southbound lanes.

Gina pounded the brakes and squealed to a stop a foot from the back of a city bus.

Shake stopped, too, several cars back, and climbed out of Vader's Road Runner.

A drunk panhandler on the corner noticed Shake. He glanced around to remind himself where he was, then tuned his pitch accordingly.

"Mi amico," he said. "Spare a little something for the troops?"

Shake tossed him the keys to Vader's Road Runner.

"All yours," he said. "Treat her right."

The panhandler looked at the keys. Looked at the car.

Shake walked up the line of cars. Gina was pounding her horn, but traffic was barely inching forward. He tapped the barrel of Jasper's .45 against her passenger window.

She slapped the horn once more, in frustration, then hit the button and unlocked the doors.

Shake slid in next to her.

"What do you say," he suggested, "we go somewhere quiet to talk?"

Chapter 22

Gina stewed and steamed all the way to Caesar's. He directed her to pull off there and park in the big garage. When she killed the engine, he held out his hand. Gina pretended for a second she didn't know what he wanted—she figured it was worth a try—then dropped the car keys in his palm. He set them on the dash but kept the gun in his hand.

She didn't think he'd actually shoot her, but she'd been wrong about these sorts of things before, so she played it cool.

Funny thing? She was glad, in a way, he'd caught her. Or maybe she was glad he was the one who caught her, if someone was going to do it.

He smelled nice, like lavender.

"Did you take a shower?"

"No," he said, "but I did use shampoo. Thanks for noticing."

"You're not gonna give me up, are you? The Whale's a bad fella, Shake, I'm not fooling."

"So you thought it would be a good idea to rip him off?"

She giggled. "You heard about that, huh?"

"I'm all up to speed on you now."

She doubted that. So did he, by the way he was looking at her. She liked that look.

"Almost three hundred large. Cash. Sweet."

"Till Moby put the word out and the Armenians dinged you in L.A."

"I mean, what are the odds? A whole big city, and that lady with the gray eyes, she and I end up at the same party?"

"You'd be surprised how the odds don't apply when you most need them to. That's been my unfortunate experience." Then he said, "No."

She worked back. "No you're not going to give me up?"

"I'm going to bring that briefcase to the gray-eyed lady you mentioned and hope she forgives and forgets."

"She's your boss?" she asked, testing him. He was a guy, after all.

"She's not my boss."

"But you work for her?" All innocent.

"Does that approach work on some guys?" he said.

Gina smiled. "She'll do that, you think? Forgive and forget?"

It was the first time, really, since she'd met him, that he didn't look calm and sure of himself. He'd managed to look calm and sure of himself—vanilla milk shake, cool like ice cream—even when she'd handcuffed him to the pipe under the sink.

"I think she harbors a certain fondness for me that may, possibly—if I'm lucky, if she's in a good mood, if professional considerations don't factor too heavily—may inform her decision."

"What are the odds, right?"

He sighed. "What are the odds Moby's bagman would find me, this entire city, in less than half a day?"

She scooted over a little closer to him and put her hand on his knee.

"So listen," she said. "Here's an idea."

He lifted her hand off his knee. He set it back on the steering wheel.

"I'm taking the stamps," he said.

"They're not stamps."

"I don't care."

"They're foreskins."

He looked at her.

"You don't want to know," she said. "It's a long story. But the important thing—"

"I'm taking them. Whatever they are."

"Don't you want to know what they're worth?"

"Definitely not."

She held up a finger. Then another one. Then three, four, and a thumb. She gave him a Queen Elizabeth wave, all wrist.

He wanted to ask. Gina knew he did. So she waited. She could wait, when necessary, with the best of them. Sure enough, after a second . . .

"Five hundred grand?" he asked.

"Five million."

She liked that his eyes didn't go wide, that he didn't whistle or say "Holy shit." He kept his cool.

"How do you know that?"

"Gets better," she said. "I have the name of the guy the Whale was going to sell them to."

"The foreskins."

"I know. It's weird. They're ancient religious relics or something. They used to keep them in cathedrals, in special relic holders."

"Reliquaries."

"Wow!"

"I grew up in New Orleans," he explained. "Everyone's a Catholic."

"Roland Ziegler is the guy's name."

Shake laughed. Gina didn't like not having any idea why.

"What?"

"Roland Ziegler is the buyer?"

"So?"

"Roland Ziegler is a ghost."

"A ghost like dead?"

"A ghost like invisible."

"Explain, please." She was enjoying this: It was like a business conference, it was like they were already partners.

"Roland Ziegler is a fugitive. The DOJ's been wanting him in a bad way for nine, ten years."

"Who'd he kill?"

"That's not why the DOJ would want you in a bad way."

Gina considered. "Money."

"Very good," Shake said. His approval gave Gina a little tingle, she was embarrassed to admit. She put her hand back on his knee. He picked it up and set it right on the steering wheel again. "He managed a hedge fund back in the nineties. I know about him because he helped the Armenians set up some burn companies."

"But that's not why the feds want him."

"No. His big play, he swindled a bunch of old folks out of their retirement savings. I heard he cleared north of a hundred million. Probably an exaggeration, but probably not much of one. The feds busted him, but he got bail and bounced before the ink was dry. He's not been seen nor heard from since."

"A hundred million. That means he can afford to buy himself some foreskins, doesn't it?"

"Did I mention the DOJ's been hunting him for nine, ten years? Did I mention he's not been seen nor heard from since? Did I mention he's invisible?"

"I know where he is."

"Panama?"

"Hey! You know?"

"That's one rumor." He shrugged. "Croatia is another one. Penang, too, I think."

"Well, Mr. Cool, I know for *certain* he's in Panama."

She told him about the index card she'd found in the Whale's Rolodex. And the phone number.

Shake laughed again. Again, Gina didn't like not knowing why.

"What's so funny, sport?"

He dug around in the glove box, found a cell phone, handed it to her. "Call the number," he said.

"Where'd you get this?" she asked.

"It came with you, the car, and all the trouble I'm in. Call the number."

"Fine," she said. She read the number off the inside of her wrist, dialed, put the phone on speaker. After a few rings, a woman's recorded voice said something in Spanish. Then the same woman's voice told them in English they'd reached Anita's Bakery in Panama City, Panama. Please place your order at the beep.

Gina killed the call. "I must have dialed the wrong number."

"It's not the wrong number. It's a telephone dead drop."

She frowned. "You have to know what to order."

"The code. That's my guess."

Gina shrugged it away. Minor setback. "We know he's in Panama for sure, then. That's something."

"A capital city of seven hundred thousand inhabitants. Throw in, once you get out of the city, remote jungles, inaccessible mountains, private islands, a culture of corruption, and a guy, with money to burn, who doesn't want to be found."

"You want me to do the math, right?"

"I hate that cliché."

"Me, too." Gina considered. "Panama. I thought there was just a canal."

"The country is a beautiful, fascinating, undiscovered gem."

"And a tailor. And a hat."

"The hat was actually invented in Ecuador."

"Do a lot of reading in the joint, did you?"

"*New York Times* Sunday travel section, cover to cover. You can understand why. I hear the food down there's good."

"Fine. We go down there and flush his multimillion-dollar ass out of hiding."

Shake started to laugh and almost said, *How we gonna do that?* Just as Gina expected. But then he stopped himself. Gina expected that, too.

Shake studied her briefly. She enjoyed the moment.

"It's not a half-bad idea," he said slowly. "But it's not a half-good one either."

"He wants these foreskins. If we put the word out, he'll come to us."

"If we're not careful, he won't be the only one."

"So we'll be careful. We'll sell out and split the take, fifty-fifty."

He studied her some more.

"Or you can just go back to your lady boss and explain what happened. I'm sure she's very fond of you. I know I am, and I've barely known you twenty-four hours."

"Well, we've been through a lot together, Gina," he said.

Gina smiled. She liked that he could tease her and at the same time still be serious (his mind turning and turning—she could see it in his eyes) about what she was proposing. She liked that he didn't seem to be trying to talk himself into, or out of, the idea but was just squaring the corners up in his mind, taking a cool, objective look at all the angles.

"If we're gonna do this," he said finally, and Gina felt a bounce of happiness, "I need to know what they—these foreskins—are really worth. If they're really foreskins. Which a large part of me hopes they're not."

"I told you already," she said, "they're worth five million dollars."

"Your source?"

Gina shifted uncomfortably in her seat. "An expert," she said.

"What I thought," he said. "Forgive me if I'd prefer some independent verification."

"So what do you suggest?"

"You're the local girl."

She thought about it while Shake took the car keys off the dash and jiggled them in the hand that wasn't holding the gun.

"That's making me nervous," she said.

"Good."

"Wait!" She remembered a regular of hers, a shy, awkward, older guy who always wore a tie and a corduroy jacket to the club. He was a professor at UNLV. "I know someone who might know something. Let's go!"

Shake just jiggled the keys in his hand for another minute. Gina had the feeling he wasn't merely trying to decide whether or not he wanted to visit this someone who might know something about the worth of the foreskins; he was trying to decide whether or not he wanted in on the $5 million. With her.

She remembered the same look on his face back in the motel room this morning—yesterday morning?—when he'd been trying to decide whether or not to give her up to Jasper.

She didn't understand his ambivalence now. This deal was a total no-brainer!

"That fucking Van Halen song," he said at last, "has been going through my head for the past fifteen minutes."

"Tell me about it."

He stopped jiggling and handed the keys to her.

"Okay," he said. "What the hell."

Chapter 23

Dawn was just starting to crack over the eastern mountains when they arrived at UNLV, so they parked in the lot by the arena to kill some time. Gina fell asleep like *that,* boom, or pretended to. Shake stayed awake. He had been in Las Vegas now for less than twenty-four hours, out of stir for less than forty-eight. He started tallying up everything that had happened to him in that time period, then gave up halfway down the list. In prison you could go weeks, sometimes months, without the slightest bump in the routine, a kind of heavy sucking boredom that was more likely to permanently damage you than a sharpened toothbrush in the shower room or a shot of bad pruno.

Shake acknowledged he had not been bored at any time during the past forty-eight hours; he could definitely say that.

He told himself that going to Panama—if these foreskins were worth $5 million, if they really were foreskins—was the smart play. He needed some leverage if he was going to survive Alexandra and Dikran and Dick Moby; that, or he needed a lot of cash to outrun them.

But it really *wasn't* the smart play—partnering up with a woman who met almost every single conceivable requirement of a person you'd never in a million years want to partner up with.

So why was he even considering this? Where had his newfound appetite for unhealthy risk come from? He wasn't sure. Maybe something had snapped in him yesterday morning, back at the Apache Motor Inn, when he'd decided to whack Jasper with the phone book. Maybe at that instant the old Shake (who eluded hard decisions whenever possible and preferred to go with life's gentle if unreliable flow), maybe that guy had died of shock and astonishment. Was even now lying dead on the floor of that motel room, a red rubber ball with teeth marks on the carpet next to his head.

Gina wasn't hard on the eyes, and the girl had a kind of sparkle he'd never encountered before, but Shake knew he'd deserve every bad thing that would happen to him if he went into this on the basis of *sparkle.*

"You're frowning," Gina said. She was awake now, and watching him. It was a little after eight.

"Let's go," he said.

They drove across campus and parked outside Wright Hall, an ultramodern tricolored building that looked more like the prison of the future than a college building. On the third floor, they found the office for Dr. Reginald Gorsch, Department of History.

Dr. Gorsch was a long-faced, long-necked guy hunched over a laptop. When he looked up from his screen and saw Gina standing in the doorway, when he adjusted his glasses and still saw Gina standing in the doorway, he swallowed several times in quick succession. Shake watched his Adam's apple bob up and down, up and down that long neck.

"Hi, Doc," Gina said brightly. "What's shakin'?"

Dr. Gorsch looked at her with yearning, then alarm.

"Oh," he said.

"Don't worry, Doc," Gina said, shutting the office door behind them. "I'm not here to get you in trouble."

Ha, Shake thought.

IT TOOK A FEW MINUTES to convince Dr. Gorsch they were not there to rob, extort, or blackmail him. It took another few minutes to assure him they did not consider his twice-a-week strip-club habit a defect of character.

"It's only research, you see," he explained urgently to Shake. "I'm thinking of writing a screenplay, and I just thought—"

"Research is important," Shake said.

"It really is!" He fiddled with items on his desk and almost accidentally stapled his hand to a *Vista for Dummies* book.

"That's why we're here," Gina explained. "We're doing some historical research and want to ask you some questions."

Dr. Gorsch brightened. "Tudor-Stuart England?"

"Not exactly," Shake said. They didn't have time to beat around the bush, so he took a calculated risk and told the truth, or at least some of it: They had in their possession some potentially valuable religious relics and wanted to know just how potentially valuable they were.

Gina held up the briefcase and did a little spokesmodel flourish with her hand.

"Religious relics?" Dr. Gorsch's long face fell. It took a while. "I'm sorry, that's not at all my area of expertise. You'll want to talk to someone with a background in medieval—"

"But I want to talk to *you,* Doc," Gina said. She put some extra-sexy English on her wink that made even Shake, at the edge of the blast radius, tingle a bit.

Dr. Gorsch swallowed. "Well, I know a *little* about the market for religious relics," he said. "There are collectors, I've heard. A very gray world. Not illegal, exactly, but the Catholic Church takes a dim view, as you might imagine. A few relics *can* be quite valuable, theoretically, but I doubt unless you've found the crown of thorns that—"

"We have a hundred foreskins," Gina said.

Dr. Gorsch looked at her. She held up the briefcase again. Another spokesmodel flourish.

"You have the hundred foreskins?" he said.

"The?" Shake said.

"You've heard of them?"

"Oh, my," Dr. Gorsch said. "Of course. They're the holy grail of religious artifacts."

"Wouldn't the Holy Grail be the holy grail of relics?" Shake asked.

"Common misconception." Dr. Gorsch, in his element now, went to one of his bookcases and started digging around. "A billionaire in London has that. Apparently the Vatican's been trying to buy it back forever. Apparently the asking price is outrageous, the *Laocoön* or something like that."

"I thought you didn't know anything about relics?" Gina said.

Dr. Gorsch snorted. "I don't." He found the book he was looking for: a big, black, leather-bound Bible. "All this is just the most basic common knowledge."

Gina gave Shake a glance. "What did I tell you? Smart guy."

Dr. Gorsch flipped through the Bible. "Here it is. First Samuel, chapter eighteen. David wanted to marry King Saul's daughter. Of course Saul would never let his daughter marry some peasant, a mere shepherd. So he told David he could marry his daughter if, and only if, David could prove his worth."

"How?" Gina asked.

"He had to go forth, alone, and bring back to Saul the foreskins of one hundred Philistine warriors."

"Which, just guessing," Shake said, "Saul knew the Philistines would not part with happily."

Dr. Gorsch nodded, then paused to absentmindedly finger his long neck like he was playing a guitar. "The Philistines, you know, have been treated quite unfairly by history. They were actually quite culturally advanced. In fact—"

"Doc," Gina said, "focus."

"Right. Yes. Well, of course it was a suicide mission. Saul knew that David had no chance of success whatsoever. But he did it, David did.

He went out, killed a hundred Philistine warriors, and brought their foreskins back to Saul."

"What did Saul do?" Shake asked. "After asking David to wash his hands, I mean."

"He told David the foreskins were only a start. Now David had to go out and kill the giant Philistine Goliath, who'd been wreaking havoc on Saul's army. Never in a million years, Saul was certain, would David survive that encounter. But if he did, if he killed Goliath, that suited Saul's purposes, too. We all know what happened next, of course."

"I like his style," Gina said.

"David?" Dr. Gorsch asked.

"Saul. He knew how to get behind the wheel of a bargain and drive it. Va-va-vroom."

Dr. Gorsch straightened his glasses and tapped away at his laptop.

"Let's see. Yes. The hundred foreskins. There's a record of their provenance up through 1939, a defrocked Jesuit in Belgium. Then the war, of course, the Nazis, and everything after that is just rumor and hearsay and collectors searching fruitlessly."

"So do you have any idea what they're worth?" Shake asked.

Dr. Gorsch grinned suddenly. "This is the most fun I've had in months. You know in the old horror movies? When the grizzled old professor with the dusty books explains how you can kill a werewolf only if you're pure of heart?"

"And have a gun with a big silver bullet."

"Ahem," Gina said.

"Right," Dr. Gorsch said. He turned his attention back to his laptop. "What are they worth? Oh, my. Hard to say. I suppose, and I paraphrase my colleagues in the dismal science, they're worth whatever a buyer will pay for them."

"Not five million bucks, though," Shake said. "Right?"

Dr. Gorsch fingered the frets of his long neck. "Possibly. According to this site, St. Agatha's vertebrae sold for two million dollars a couple of years ago. Your foreskins would bring at least that, I'd think. Probably much more. They're more unusual, and they've got to be at least eight, nine hundred years old."

Shake opened his mouth, but Gina beat him to it.

"Wait a minute," she said. "I'm no college professor, but . . . David and Goliath? I'm pretty sure that was a lot longer than eight or nine hundred years ago."

Dr. Gorsch looked at her blankly. "Well, of course."

"But then—"

"Your foreskins aren't *real,*" Dr. Gorsch said. "Well, of course they're real foreskins, but they're not the actual ones David removed from the Philistines. Probably they're from monks, or medieval peasants who were paid for their service or who thought they'd improve their odds on Judgment Day."

"They're fakes?" Gina said.

"Most religious relics are." Dr. Gorsch chuckled. "You don't think that billionaire in London has the actual Holy Grail, do you?"

Shake had thought so, actually.

"But—"

"It has no effect on the value," Dr. Gorsch said. "What matters is the rarity of the counterfeit, the age, the quality. The narrative behind it. You have to understand, these relics were venerated for centuries and centuries. In some cases they were created by men and women who later *became* saints. City-states went to war over purloined relics. They might be fake in the strictest sense, the motives behind them might have been venal at the time—you know, one trying to advance one's prospects to become a cardinal—but eventually the counterfeits themselves became singularly unique religious artifacts of great historical significance. Sometimes the fakes are more valuable than the real relics, depending on the circumstances."

Shake took a second to wrap his head around all that. He would have suspected that Dr. Gorsch was fucking with them, except that Dr. Gorsch was clearly not the kind of guy who fucked with anyone. Still . . .

"You're fucking with us, aren't you?"

"What? No!"

"Ahem, ahem, ahem," Gina said. "Our foreskins?"

"Very rare," Dr. Gorsch said. "Very unique. The bones of saints were everywhere back then. Mark Twain, if you recall that amusing passage in *Innocents Abroad,* claims there were enough nails and pieces from the true cross in the cathedrals across Europe to build a small town. But your foreskins—there's never been a record of anything else remotely like them. Whoever came up with the idea of faking such a relic, he had extraordinary imagination."

"Or extraordinary something," Shake said.

Dr. Gorsch jumped to another site on his laptop. Scanned the page.

"Hmmm," he said. "Apparently many scholars think the man behind the foreskins might have been the Coeur de Lion himself."

"The Lion Heart?" Gina asked.

Shake turned to her. "You speak French?"

"*C'est en forgeant qu'on devient forgeron,* sport."

"Richard the First," Dr. Gorsch continued. "Yes. That's why the foreskins would have been so valuable right from their creation." He continued to tap away at his keyboard. Blue light from the screen flashed in the lenses of his glasses. "According to this—interesting—Dante himself might have owned the foreskins at one point. Machiavelli lost them in a card game to Pope Clement VII. They ended up eventually with Julius II, who traded them to France so they'd stay on the sidelines when he marched on Bologna. By the time Martin Luther came around, they were so famous, so beloved, he didn't dare burn them with all the other relics."

"Okay," Shake said, "I'm following. But five million? You're sure?"

"Well, no," Dr. Gorsch said, "but I think that's a fair ballpark figure."

"I like that ballpark," Gina said. So did Shake, though he knew better than to get his hopes up yet. And, he reminded himself, if what was in that briefcase really *was* worth $5 million—Alexandra wouldn't stop looking for it.

Shake noticed that Dr. Gorsch was staring at the briefcase in Gina's hand.

"May I, do you think," he said, "just for moment, perhaps . . . ?"

Shake considered, then nodded to Gina. She popped the snaps and turned the briefcase toward Dr. Gorsch.

Dr. Gorsch looked nonplussed. "I don't understand," he said.

Shake leaned over to see for himself. The interior glass case—with the foreskins—was gone; the briefcase was empty.

Shake turned to Gina. She stared down into the empty briefcase like she was about to laugh, to throw up, to burst into tears. Shake didn't think anyone, not even someone with the advanced deceptive skills of Gina, could fake all three of those at once.

"There's no way!" Gina said. "Fuck! Fuck! I had it with me the whole time, I never once even—"

She stopped. Shake waited. Gina closed her eyes.

"I'm going to murder him," she said, so softly that Shake could barely hear her.

Chapter 24

Gina tossed Shake the keys to the Town Car so he could drive. She was steaming, so mad at herself she could barely stand it. They hauled ass across town to the strip mall and parked a few doors down from Marvin Oates Fine Jewelry and Pawn. The shop was supposed to open at ten, but by eleven there was still no sign of life.

"He's gone," Shake said.

Gina remembered pushing open the exit door to smoke. She remembered thinking she saw something in the shadows, by the alley Dumpster. She'd had her back turned to Marvin Oates for like all of two flipping seconds.

How could she be such a dipstick to let that creep steal her foreskins? Right from under her nose? She resolved to quit smoking at the earliest opportunity. Dangerous, stupid habit—see where it got you?

She'd started smoking at age thirteen, because her other friends were too chicken to try it. Because she'd watched Faye Dunaway in *Bonnie and Clyde* on TV. Because it was five minutes every evening, sitting out on the porch steps, when she and her mother had something in common.

"You don't think he'll show up eventually?" she asked.

"Would you?" Shake said.

"I'd go to Panama."

"Exactly."

"Maybe he didn't," she said. "Maybe he left them inside, and he overslept, and he's just running late this morning."

Gina shut up. She was out of straws to grasp at. "He's not the brightest star in the sky," she said.

"What's that make you?" Shake said. The way he was looking at her—the twinkle in his eye, a smile tugging one corner of his mouth—he was enjoying this way too much.

"What's that make *you*?" she fired back.

"Fair point."

"How far ahead of us is he, do you think?"

"Let's find out," Shake said.

They drove a mile or so west and found an Internet café. Shake paid for half an hour on one of the computers, and Gina pulled up the flight schedules. A Continental nonstop had left Las Vegas at 7:00 A.M. It was due to arrive in Panama City, Panama, at 6:00 P.M.

Gina pulled up more flights. Looked at her watch. Shitburgers.

"The best we can do is a four-o'clock through Dallas that doesn't get us in till tomorrow morning."

"Shitburgers?"

"Did I say that out loud?"

"I doubt he'll be able to find Ziegler and make a deal by tomorrow morning," Shake said.

"So you're saying we still have a shot."

"I'm saying I don't have any other options."

She nodded. Shake's gray-eyed lady boss. He didn't say anything for a second. Gina started to worry he was remembering he *did* have another option, which was to give her up to the Whale, or to his boss, and try to save his own butt.

But then he said, "I'll need a passport."

"I know someone you can go to," she said. "How much money do you have?"

"How much of *my* money do *you* have left?" he asked.

"Sheesh. Ever heard of bygones? Letting them be?"

"How much?"

"Enough to cover a passport. It'll be my treat." She swept her hand magnanimously across the Internet café.

"Generous," he said. "But then how are we gonna pay for the plane tickets?"

Oh. Gina hadn't thought of that.

"Well, we can—"

"Forget it," he said. "I found a couple of grand in a shoe."

"Your shoe? What?" She'd searched his shoes, back at Treasure Island yesterday morning.

He was already heading toward the exit. "We'll go dutch," he said.

Chapter 25

The passport acquisition went off without a hitch, which in light of recent events Shake found a refreshing change of pace. The old guy Gina sent him in to see—while she slouched down in the front seat of the Town Car, the brim of her baseball cap pulled low—had a monster, state-of-the-art computer-scanner-printer rig in the basement of his smoke shop.

"I've got to give you an old one," the guy explained to Shake. "Issued in '05, but that still gives you a few years before it expires. The new ones they changed to, holographs and shit and embedded biometric microchips, those fuckers I got to contract out now, piecework, you know, and it's a total pain in my ass. My profit on those fuckers don't make it hardly worth the pain in my ass."

He scowled as he snapped Shake's picture with a digital camera.

"That's the federal government," Shake said, "always screwing it up for the workingman."

"You got that right," the guy growled. Twenty minutes later, Shake walked out of the shop with a passport.

At the airport Shake told Gina to wait in the car again, short-term parking, while he went inside to buy tickets. They needed to keep her public exposure in Vegas to a minimum.

"How do I know you won't just get on the plane by yourself and ditch me here?"

"The thought's occurred to me," he admitted. As it continued to. "But I'm not going to ditch you."

"You mind I ask why?"

"I'd tell you if I knew."

He went inside and bought tickets. Half an hour before their flight was scheduled to depart, they blew through security, no waiting, hit the gate just as the plane was about to board.

"Hey!" Gina said when she saw her boarding pass. "This is coach!"

"We're on a budget this trip," Shake said.

She scowled at him, but before she could respond, they were joined in line by a big group of middle-aged men in suits. A dozen of them, faces flushed and ties loosened, laughing too loudly, slapping one another on the back, glancing around the gate area to gauge the effect of their contagious (they assumed) bonhomie. Each one wore a small purple name tag stuck to his lapel.

Shake stole a glance at a couple of their boarding passes. Checked the row numbers against his boarding pass. Winced.

"How long is this flight?" Shake asked Gina.

"You're right," she said, a serious, responsible look on her face. "First class is an extravagance we can scant afford."

"I don't sound like that."

"Mmm-hmm."

The purple-tagged businessman in line right behind them shoved a big, beefy hand at Shake.

"Hey, there," he said. "George Pirtle."

Another purple-tagged businessman peered over his buddy's shoulder and grinned at Shake. "Like 'turtle,' but with a *p* instead of a *t*."

This triggered, among the purple-tagged businessmen in the vicinity, a fresh round of booming hilarity and backslapping. A couple of them started chanting, "Turtle, Turtle," but that died out when a female flight attendant walked past. She triggered a round of snickering and rib-nudging.

Shake winced again.

"I'm sure first class is just as bad," Gina said, and gave him a snickering rib-nudge.

FIRST THING: FUCKING FLIGHT IS CANCELED. After the plane sits on the tarmac for four hours at LAX. Four hours! Almost the time it takes to drive to fucking Las Vegas! To drive and stop for a hamburger along the way!

Second thing: No more flights to Las Vegas tonight. To Las Vegas? The fucking tourism capital of the entire world?

"There are no more available seats on any other flights tonight," the airline person at the counter clarified.

"Then you should clarify that first time," Dikran told him.

So he could drive and get there in four, five hours. Or he could wait till the first flight in the morning and get there in ten. Dikran called and checked with her. She sighed and said, "Just take the first flight in the morning, Dikran, I don't care. Just find him, yes? Et cetera?"

Oh, yes. Dikran would find him. And the et cetera to follow would be pleasurable beyond imagination. That ass-lick. Dikran didn't want to wait. So he went downstairs to the rental-car counters, because he'd left his car at home and taken a blue van to the airport.

Third thing: No rental cars available. At LAX? Biggest fucking airport on the West Coast?

"Sorry."

Sorry.

Fourth thing: First flight in the morning is delayed. Two hours on the tarmac.

Fifth thing: First flight in the morning is carrying a girls' college softball team to a tournament in Las Vegas. Occidental College girls' softball team. Twenty girls, all around him, tan buttery skin and glittery blond fur on their cheeks. A smell like fruit and candy and buttery tan skin. The smell drives the Little Soldier in Dikran's lap mad.

All this bad luck: Dikran felt furious, like poison was steaming from his pores. God wanted to punish him. Well, Dikran wanted to punish God back.

The plane stopped. The bell dinged at last. Dikran snapped off his belt. The college softball player next to him reached into the overhead bin for her bag. Her shirt rode up when she reached, and now suddenly he stared at a slice of buttery tan stomach skin. A gold ring in the belly button. The Little Soldier—fucking testosterone patch!—begged Dikran to touch that belly button. Just a touch—she would never notice. With your tongue, Dikran, quick.

He looked quickly away. Counted backward from ten like she had advised him to do when such issues arose.

Belly Button Girl moved up the aisle, and Dikran followed. He trudged with all the other passengers out of the airplane and into the plastic tube, then out of the plastic tube and into the airport. Trudging, trudging, slowly, even now, because at the head of the line like a parade marshal was an old person in a wheelchair.

Belly Button Girl in front of him, the skin on her back between pants and shirt, it was buttery tan skin, too, like her stomach, with a little tattoo there, right where—

Dikran looked quickly away. Counted backward from ten again.

Ten, nine, eight, seven—

Dikran stopped counting.

He squinted to sharpen the focus of his eyes.

The gate next to this gate. These people trudging from the airport *into* a different plastic tube, *onto* a different airplane.

The girl.

And. Dikran shivered with joy. Next to her in the line: *Shake.* That ass-lick! Right there in the airport next to him!

Moving into the plastic tube. Nowhere to hide.

"LET ME GUESS," GEORGE PIRTLE SAID.

He was seated on the aisle, with Gina at the window and Shake squeezed between. Three of his purple-tagged buddies occupied the row directly in front of them, another three the row directly behind.

"You two are newlyweds."

"In a manner of speaking," Gina said.

"Thought so. In my line of work, you gotta be able to read a person like *that.*" He snapped his fingers, grinned, and waited for them to bite. When they didn't, he said, "Friendmaking! People who don't know better call it sales, but it's not about product. I've got great product, sure, do not get me wrong. Want to guess?"

"Buttercup," Gina asked Shake, "do we have any of that Dramamine left? I don't want to blow chunks again like last time."

Shake squeezed the bridge of his nose. "Sorry, sweetpea. Just try not to miss the bag this time."

"Feline nutritional systems," George Pirtle continued, unfazed. He let that sink in.

"Cat food?" Gina said.

"Cat food? Oh, no. No, no, no. Exactly *not* cat food. Much, much *more* than cat food. I have an analogy I like to use—"

"Turtle!" One of the guys in the row behind stuck his head over. "Introduce us to this lovely young lady."

George Pirtle shot him cold daggers for the interruption but went ahead and ticked off the names of all six purple-tags, fore and aft. The last guy, the one seated directly in front of Gina, was named Ted Boxman.

"Like 'cocksman,'" Pirtle said, "but with a *b* instead of a *c.*"

This triggered, among the purple-tags, both laughter and snickering, both shoulder-slapping and rib-nudging. Only the Cocksman himself did not join in. He closed his eyes and leaned his forehead against the seat in front of him.

"You guys headed to what? A sales conference?" Shake couldn't figure out the purple tags on their lapels. Printed in small letters above George Pirtle's name was: BUILDING BRIDGES INTERNATIONAL.

George Pirtle gave Shake a sly look. "You might say that," he said. He waited again for Shake or Gina to bite. They didn't.

"Ladies and gentlemen." The captain's voice crackled over the public-address system. "The tower informs me traffic's stacked up a little out there on the runway, so looks like we're gonna have a short delay."

"Back to that analogy," George Pirtle said. "What cat food is to our enhanced feline nutritional system—"

Shake unbuckled his seat belt.

"We can get a drink in the terminal?" Gina asked.

Shake stood up. "Please."

DIKRAN NUDGED BELLY BUTTON GIRL to the side. She sat down on the floor of the airport and looked up at him with wide eyes.

"Hey!"

"Hey," he agreed. He pushed through the people toward the other gate. Nudging.

"Sir!" a flight attendant yelled to him. "Sir! Please wait your turn!"

Okay, Mr. Fancy-Pants Flight Attendant, Dikran thought, *if you can* make *me wait my turn, I will.*

But then—he was almost to the front of line, almost to the parade marshal in the wheelchair—Dikran noticed a man turn to see what the commotion was.

The man was calm. He wore a nice suit but had a big, heavy wrist-watch on his wrist. A thick wrist. Too thick. Too calm.

Dikran stopped nudging. He was no genius, he knew, but when it came to some things—certain important survival things—his senses were finely tuned. He would be dead a hundred times over by now, one of those rotting bodies in the cargo container back in Armenia (summer of 1983, remember?), if this had not been so.

The calm man in the suit was a federal air marshal, armed.

"Sir! Please return to your place in line!"

Dikran would like to pop the frantic little fancy-pants flight attendant's melon. Instead . . .

"I'm so sorry, sir," he said politely. "Of course. Please pardon my eagerness for our arrival."

The flight attendant puffed up with triumph. After a second, like he was a pasha, he deemed Dikran worthy of conditional forgiveness and nodded curtly.

Dikran returned to his place in line. Shake was on the plane now. Dikran waited. Waited. *Fuck fuck fuck!* Finally the old person with the wheelchair was wheeled away and the line moved fast.

The federal marshal was standing by a trash can. Watching Dikran.

Dikran gave him a quick, shy smile as he passed. *Fuck you,* he thought. *You think I'm an idiot?*

He walked fast to the other gate. He went to the counter. Shake's plane still sat at the gate. The sign said DELAYED.

Dikran told God all was forgiven, and more.

SHAKE HAD JUST SQUEEZED PAST George Pirtle and into the aisle when the PA crackled again.

"Good news, folks," the captain said, and bells started dinging all over the plane.

Chapter 26

I like to go on that plane now," Dikran said to the agent. He pointed.

"I'm sorry, sir," this one said, a black one. "We've already closed the gate for that flight."

"It's okay," Dikran assured him. "I have money."

"Federal regulations." He shook his head as if saddened by federal regulations. "It's departing now."

Dikran saw, through the window, Shake's plane start to roll away from the gate.

Fuck fuck fucking!

Dikran roared and swept stacks of airline schedule pamphlets and offers for airline credit cards off the counter.

A man in a beard, sitting nearby, tucked his beard down and looked at Dikran over the top of his glasses.

"What you looking at?" Dikran asked him. "You want me to put fist so far up your ass that—"

One of the buttery softball girls walked past, trailing candy and fruit. Dikran watched the backs of her legs moving.

The black agent had his hand on his telephone. Dikran gathered up the airline schedule pamphlets and airline credit-card offers and returned them to the counter, neater than before.

"I apologize, sir," he told the black man. "I am no trouble, I promise."

Eye to eye for a moment. Then the black man took his hand off the telephone.

"You need to chill out, brother," he said.

If only this man knew how Dikran wished he could. He rubbed his temples and shook his head. He pointed to the patch on his arm. "This fucking medicine," he explained.

The black man nodded wisely. "Get you some chewing gum. A lollipop or such. That'll help you kick the cravings."

Really? Dikran felt dubious. He watched Shake's plane pivot, straighten, roll forward out of sight.

"You with that group headed to Panama?" the black man said.

Dikran went to a quiet spot and called her on his cell phone.

"He's on a plane," he said. "Panama?"

He heard her laugh to herself. "Of course," she said.

Dikran went back to the counter and bought a ticket for the next flight. It left in six hours and flew through the night.

The fancy-pants flight attendant from his airplane emerged from the men's room. He rolled his suitcase up the smooth concourse.

Ah.

Dikran smiled. He followed the fancy-pants flight attendant to the parking garage, to his car. The flight attendant was on his cell phone. Laughing into it. Dikran crept like the soft flow of water up from behind and cupped the flight attendant's head in his hand and smacked the head against the door window. The glass cracked a bit, but glass in cars these days was much stronger than it used to be, for safety reasons, and did not shatter as it might have years ago.

The flight attendant fell to the oily, smooth cement floor. Dikran kicked him until he stopped bubbling and pleading. Then he piled the broken pieces of the fancy-pants flight attendant into the backseat and arranged clothes from the suitcase on top to hide what was beneath.

He would fly through the night and be in Panama right behind that ass-lick.

Dikran felt much better.

Chapter 27

Jasper was tired. It was coming up on the second midnight since the morning this all started. That meant he hadn't slept in . . . He was too tired to calculate. That meant he hadn't slept in a long-ass time.

He'd been all over town. Most places twice. He'd tapped every source, called in every marker, made threats, promised favors, answered probably a hundred calls on his cell phone from people who thought they'd seen Gina or the guy but turned out they really hadn't.

Jasper, you asked him what he thought, he thought Gina and the guy had most probably left town already. The guy, Shake, had struck Jasper as intelligent. Gina certainly was.

The way to catch intelligent people was to slow down, think it through, find a shortcut through the canyon—Jasper, growing up, had loved those old westerns—and get to one of their ideas before they did.

You asked Jasper what he thought, he thought it was a waste of crucial hours, humping all over town, back and forth, asking bellhops and busboys had they seen this girl in the picture?

But that's the way Mr. Moby wanted it done, and you know he wasn't going to ask Jasper what Jasper thought, not until there was a mountain of ice and hell under it.

Jasper took a minute outside Mr. Moby's office and checked again; were there any options he might have left in his life that didn't involve what he was about to do? There weren't. This was where he was, nowhere else. He knocked on the door, and Mr. Moby said come the fuck in.

Mr. Moby glanced up at Jasper, saw his face, didn't need to ask.

"You want me to go to L.A.? Try there?" Jasper said.

"Why would I want you to try L.A.?" Mr. Moby said. Not, though, with his usual poison. Jasper saw he was distracted, watching the TV on top of the cabinet. "Look at this."

Jasper looked. On TV was a tape of the security feed from the camera in the lobby. A high-angle shot looking down on the heads of customers coming and going, girls coming and going. One head stayed where it was. The lobby bouncer on the tape was Rock Star, the long-haired one Jasper couldn't abide, the one reminded him of an evil baby Whale.

"Last night?" Jasper said.

"Yeah. Just watch." Mr. Moby hit a button on the remote, and the picture stopped moving. "What do you see?"

Jasper saw a couple of customers and Rock Star and—just coming in the door—a girl in a black wig with braids.

Son of a bitch. Gina.

"Uh-huh," Mr. Moby said.

"She was here last night? What was she doing here last night?"

In his surprise, Jasper asked what Mr. Moby would generally consider dumb-fuck questions. Mr. Moby, though, was too locked in on the TV screen to notice or care.

"I'm going to find out," he said. "But that's not the thing right now." He pushed a different button, and the picture jumped ahead a few frames, then stopped again. The girl in the black wig was definitely Gina. "What do you see now?"

The girl behind Gina, with Gina, her hand on Gina's hip, pushing her forward past the bouncer.

Lucy.

"The accomplice," Mr. Moby answered for Jasper. His face was grim.

Jasper felt his chest tighten. *Easy, easy,* he told himself. Lucy was Mr. Moby's favorite, after all. She could irritate him and get away with it like no other girl Jasper had ever seen. They'd been together almost two years. Mr. Moby had genuine human feelings for her.

"We should talk to her, I guess," Jasper said. He hoped his voice didn't sound to Mr. Moby the way it sounded to himself.

"Nothing to talk about," Mr. Moby said. "She won't know shit, guaranteed." He watched the tape again. From the corner of his eye, Jasper searched Mr. Moby's face for some flicker of genuine human feeling. There wasn't any.

"You just saw this?" Jasper asked.

"About an hour ago. You weren't here, so I sent that longhair on ahead to her place. He's probably wrapped the show up, but get your ass over there and make sure he didn't fuck it up."

Jasper's heart tightened some more, too much. It felt as though the threads of a screw were being stripped.

An hour ago.

"Yes, sir," he said.

JASPER DROVE FAST. Shake had taken his .45 after he'd hit him with the door, but Jasper still had his backup piece. He put it on the seat next to him. Jesus help the cop who pulled him over right now. Jasper was glad for the cop's sake that no cop pulled him over.

Jasper flew across the parking lot outside Lucy's apartment house. He'd decided what he would do. If Rock Star hadn't finished yet, if it wasn't over yet, Jasper would tell Lucy he suspected he loved her and did she, in light of that, want to go away with him somewhere far away?

He would promise to keep Lucy safe and respect her and treat her as an intelligent, equal human being. He would do his best to make her happy. What *she* considered happy, not what he did, which was a fundamental mistake he thought a lot of men made. He would try to be a good man, something at which he had no real practice but for which, when it came to her behalf, he had a sincere desire.

Jasper flew up the stairs to Lucy's apartment. That's what he'd decided to tell Lucy. He was prepared to face the consequences. The consequences would be Mr. Moby.

An hour ago.

If it wasn't over yet.

Lucy's door was closed. Jasper kicked it open, one kick, the wood splintering around the lock.

Rock Star, sitting on the sofa, jumped a foot in the air and looked up at Jasper with alarm.

"Fuck!" Then, when he saw it was Jasper, he said, "Fuck," in a different sort of way, like he was relieved and annoyed and laughing at himself. "You scared the shit out of me, J!"

"Where is she?" Jasper said.

Rock Star shrugged. "She's not home yet."

Jasper felt a surge of relief like a wave lifting him onto his toes.

He was calm again; he had returned home to himself, a deeply reassuring sensation.

"Glad you're here, my man," Rock Star said. But Jasper could see that something was bothering him. He clicked too fast through the channels on Lucy's TV. "But hey, listen, if it's cool with you, Mr. Moby said I could handle this, you know? I was hoping this was going to be, like, my first real gig, you feel me?"

"I feel you," Jasper said.

"Primo!" Rock Star said, bouncing around with delight and relief. He flipped some hair out of his eyes so he could see the TV. "Not that I don't want you to *participate,* my brother. I mean, we're going to have some *fun.* Party like it's 1999, hee-hee."

Jasper considered. "Phone book around here?"

"What? I don't know."

"Never mind." Jasper decided to do it old-school, with the butt of his backup piece. He knocked Rock Star off the couch and tossed Rock Star's gun away. Rock Star tried to crawl off and escape. He was quicker than Jasper expected, but his head was scrambled from the whack Jasper had given him, and he crawled the wrong way, into the bathroom instead of out the front door, and hit a dead end.

Jasper followed him into the bathroom and whacked him again. He found Rock Star's cell phone and dialed Mr. Moby.

While the phone was ringing, Jasper told Rock Star, "Tell him it's done. Tell him, 'Me and Jasper will take care of the aftermath.' You say another word, I'll kill you."

Rock Star managed to nod. Mr. Moby answered. Jasper put the cell phone close to Rock Star's bloody, broken-up mouth. With his other hand, he held his gun pressed into Rock Star's stomach.

"It's done," Rock Star said. His voice sounded strange, because of the broken-up mouth, but Jasper didn't think Mr. Moby would notice. "Me and Jasper will take care of it."

"The aftermath," Jasper murmured.

"The aftermath," Rock Star said into the phone.

"Good," Jasper heard Mr. Moby said. He clicked off.

Jasper smashed the phone on the floor, then put the pieces back in Rock Star's pocket.

"Different circumstances," he explained to Rock Star, "I'd kill you. But I have business that's not going to wait, so that's your good fortune. You feel me?"

Rock Star nodded. He was crying a little.

"You gonna disappear. I'm gonna tell Mr. Moby you didn't have the stomach for the job. I'm gonna tell him not to worry about you, you'll keep your mouth shut. But he might send someone looking for you anyway, so you best really disappear. It comes down to your word or mine, he'll take mine. But I'll kill you first. You understand?"

Rock Star nodded.

Jasper considered for a second, then changed his mind—he decided there was no shame in that, if the change was well reasoned—and shot Rock Star in the head.

He carried the body to the trunk of his car. Then he went back upstairs to tidy up. He turned the sofa back right side up and picked Rock Star's gun off the floor. When he straightened up, Lucy was standing in the doorway.

All right, son, Jasper thought, *here it is; here's your chance.*

"Lucy," he began slowly.

But she was looking at the splintered wood around the lock on the door. She was looking at the gun in Jasper's hand. When finally she turned her eyes up at him, there was the worst kind of stunned horror in them, the worst kind of searching question.

You? How could you . . . ?

She thought he was there to kill her.

Oh, no. Oh, no, no.

"Lucy," Jasper said, "you don't understand."

But she was already turning and running, and Jasper, his heart tight beyond anything he'd ever experienced yet, knew he'd never catch her.

LUCY DROVE AND DROVE AND DROVE, until the fuel light flashed. A hundred and fifty miles east of Vegas, she pulled over at a truck stop to fill back up.

She was still shaking.

And yet—the cold rush of a desert wind blowing through her—she felt exhilarated. She felt liberated.

The scales had fallen from her eyes. Lucy remembered the story from Mass as a child. Paul? Standing back there in the doorway of her apartment, she'd been able to see clearly for the first time.

Providence—in the form of Jasper, come to murder her—had given her that gift.

So many years she'd wasted—waiting, pretending, wishing.

Waiting for the courage. Pretending the life she led wasn't *all* bad. Wishing for a savior to drop a bucket down from the sky and save her from stormy seas.

How many times over the years had she thought about leaving? How many times had she come so close?

There was no good in the life she led. There was nothing good in it at all.

Understanding that, finally, was the kick in the ass she needed.

She'd go to college. She'd meet a nice man. Or woman. She wasn't sure about that yet, but so what?

Lucy, pumping gas in the middle of the night, at a truck stop in the middle of the desert, unsteady on her big heels and wearing a short, short crimson dress that snapped in the wind around her thighs, laughed.

She had nothing. She had a couple of hundred dollars in her purse. A nice watch she could sell.

She had, at last, everything.

JASPER TOOK CARE OF THE AFTERMATH in the trunk, then drove back to the club. Mr. Moby was in a poisonous mood. When Jasper told him that Rock Star had bitched out and bolted, Mr. Moby said, "Thank fucking God I got you, Jasper."

That made Jasper feel proud and ashamed.

"We're gonna find that whore," Mr. Moby said. "And we're gonna find that asshole ex-con who fucked all this up in the first place."

Jasper, in a poisonous mood himself now, nodded. He was on exactly that same page. Oh, yes he was.

Chapter 28

The connecting flight to Panama City was two hours out of Dallas when a storm system blew up from the Gulf and they had to return to DFW. Shake and Gina spent most of the night in the airport terminal there, half sleeping, propped up in the hard plastic chairs. So did George Turtle, Ted the Cocksman, and the entire hard-drinking, backslapping Building Bridges gang. Who, as luck would have it, were headed to Panama, too. Shake learned everything there was to learn about enhanced feline nutritional systems. Gina asked Shake in a whisper if she could borrow his shoelaces to hang herself. Shake told her she'd have to wait till he was done hanging himself.

The next day, around one, they finally landed at Tocumen International, Panama City, Republic of Panama.

The silver lining, Shake calculated, was that the storm system had delayed all flights to Central America, so if Alexandra or Moby had already figured out where they were headed—and the odds of that were pretty good—they'd still be at least half a day behind. Marvin Oates and the foreskins, on the other hand, would now be at least a day ahead.

They cleared customs and parted ways with the Building Bridges contingent at the luggage carousels. Gina was so giddy to part ways she gave several of the purple-tag boys big enthusiastic hugs.

Shake went to find a place to change their money. He discovered that the official unit of currency in Panama was the good old American greenback. His second surprise, as they took a cab in from the airport, was Panama City itself. It wasn't what he'd expected. Rising up from the brilliant green rain forest, perched on the edge of the Pacific, was a true city—dozens and dozens of gleaming skyscrapers, plus dozens and dozens more in the midst of construction. It was nothing like Shake's one other experience with Central America—grim, grimy little San Salvador, where years ago he'd once spent a few days helping a friend liquidate his export-import business. Shake did not recall that trip with affection.

He rolled down his window. The heat here was intense and wet. And the smells. In Las Vegas, desert dry, the smells tended to be of the inorganic sort: car exhaust, baking asphalt, the chlorine pumped into the giant fountains, lagoons, and canals outside the hotel-casinos. Here the smells seemed richer, sweeter, more jungly: life blooming, life rotting, the rain about to fall and the river about to flush it out to sea.

And plenty of car exhaust, too.

Overall, Shake liked it.

The cabdriver tapped his horn a few times and gunned around the bus in front of them. The driver of the bus beeped back. Shake had noticed that although the traffic and drivers here were the worst he'd ever encountered in his life, the horn-honking was much more expressive than in the States, civil and musical. That was another thing he liked about Panama.

And the buses, too. Rickety old American school buses, each individually painted wild colors, with psychedelic stripes and flames and movie scenes and portraits of doe-eyed Spanish beauties and the names of these women written in elaborate cursive script. Even the front windshields were painted, leaving just a narrow strip of glass free for the driver to see out, like a soldier peering through the gun slit of a concrete pillbox.

The cabdriver saw Shake looking at the bus they'd just passed.

"Diablos rojos," he said.

"Red devils?" Shake asked after a second.

"Because the driver are so crazy driver." He shook his head with resigned exasperation, then tapped a quick rhythm on his horn and gunned around another bus, narrowly missing a cast-iron street lamp.

"I like Panama so far," Shake told Gina.

"You know what this humidity is going to do to my hair?" Gina asked. "And if there are giant cockroaches, I'm warning you now, I'm gonna freak."

Gina picked a hotel from the guidebook Shake had purchased at the airport. Shake told the cabdriver to drop them off a couple of blocks away. Just in case.

"Have fun at Carnaval," the driver told them. Shake remembered: Fat Tuesday was in two days.

He followed Gina into a hotel that looked okay from the outside. Inside, the place was better than okay—hushed marble elegance and fresh orchids everywhere. It was definitely not coach class, and Gina seemed to approve.

"Good day," the desk clerk said in English.

"We don't have a reservation," Gina said.

"It is not a problem," the desk clerk said. "One room or two?"

"Two," Gina said.

"One," Shake said.

The clerk waited, pleasantly nonplussed.

"You worried I might decide to screw you?" Gina asked Shake. "Or you're hoping I might decide to screw you?"

"One room, please," Shake told the clerk.

"I'll consider that a yes," Gina said.

"I will just need a credit card, please, to secure any incidental expenses."

To Shake's surprise, Gina produced a MasterCard.

"Don't run it," she told the clerk. "We'll pay cash when we check out."

"Of course. I will just keep the number on file."

He took the card from her and read the name on it. He looked at Gina. Then Shake.

"Mr. Ted Boxman?"

"Like 'Cocksman,'" Gina explained, "but with a *B* instead of a *C*."

THE ROOM WAS BANANAS, Gina saw with glee, almost as luxe as the one she'd had at the Peninsula in L.A. There was a private balcony with a view of the sea and a giant bathroom with an old-fashioned claw-foot tub.

Gina bounced on one of the two queen-size beds. She decided, actually, this room had the edge over the Peninsula. Better sheets, more character—a whiff of colonial charm—and, best of all, she wasn't paying for it with her own money.

She watched Shake check out the balcony, watched the muscles moving beneath his shirt as he leaned on the railing, and reflected that . . . well, yes, she guessed she really hadn't paid for the room at the Peninsula with her own money either. She'd paid out of the three hundred grand she'd lifted off the Whale.

That seemed so long ago. Funny how things turned out. She'd been so excited by three hundred grand. And now, twists and turns, some scary moments in there, here she was looking at a payday of $5 million, maybe more.

Or . . . well, half that. She couldn't forget she had a partner now.

She wondered how Shake would look in a nice suit. Very good, she suspected. He had the kind of body she liked on a guy. Lean, shoulders broad but not overbearing about it, a guy who would have been good at sports if he'd been into that whole scene. Which he wouldn't have been, thank God. Shake was a little bowlegged, but there was a certain charm to that. She wondered what he'd look like *out* of a suit, out of everything. Good abs, she suspected.

"This room is bananas," she said.

"Nicest place I've never been drugged and robbed in," Shake said over his shoulder.

"Sheesh. You gonna hold that against me forever?"

"I need a shower."

"Me, too. Then after that I want to buy some clothes." She held up the MasterCard and twirled it across her knuckles, the way a blackjack dealer in New York had taught her long ago. "Before Cat Food discovers that his card is missing."

"Cat Food was the other one."

"Wait. Which one was the Cocksman?"

"No idea."

He entered the bathroom and shut the door behind him. She heard the shower start to run.

"You don't have to shut the door!" she called. "I wasn't gonna peek!"

She had been totally gonna peek.

THE MAIN SHOPPING DRAG, the Via España, wasn't very big and had nothing on Rodeo Drive—no Fendi, no Prada, no Dolce & Gabbana. But a high-end local boutique caught Gina's eye (when in Panama, right?), and she dragged Shake inside.

She came out of the dressing room in a green dress that fit just, just right.

Shake was sitting on a leather sofa, sipping mineral water a salesgirl had brought him.

"You like?" Gina twirled on the ball of one bare foot. "And don't bother with that 'I'm deliberating' act you always do."

Shake deliberated.

"Not bad," he said.

Gina smiled and twirled again. He was so full of shit. She knew he knew she knew it.

THEY CHANGED CLOTHES BACK at the hotel and then Shake asked the concierge to recommend the best restaurant in Panama City.

"Manolo Caracol," the concierge said without hesitation. "It is beautiful."

"The best *food* in Panama City," Shake clarified.

"Manolo Caracol," the concierge repeated.

Shake, skeptical, crossed the lobby and asked the desk clerk for a second opinion.

"Manolo Caracol," he said. "Without question."

The restaurant was in Casco Viejo, the old quarter of town. Casco Viejo was safe for tourists, but it was surrounded by rough neighborhoods, and the desk clerk advised them to take a taxi.

"What's the best restaurant in Panama City?" Shake asked the cabdriver. "The best food?"

Gina told him to shut up already.

"Food is important to me," he said.

"Eurasia is very, very good," the cabdriver said.

"Where's that?" Shake asked.

Gina pushed herself in front of Shake. "Casco Viejo," she instructed the cabdriver. "A place called Manolo something something. And please ignore my friend for the rest of the trip."

Chapter 29

Ted traced the seam of the tablecloth with the tines of his fork and watched the ice melting in the exotic-looking but not great-tasting drink Nerlides had ordered for him and waited for her to return from the ladies' room.

The restaurant was practically empty, just one other table occupied, on the far side of the room. And the waiter, slouched at the bar, glaring at him.

Ted was pretty sure it wasn't just his imagination, the waiter glaring at him.

The restaurant didn't seem very clean, and the food hadn't been very good. But he tried not to be judgmental, because that was a quality he didn't admire in other people. Maybe what was happening was that he was just imposing his own cultural values on Panama. His father, for example, refused to even try mushrooms. Once, at Golden Corral, Ted had brought him a slice of blueberry pie from the buffet because there was no more cherry. His father had taken a tentative, dubious bite.

"Do you like it?" Ted had asked. He'd been taking his father to dinner almost every night for the past year, ever since his mother passed away, because his younger brother—

Ted stopped that thought. He had edged again into judgmental territory.

"I don't know if I like it or not!" his father had barked. As if to say, *How am I supposed to know if I like the taste if I don't know what it is?* Ted had found that revealing and amusing. Well, as amusing under the circumstances—another dinner with his father at Golden Corral—as he could expect something to be.

The waiter glared at Ted. The ice in his drink melted. Nerlides remained in the ladies' room.

What am I doing here?

It wasn't the first time, in the past twelve or so hours, Ted had asked himself this question. It was more like, like, the two-hundredth time.

He thought about Vivian. He tried not to think about Vivian.

He wanted nothing more, right now, than to lay his forehead down against the tabletop in this restaurant in Panama and not feel—thinking of Vivian, gone forever, twenty-six months now—like he was going to have diarrhea.

What am I doing here?

He'd asked that on the plane. In the van on the way to the hotel. Just about constantly throughout the entire duration of the lunch orientation. The Building Bridges "facilitator" was a guy named Frank who spent the first part of the orientation detailing his professional background. He had been a successful golf pro, a successful home builder and developer, and a successful radio talk-show host. Frank explained that the orientation was to illustrate vividly that groups like Building Bridges, popular misconceptions aside, weren't for losers. They were for quality individuals. Guys who knew what they wanted and weren't afraid to "move the ball down the field."

A lot of the other guys nodded. Ted's friend, George Pirtle—his, really, *acquaintance,* George—nodded and said, "Amen, brother."

This was George's third "tour of duty," as George called it, with Building Bridges. He'd been to Thailand and the Ukraine, too.

Ted knew George from work. Ted was the marketing director for the Oklahoma City Convention & Visitors Bureau. He had the thankless and surprisingly low-paid task of trying to lure conventions and visitors to a city that, while a nice place to live, really had nothing much to entice conventions and visitors, at least not compared to places like Las Vegas or even Dallas. George was a member of the Greater Oklahoma City Chamber of Commerce, of which the Convention & Visitors Bureau was a subsidiary component. George had come to Ted a few months ago with a scheme to lure Chinese tourists to Oklahoma City, now that tourism restrictions in China had been lifted. It had involved cat food and the construction of a frontier cattle town in the vein of Colonial Williamsburg.

"These gals you're going to meet," said Frank, the facilitator, at the lunch orientation, "they're very, very different from the women back home."

"Amen, brother."

"They appreciate a man for what's on the inside. Not how fat he is or bald or does he have six-pack abs. They don't care if you make a hundred K a year or not."

George had talked him into this trip by hammering away at Ted until Ted had the epiphany that George wasn't ever going to stop hammering away, ever, unless Ted said okay. So Ted said okay. He was too exhausted to face the alternative; he'd only been sleeping a few hours a night since he'd lost Vivian.

"Good," George had said when Ted finally said okay. George's tone was suddenly quiet and serious. "You've got to move on with your life, Ted."

Ted supposed that was right.

Frank the facilitator had told them, with a sly smile, that while old-fashioned in all the good ways, these Latina gals were also adventurous in the boudoir, if you knew what Frank meant, much more open-minded than the women back home.

Almost all the men in the group were grinning and nodding.

What am I doing here?

At that point of the lunch orientation, Ted had seriously considered slipping out of the banquet room and catching a cab back to the airport. But then he started thinking about Vivian again, and before he could rouse himself to action, fifty or sixty Latina women filed into the banquet room for the first of the four mixers, the Day One Happy Hour Mix-N-Mingle.

Frank had assured them that at the mixers the ratio of potential Latina marriage partners to quality American individuals would never be less than three to one, and usually even better than that.

Most of the Latina women, Ted guessed, were in their twenties. Most of the men in the Building Bridges group were in their forties or fifties. There were several guys who looked a lot older. Ted was one of the youngest, at thirty-four.

The women weren't allowed to approach the men, so the men moved from table to table at their own pace and discretion. Four women sat waiting at each table.

Like the stations of the cross, Ted heard one guy say with a grin, and all the guys around him laughed.

There weren't enough translators to go around, about one to every three tables, but Frank the facilitator assured everyone that communication—"real communication, I'm talking about, not just words"—wouldn't be a problem.

Ted should have slipped out of the banquet room when he had the chance. Once the women arrived, though, he found himself swept along—story of his life—in the inexorable current of activity, found himself swept into a hotel shuttle van with a group of guys and Latina women, found himself swept along on a self-guided walking tour of the old town, found himself finally at dinner in an almost-empty restaurant with a "date" George had insisted on asking out to dinner for him.

What am I doing here?

Nerlides, his "date," returned from the ladies' room. Ted stood politely up. Nerlides laughed like this was the funniest thing in the world.

"Hubba, hubba," George had whispered to him during the walking tour, after Nerlides without any sort of preface had linked her arm through Ted's.

Ted supposed Nerlides could be considered attractive. He knew that a lot of men liked the kind of body she had. But she also frightened him a little. Her eyes never really seemed to focus, and she laughed an awful lot. On the walking tour, she'd laughed and pointed when they passed a dog that had been run over by a car.

The waiter at the bar was *really* glaring at Ted now. It was definitely not his imagination. He wondered if the waiter thought Nerlides was a prostitute.

She talked loudly and constantly, all in Spanish. She was, Ted thought he gathered, from Cartagena, Colombia, not Panama. Occasionally he would catch an English word or two. "Shopping," several times. "Breast revision," once.

Was she? Ted wondered, alarmed. A prostitute?

What am I doing here?

He was resolved. This was it. He'd ask for the check and bid Nerlides, politely, good night. He'd take a cab back to the hotel and pack and call the airline and fly home first thing in the morning, even if doing so cost him a fortune to change his ticket and he lost the deposit he'd already put down with Building Bridges. Ted didn't care. He was tired of being swept along with the current. He was not going to marry this woman and pay for her breast revision, whatever that was.

He didn't have to move on with his life. He didn't have to pretend Vivian had never been a part, the better part, of the better part of his life. And he definitely wasn't going to submit George's stupid proposal for a fake frontier cattle town to his boss, no matter how George hammered at him about all the Chinese tourists who were just dying to come to Oklahoma City.

What am I doing here?

I'm leaving, that's what.

Ted Boxman felt a lot better. He motioned to the waiter and reached for his wallet.

CASCO VIEJO REMINDED SHAKE of pictures he'd seen of Havana, Cuba. Charm and crumble in equal measure. Paint peeling from buildings the colors of the tropical rainbow, guava and mango and papaya. Cobblestone streets, wooden shutters, and wrought-iron balconies. Old churches and wet laundry strung between windows. What the French Quarter in New Orleans might once have looked like, long before Shake's time, before the titty clubs and T-shirt shops and two-for-one Hurricanes in commemorative glasses.

A girl in a bright mango dress leaned over a third-floor balcony and dropped a coin to her little brother on the street below, expertly threading the snarl of electrical wires between them. The little brother caught the coin and ran off toward a snow-cone vendor down the street.

The restaurant was in a restored colonial building. Wooden tables and white stucco walls, the kitchen out in the open under a copper smoke hood. Shake was relieved. It *was* a beautiful place, as promised, but not in the way that would have made him worry about the food.

Walking to their table, he caught a glimpse of himself in a mirror. Shake couldn't remember the last time he'd been in a suit, let alone a suit that fit properly. He'd shaved and, at Gina's gentle insistence, had his hair trimmed; the girl who'd trimmed his hair, in the salon in the lobby of the hotel, had also plucked a few dark wiry hairs between his eyebrows. The process, she'd assured him in musically accented English, was, like many things in life, painful but necessary.

Shake drew her chair back so Gina could sit. Aside from the glimpse of himself in the mirror, the quick appraisal of the crowded restaurant when they'd arrived, he hadn't been able to take his eyes off her. Nor, he admitted, had he really wanted to. She wore a silk dress, dark green, the one from the store. It was cut in such a way that left much to the imagination but at the same time guided the imagination in some very intriguing directions.

Shake asked for the menu. The waiter said there wasn't one. The chef cooked what he felt was good, the waiter brought it to you, you ate it. Shake wasn't sure what he thought about this, but he didn't say anything.

"So tell me more about this Ziegler guy who wants to buy the foreskins," Gina said after the waiter had filled their wineglasses.

Shake didn't have much more to tell. "He started out legit, New York money, but preferred the shady side of the street. He pulled off his first big scam in the midnineties. The old people I told you about?"

"Details," Gina said.

"Your basic pyramid scheme. He cruised Florida and Arizona, went after the retirees, wowed them with his degree from Wharton and a lot of high-tech mumbo jumbo. Bled them dry, then blew the country."

"They caught him?"

The first course arrived. Fried plantains almost lighter than air, with some kind of a garlic mayonnaise. A combination Shake wouldn't have dreamed up in a million years, but it was very, very good.

"Eventually. He came back for a second helping, but they grabbed him this time. Few days before his trial, he welcomed the Lord Jesus Christ into his heart."

"They fell for that?"

"Probably not. But he cut a deal where he promised to help the feds track down other white-collar criminals. It was tricky stuff, a lot of what was going on. You practically had to have an advanced degree in economics just to understand you'd been robbed. The guys at Justice were just cops, working stiffs who knew how to hide a wire and fill out an incident report. Most of them were out of their league when you went two places past the decimal. Ziegler offered to use his powers, you know, for good not evil."

Gina giggled. "They fell for *that*?"

"He played ball for about a year. Alexandra told me the feds were thrilled. Bust after bust after bust. It rained Cayman accounts."

"There's always," Gina said, "a 'but then.'"

"But then," Shake continued, "after Ziegler had used the resources of the federal government to put all his closest competitors and personal enemies behind bars, after he'd learned everything he could about how his closest competitors and personal enemies and the federal government worked, he disappeared."

"He decided it was more fun to use his powers for evil."

The next course arrived. Two kinds of ceviche. The octopus was warm, with roasted peppers and tomatoes, almost Tuscan. The sea bass was cold, with an explosive citrus-cilantro wallop. Both were ridiculously fresh. Shake closed his eyes while he chewed.

"He stayed busy," Shake said. "He landed another huge score a few years ago. Something with server farms and bank routing codes."

"How did that one work?"

"I didn't know this was a private tutorial."

"I like to live and learn." Gina tapped a fingernail thoughtfully against her teeth. "So, the elusive Mr. Ziegler. You really think he'll just come to us?"

"I'm hoping," Shake said. "It's your buddy Marvin Oates I'm worried about. If we can't find him, if we can't find the foreskins—"

"It's not going to be a problem."

"You say so."

The waiter brought the next course. Duck in a sweet, dark, smoky sauce, mole meets Kansas City barbecue. This was serious stuff. Shake held up a palm to forestall the next round of discussion, and they ate in silence.

The ginger prawns were even better than the duck, and the grilled dorado with lemon was even better than the prawns. There was also pork loin with sautéed bok choy, clams with butter.

"Wow," Shake said after they'd finished dessert. Shredded coconut flavored with a sweet heavy syrup, plus a miniature flan and green tea with cinnamon.

"Beats the food in stir?"

He smiled. "You ever do time?"

"Does working for the Whale count?"

"What did you do before that?"

"You name it. Worked at Starbucks. Sold cell phones at the mall. Cocktail waitress. Various entrepreneurial activities of the less-than-legal sort, when the opportunity arose. I never turned tricks, if that's what you're thinking."

"I wasn't thinking that."

"I wouldn't ever do that. I didn't even like giving lap dances.

Sex should be all about fun, not profit. Or fun *and* profit, not just profit."

"What about love?"

"Sex should be about fun, profit, and love? Or fun and profit, but not love?"

"Well, that's one of the great conundrums, isn't it?" Shake said.

The waiter brought espressos and the bill, which came—with tax, tip, and the wine—to under seventy-five bucks. Shake wondered how long it would take him to learn Spanish and find an apartment down here.

"I bet you had fun stealing the Whale's three hundred grand."

"That's different." Gina giggled. "What about you? Besides the driving?"

"I was a cook."

"Aha."

"You have to have something to show your PO," Shake said, "and most kitchens don't care where you come from, as long as you get there on time and don't stab the waiters."

"When I was young, like seventeen, I was a topless shoeshine girl. That was my introduction to the adult-entertainment industry. My first day, I went up to this guy's hotel room, right, and it turned out I was really supposed to give shoeshines. I thought I was just supposed to look cute and topless and maybe do a little dance."

Shake laughed. "What did the guy say?"

"He was apologetic. He said he had a big job interview in the morning and wanted his shoes to look really good."

"So tell me."

"About the various entrepreneurial activities of the less-than-legal sort?"

"I like to live and learn."

She shrugged. "Mostly small-time stuff. I wouldn't even really call them cons. Pretending to be some rich guy's daughter's friend, while she was away in Europe for her junior year abroad. That sort of thing. I did a couple of honey traps, with this friend of mine, but those take forever to set up right."

"You've a had a full life," Shake said, "a girl your age."

"Twenty-six," she said. She hawk-eyed his reaction. "Well? Don't lie or I'll know it."

"I was thinking twenty-four," he said, which was the truth.

She seemed satisfied. She sipped her espresso. "So you were nineteen, huh, your first time?"

"Good memory."

"What happened?"

Shake knew what she meant. He thought about it. "I fell in with the wrong crowd," he said. "What's your story?"

She glanced away from him, which wasn't like her at all.

"I was born into the wrong crowd," she said, "if you know what I mean."

Shake did. And for a splinter of an instant, looking across the table at her, the candlelight softening the angles of her face, he thought he glimpsed a young woman more complicated, sadder and sweeter, than she'd ever admit.

Or maybe that's just what she wanted him to glimpse. Shake wasn't sure.

She turned back to him. Smiled. Winked.

"How about a nightcap before bed?"

Chapter 30

The waiter went to the back and brought out the restaurant manager. Now Ted was being glared at by three people: Nerlides, the waiter, and the restaurant manager, who was short and unshaven. He smelled pungently of sweat and cigarettes.

The waiter and the manager talked rapidly and angrily at Ted in Spanish. Then Nerlides talked rapidly and angrily at Ted in Spanish. She seemed to be under the impression she was translating.

Ted kept trying to explain—English, mime, the few Spanish words he knew—that he had somehow lost his wallet, but that it was going to be okay, he intended to pay, he had not noticed the missing wallet earlier because the shuttle van from the hotel had been complimentary, the wallet was just probably back at his hotel room, and Ted was in no way attempting to pull a fast one on the waiter, the manager, or Nerlides.

He tried to make them understand that he would go back to his hotel room, find his wallet, and return to pay the bill. He took a step toward the door to demonstrate.

"Ai-ai-ai!" both the waiter and the manager said, or something like that, and they each grabbed one of Ted's arms to stop him. They marched him, Nerlides following along, to the back of the restaurant. Through the suffocatingly hot, cramped kitchen to a suffocatingly hot, cramped office off the kitchen.

The manager pointed to the telephone on the desk next to the computer and made Ted understand that he'd better call someone to bring him some money, *pronto,* or he, the manager, would call the police and have Ted arrested.

Ted couldn't believe that this was happening to him. He was soaked with sweat. He didn't know who to call. He couldn't call the hotel. George would still be on his "date." Ted didn't know Frank the Facilitator's last name. The other guys, even if he remembered their last names, would still be on *their* "dates." He couldn't call his credit-card company, because that number was on the credit card in the wallet he didn't have with him. He couldn't call his brother, of course. He could call Hannah, his favorite colleague at the Chamber of Commerce, but how mortifying would that be? And what could she do, ten o'clock at night, from the United States? What if her surly husband answered?

It was incredibly difficult to think clearly in this suffocatingly hot, cramped office, with three people glaring at him and yelling in Spanish. Ted understood now, in a way he never had before, how the contestants on *The Amazing Race* would sometimes make what he, Ted (at home on his comfortable couch in his comfortable house, a glass of iced tea in his hand), would consider somewhat questionable decisions. Like walking thirty blocks to the Hermitage instead of taking a cab—when they were in a race, after all.

"PayPal!" Ted said in desperation, and pointed at the computer.

All the Spanish yelling stopped. The restaurant manager nodded. "PayPal," he said, giving Ted what might pass for a friendly clap on the shoulder. *"Bueno."*

Ted sat down at the computer, wiped his sweaty palms on the legs of his trousers, and thanked God he remembered his password. He e-mailed eighty-four dollars from his account to an e-mail address the restaurant manager wrote down on the back of an envelope. Then he logged off, cleared cookies and history to be safe, and exited Explorer.

The waiter and Nerlides had wandered off. The manager pulled up a chair, and together he and Ted waited for the transaction to process. When the eighty-four dollars showed up in the manager's account, fifteen minutes later, he clapped Ted on the shoulder again.

"Vámonos," he said.

Ted stepped outside the restaurant and took several deep breaths of night air that wasn't cool, exactly, but at least immeasurably fresher than what he'd been breathing in the restaurant office.

A cab waited at the curb. Ted remembered, just in time, that he didn't have the money to pay for it.

He started walking. The hotel wasn't too far, only a few miles away, he calculated. He'd always had a decent sense of direction, and it felt good to be moving. He tried to think what could have happened to his wallet. He assured himself, without really believing it, that this would be a funny story he could tell people someday.

He noticed that the neighborhood had begun to change. Less light and music now, fewer restaurants and clubs. Actually, there were no longer any restaurants and clubs at all. Just run-down gray apartment buildings and, from the alleys, the sour smell of garbage.

Ted walked faster. He stepped around a hole in the sidewalk that someone had tried to fix by stuffing a red plastic Coca-Cola crate into it, but the hole was bigger than the crate. Up ahead, on the other side of the street, three young guys sat on the hood of a parked car, passing a joint back and forth and drinking cans of beer. When they noticed Ted, they slid off the hood of the car, hitched up their pants, and strolled across the street. They timed their stroll so they reached the next corner just before he did.

"Hola," Ted said, in what he hoped was a gruffly nonchalant way. He tried to edge around the guys, but they edged with him.

The tallest young guy said something to Ted in Spanish.

"No habla español," Ted explained. He edged some more. So did the

young guys. The shortest young guy offered Ted the joint, and Ted saw that the middle young guy had a knife.

Ted remembered then, a sharp click of revelation—the very attractive woman from the plane, the surprising round of hugs at the baggage carousel, the way she'd squeezed his bicep, the way her other hand had brushed across his—

"Give us your wallet," the young guy with the knife said, in perfect English.

Chapter 31

When they got back to the room, a little after midnight, Shake asked Gina which bed she wanted. He wanted the one by the window, but he tried to be a gentleman whenever possible.

"Just shut up," Gina said. She got behind him, and he felt her put a shoulder to his back. She guided him to the big leather chair. "Sit."

He sat. She turned the radio on and fooled with it until she found some bass-heavy hip-pop thing with a girl singer spelling out the words she'd just sung. Shake probably wouldn't recognize it if he heard it a hundred times. But he liked it; he liked the way Gina, in that sea-green dress, her back to him, let the beat start moving her.

The beat moved her over to him. She faced him, still moving, smiling a little, and flicked one of the dress straps off her shoulder.

"Whatcha doin' there, sport?" he asked.

She turned around, flicked the other dress strap off, peeked at him over her shoulder with a look that was at once both playfully wholesome and the playfully complete opposite of wholesome, whatever that was. The whole time Gina kept moving to the beat, swimming along with it.

"I lied," she said. "Sometimes I do like giving lap dances, when it's for fun."

"And profit."

She didn't answer. She slid up against him, then back down. Shake breathed her in. Her lips, those lips, almost brushed his when she slid back up. Almost, but not quite.

It took every ounce of willpower he had, seriously, to put his hands on her shoulders.

"You're not supposed to touch, mister, but I suppose we can make an exception."

He moved her gently away from him. Arm's length.

"We're gonna keep this professional," he said.

"Why?"

Good qucstion.

She kept moving to the beat, moving beneath his hands. Which wasn't making things casicr.

"Which bed do you want?" he asked.

She stopped moving to the beat and looked at him. She wasn't surprised, exactly. Maybe disappointed by his resistance. Maybe pleased. Shake couldn't be sure.

"You don't trust me, do you?" she said.

"I don't really trust anyone."

"I can't really be trusted," she said.

"A perfect match."

She went and turned the radio off and plopped down cross-legged on the bed by the window.

"Shake?" She tugged her dress straps back up, one, then the other.

"Gina?"

"I'm not sure I trust me, and I *am* me, you know?"

He thought he knew what she was trying to tell him, and he appreciated it.

"I know what I'm getting into," he said. "No warranty, expressed or implied."

She blew a strand of hair out of her face. For one second, Shake came alarmingly close to standing up, walking across the room, and kissing her.

Instead he said, "We need to get busy tomorrow morning. If we're gonna find those foreskins, we've got a lot of work to do."

She laughed. "I seriously doubt it."

"What's your brilliant plan? There are probably a hundred hotels in Panama City your boy Marvin might be holed up in. We have no idea what name he registered under, and we can't just—"

He stopped. She was waiting very politely, hands folded in her lap, for him to finish.

"You're saying he's *that* dumb? He'd use his own name?"

"I'm saying," she said.

Shake grabbed the phone book from the desk.

"I thought you said there were probably a hundred hotels in Panama City." She eyed him dubiously. "You're gonna call every single one?"

Shake smiled and flipped the phone book open.

"I'm not that dumb," he said.

Chapter 32

Why in the fracking world, Marvin Oates wondered, if you had hundreds of millions of dollars, would you choose to relocate to this steaming, sweltering, filthy, probably malaria-ridden swamp of a country? Where the street numbers made no logical sense whatsoever and the street names seemed to change every time you crossed an intersection? Marvin had ditched his rental car after about ten minutes. But even the cabdrivers had no idea where anything was. The last cabbie—*who lived here, in Panama City!*—had asked if he could borrow Marvin's map. Which was a piece-of-shit map to start with.

Hadn't Roland Ziegler, that millionaire dipshit, hadn't he ever seen the *Lord of the Rings* trilogy? Hadn't he heard of, oh, say, New Zealand? That's where Marvin would go if he had a couple of hundred million bucks and was on the run from the feds. Or somewhere at least like Tunisia, maybe, where the heat was dry, where it didn't seem like every step you took you were being cooked from the inside out, like fracking dim sum.

Marvin slogged back down the block he had just slogged up. Number 276 was next to Number 214, which made perfect sense. He slapped at what felt like a mosquito on his forearm. On the plane down, he'd read a history of the Panama Canal. It said there were two kinds of mosquitoes. The kind that carried malaria was the one kind, and the kind that carried yellow fever was the other.

Great.

This morning before leaving the hotel, Marvin had doused himself with crop-duster quantities of DEET, but the humidity had the sweat running off him in rivers, the DEET running with it.

The guy at the hotel had asked Marvin, when he checked in, if he wanted to sign up for a day tour to the rain forest, to see the sloths.

Jesus fracking Christ.

There was actually a third kind of mosquito, too, he remembered, the one that carried dengue fever.

Marvin scowled. Things had started out so well. He'd been brilliant, if he did say so himself, when the blond chickie showed up with that briefcase of hers. Marvin had played it cool, stayed cool, gave nothing away. And the foreskin nab itself—that had been a masterwork of decisiveness and crafty improvisation.

Ziegler, though, the potential buyer, had been harder to find than Marvin had expected. Marvin had been slogging around this hot, hellish swamp of a city for two days now and hadn't turned up a single lead.

He slogged an extra block in what he knew for certain was the wrong direction, but he didn't have any other bright ideas, and the place he was looking for was the last one on his list for the day. And hey, of course, sure enough, there it was, the shop, in exactly a spot where it shouldn't have been.

Marvin pushed through the door. A bell *tink*ed once. He sucked in a big blast of could-have-been-colder A/C and glanced around. Polished wood floor, spotless glass cases, oh-so-tasteful framed art.

Yeah, yeah, yeah, whatever. You couldn't compare an absurdly pretentious place like this to Marvin's establishment back in Vegas, which was for the *serious* collector of antiquities. This place, clearly, peddled overpriced, dime-a-dozen crap to dilettantes, rich tourists, and local Botox-swollen trophy wives.

Even the clear, whiskey-colored light filtering in through the big windows felt expensive.

A girl with jangling bracelets jangled over to him, smiled, said something in Spanish.

"I want to talk to your boss," Marvin told her. He looked around for a chair. His feet felt like they'd been battered and fried. Like they were made of soft cheese that had been battered and fried.

"Of course," the girl said. She jangled away.

A couple of minutes later, the boss came out. He looked like he was trying to look like Clark Gable—black hair slicked back, skinny black mustache, a dark suit he probably thought was in just the most perfect understated taste. The cuff links probably cost even more than the suit.

"Marvin Oates, Las Vegas," Marvin snapped. He said it like he expected the guy to know who he was. He didn't really expect him to, but in his experience it was tactically smart to put your opponent immediately on the defensive.

"Ah! Of course," the guy said, with such genuine feeling that it threw Marvin for a second. Maybe the guy *had* heard of him. It wasn't out of the question, after all. It wasn't like, in the world of serious collectors, Marvin was some nobody. What with the Internet and all. "Such a pleasure, Señor Oates. My name is Antonio Cornejo. At your service."

"Fancy digs," Marvin said in a collegial way. "Overhead must butt-fuck you to death."

"I'm sorry?" Cornhole said. Apparently his English wasn't as good as he thought it was. "In what way may I be of assistance, Señor Oates?"

"I'm looking for this collector guy, heavy into religious relics, Roland Ziegler."

The jangly shopgirl and the only other customer in the place, a bent old man browsing the cases, both glanced up when they heard the name.

"Roland Ziegler?" Cornhole mused. "Hmmm. I'm afraid I'm not familiar with someone of this name."

"C'mon," Marvin said. "Millionaire collector, world-famous fugitive, hiding out in Panama the last three years, you're saying you've never heard of him?"

"I'm afraid not."

"You're afraid not."

Cornhole pondered. "Have you, Señor Oates, tried the telephone book?"

"Of course I have," Marvin said, insulted. He stood there, stumped. He wished there had been a chair to sit in. It was almost five o'clock, and he was starving.

"Forget it," he said finally, and stomped out of the shop. He slammed the door open so hard on his way out that the bell *tink*ed twice.

DINNER DID NOT IMPROVE MARVIN'S MOOD. He added up all the money he'd blown already on this stupid, misbegotten trip. Airfare, rental car, hotel, cabs, meals. Factor in the revenue dripping away minute by minute with his shop shut down, and Marvin wondered if he should wish he'd never come across those foreskins in the first place.

But that was dumb-ass. Those foreskins were worth millions. He just needed to be smart about this. Smart and patient. He needed a nice cold soak in the tub and a good night's sleep.

He slogged back to his pit of a hotel and slogged up the stairs—the elevator was out of order, of course. By the time he got to the third floor, it looked like he'd already taken a bath.

He took a hit off his inhaler and unlocked the door to his room. The housekeeper had drawn the blinds, for no apparent reason, and the room was dark. He slogged across and yanked open the blinds. Late-afternoon sunlight poured in, and that's when Marvin saw her, sitting in the chair by the bathroom. Smiling at him.

"Frack." He sighed.

Chapter 33

Remember me?" Gina said.

Marvin whirled to flee, but Shake had figured on that and positioned himself by the door. He stepped in front of Marvin, grabbed him, marveled for a second at the buggiest bug eyes he'd ever seen, spun Marvin back around.

Marvin looked at Gina. "Listen, I don't have your—" He stopped himself. Took a hit off his inhaler. "What do— What are you doing here?"

"You think," Gina asked Shake, "I should have gone with 'So we meet again'?"

Shake thought "Remember me?" had been fine, not too forced. He told her so.

"Listen," Marvin said.

"Don't have my *what,* Marvin?" Gina said. "Finish your sentence and you can have dessert."

"Those foreskins aren't yours!" Marvin said, transitioning smoothly from fake bug-eyed innocence to genuine bug-eyed petulance.

"They sure aren't *yours*."

"You had no idea what they were worth. You wouldn't know a Philistine from a philharmonic."

Gina looked at Shake.

"One was an ancient tribe in the Holy Land, more culturally advanced than most people realize," Shake said. "The other one's an orchestra of some sort."

"See," Gina told Marvin. "I knew that."

"You can't make me give them to you."

"Yes," Gina explained kindly, "I can. My boy here, Shake, just got out of the joint for beating a guy to death with his bare hands. Isn't that right, Shake?"

Shake shrugged modestly. "I used a sock filled with gravel part of the time."

Marvin took a nervous look at Shake and deflated. "How did you find me?"

"You left a trail, you big slug," Gina said. "Tip for next time? Use a fake name."

"You called all the hotels in Panama City?"

"We called the rental-car places at the airport," Shake said. "All seven of them."

"Remember when the nice lady at Avis asked you where you were staying while in Panama City?" Gina explained.

"Oh."

"Where are they?" Shake said.

"I don't have them here," Marvin said. "You think I'm a total moron?"

Shake and Gina considered.

"The bed," Gina said.

Shake lifted the dust ruffle with his foot and peered underneath. Then he reached down and pulled out a big padded envelope.

"Frack."

Shake opened the padded envelope and slid out the slender glass case. He examined the rows of foreskins. It was hard to believe they were worth $5 million. It worked out to fifty grand per. He wondered what, back in the day, each monk or peasant had been paid for his contribution. What the procedure had been like. All at once, like an assembly line, one guy with a knife? Shake winced. He was glad he'd been born at a period in American history when the circumcision of infants was routine, no matter what your religion, so you were too young to ever remember it happening.

"We're in business," he told Gina.

He started to open the glass case to get a better look.

"Don't open it!" Gina and Marvin hollered at him.

"Roger that," Shake said. He eased the glass case with the foreskins back into the padded envelope. He slipped the padded envelope into a leather day pack they'd bought and brought along for just this eventuality.

"I want a finder's fee," Marvin was saying. "Ten percent. I demand a finder's fee."

"Count on it," Gina said. She followed Shake out the door. Halfway down the stairs, Shake could still hear Marvin kicking the walls of his room.

Chapter 34

They covered three of the shops on their list in an hour. Shake was surprised there was such a big market for antiques. Or rather, as he'd been corrected by the owner of one such shop, a haughty middle-aged woman with the profile and manner of a Roman emperor, "antiquities."

They hit the fourth one just before it closed for the day.

"Buenos tardes," Shake told the shop clerk, a girl in her late twenties with hair corkscrewing in every different direction and enough metal bracelets to sink a ship. Or build one. A small, pale scar parted her upper lip, which made her even more attractive than she already was.

"How may I help?" she asked.

"We'll take one of you to go," Gina said with a wink.

The girl smiled back, confused.

"We're just browsing," Shake explained.

"I will bring the proprietor to you," the girl said.

Shake and Gina moseyed over to the nearest glass case. Inside, on a bed of crushed crimson velvet, were several necklaces that even Shake could appreciate as beautifully crafted and seriously old.

A courtly guy with a rakish black mustache had glided noiselessly over to join them at the counter.

"The French," he said, "when they came to build the canal, there was such enthusiasm, such certainty of success, they brought their families with them, all their most prized possessions." He touched one long, reverent finger to the glass of the case. "Alas."

"The French?" Shake asked. He had been under the impression it was the Americans who built the Panama Canal. Then again, he also hadn't known the difference between antiques and antiquities, and had thought that some guy in London owned the real Holy Grail.

"You have not yet seen the statue of Ferdinand de Lesseps? It is a fascinating story."

The rakishly courtly guy introduced himself—Antonio Cornejo, proprietor—and told them the story. How it was the French who started the canal in the 1870s, with grand plans based on even grander delusions. De Lesseps was the charismatic entrepreneur who'd built the Suez Canal a decade earlier. But the Egyptian desert had been flat and dry, and the Panamanian jungle, the Panamanian mountains, were definitely not that. Malaria and yellow fever killed tens of thousands of canal workers. The French company bled money, then went bust, which caused a national financial panic, ruined thousands of small investors, and brought down the government. Later on, it was discovered that de Lesseps's canal company had spent massive amounts of money to bribe newspapers for favorable editorials and pay off high-ranking government officials. In the end, the French didn't finish even a tenth of the canal they'd set out to cut.

Give it up to the French, though. A couple of decades later, it was another charismatic French hustler, Philippe Bunau-Varilla, who convinced Teddy Roosevelt and the Americans to forget about the canal they were planning to build in Nicaragua and pick up where the French had left off. Bunau-Varilla arranged for the Americans to buy what remained of the French canal company. In which, just a coincidence, he happened to own a shitload of stock.

"Mais oui," Gina said, and Shake remembered she could speak French. He didn't want to guess what other hidden talents she had.

He remembered what she'd looked like last night, sliding the strap of that green dress off her shoulder.

"Your American Congress had been fixed on Nicaragua," Cornejo said, "but Bunau-Varilla frightened them with the prospect, in that land, of erupting volcanoes. He gave each congressman a postage stamp of the time, from Nicaragua, to illustrate his thesis."

"There was a picture of a volcano on the stamp?" Shake guessed.

Cornejo nodded and led them to another glass case. He pointed to the very stamp.

"A beautiful addition to any collection," he said.

"Actually," Shake said, "we're not interested in stamps."

"We're interested in something like *that.*" Gina pointed to an old rosary coiled on the velvet. Set into the center of the cross was a small glass bubble. Inside the small glass bubble was a tiny pale splinter of what appeared to be bone.

"Mais oui," Cornejo said. He started to unlock the case. "The young lady has exquisite taste."

"It'd go great with our foreskins," Gina said. Cornejo stopped moving. Shake could hear him breathing.

"I thought we were gonna sell those damn things, buttercup," Shake said.

"Foreskins, did you say?" Cornejo asked.

"Just some silly old Catholic thing Grandmama left us when she passed on. Back in Belgium? They're supposed to be quite old, but who knows?"

"We'd like to find a home for them," Shake explained, "but that's hard to do without a good broker, you know."

Cornejo smoothed his tie. He'd forgotten all about trying to sell them that rosary or anything else.

"You must," he said, "entrust only a gentleman in such matters, where discretion is of the utmost importance."

"We're at the Bradley Hotel," Shake said. "Mr. and Mrs. Boxman. You'll give us a call if you hear of anything?"

"Most certainly," Cornejo murmured, distracted by the effort, Shake suspected, of calculating the commission on a $5-million deal.

Chapter 35

It was dark by the time they left Cornejo's shop and began the stroll back to their hotel. The streets were crowded. Salsa pumped from jerry-rigged PA systems on the balconies and Carnaval revelers were out in force, drinking and dancing and laughing. A lot of people were in costume—homemade devil masks were popular, as were feathers and tropical wraps dyed vibrant shades of crimson, indigo, sunshine yellow. Everyone seemed local, and every five feet or so, someone stopped Shake and Gina to offer them a beer or a dance or a greasy paper plate of tapas. Shake compared this to what the Mardi Gras back in his hometown of New Orleans had become—drunk out-of-town idiots flashing their tits at other drunk out-of-town idiots—and did not find it lacking.

"This is nice," Gina said. "It feels real."

It was like she'd read his mind. Shake hoped she couldn't really read minds, or he was in over his head for sure.

Yes, I know, he acknowledged wearily to himself. When it came to Gina, he knew he was already in over his head.

"Look." Gina pointed to the full moon floating over the water.

"Blue moon," Shake said.

"It's yellow."

"Second full moon of the month," he explained. "Very rare."

She slipped her arm through his. "What are the odds?" she said.

"Long," he admitted. "You can't have two full moons in February, not even a leap year."

"I was talking about us."

"Maybe even longer than that. I'm not sure."

She smiled. "Maybe there are forces bigger than us at work here."

Before Shake could answer, a guy pushing through the crowd, moving fast in the opposite direction, bumped hard into him.

"Sorry," Shake said, because he was smart enough, in situations like this, to avoid confrontations with bumpers who outweighed him, as this guy did, by a hundred pounds or so.

Shake continued on for several steps then stopped. Wondered. Turned.

The guy who outweighed him by a hundred pounds had stopped, too. Had wondered. Was turning.

The guy who outweighed him by a hundred pounds. Who had a bald head shaped like a bullet. Who had a face like a bullet flattened against a concrete wall.

Dikran.

He and Shake stared at each other. With a disbelief, Shake guessed, that was mutually profound.

Then Dikran pulled a gun tucked against the small of his back. Shake grabbed Gina, who was eating a tapa and dancing with a devil.

"What is it?" she asked.

"A force bigger than us," Shake said.

SHAKE LIKED THAT, THAT GINA didn't have to be told an important thing twice. *Run.* They ran. The heavy crowd slowed them down, but

Shake knew it would slow down Dikran—larger, less nimble—even more.

Unless, of course, he decided just to bulldoze right through the Carnaval revelers, slamming them aside. Which was exactly what, Shake confirmed with a glance over his shoulder when he heard the alarmed shouting start, Dikran was doing.

He didn't think Dikran would open fire on a crowded street. Not because he'd be afraid of accidentally hitting innocent bystanders, but because he'd be afraid of accidentally killing Shake before he had a chance to go to work on Shake with a pair of needle-nose pliers and a quart of drain cleaner.

"Run faster," Shake told Gina.

They cut down another crowded street. Dikran was about fifty feet behind them. He wasn't gaining, but they weren't losing him either. They reached the corner and turned onto a wide avenue. But *fuck,* there was no way to cross it. A Carnaval parade was in full swing, inching down the avenue—homemade floats on the backs of flatbed trucks, strutting salsa bands, platoons of dancing marchers in matching costumes. Shake pulled Gina up the avenue, trying to find a gap in the action they might be able to dart through.

Dikran rounded the corner and spotted them.

"Come on," Shake said. They plunged into the middle of the parade, into the middle of what seemed like a fifty-piece salsa band. Spinning, gyrating, knocking Shake sideways. He ducked, squeezed, turned, got pressed between two musicians playing instruments he didn't recognize. Almost got impaled by one of those instruments. Shake spun to avoid that fate and collided with a tall, salsa-dancing woman in an even taller, teetering, flame-red turban. This was the group following the musicians: an entire battalion of tall, salsa-dancing women in turbans. The first turban woman shoved Shake playfully aside, into another turban woman who grabbed him and swung him around. A third turban woman joined the fun and started grinding Shake from behind.

He'd lost Gina. He'd lost Dikran. Shake didn't even know exactly what direction he was facing. In the madness he spotted Gina's hand and grabbed it, pulled her finally out of the parade and across the avenue.

The far side of it, thank the lucky blue moon that really wasn't one. Shake, no time to look behind him for Dikran, pulled Gina toward a *diablo rojo,* a few yards down the side street, that had just lurched to a stop. The bus was painted purple and green and orange, with a bus-length portrait of what appeared to be a man in pinstripe pajamas backstroking through a sea of baseballs.

Shake wondered if he'd feel Dikran's bullet before it blew his brains out.

"*Really* run now," he said.

He dragged Gina behind him up the steps of the bus just before the doors creaked shut.

Shake looked out the window as the bus pulled away. Dikran was only a few yards behind. He lumbered after the bus for longer, and at a faster clip, than Shake would have thought possible. Then the bus picked up speed, and the giant bald bullet head fell bobbing behind. Just before the bus rounded a corner, Shake saw Dikran slow, wobble over to the curb, bend over with the gun against his knee, and puke from exhaustion.

Shake bent over, too, with exhaustion and relief.

"What are the odds?" he said, and turned to Gina.

It wasn't Gina. Shake discovered that the hand he'd been holding belonged to a tall woman in an even taller turban.

And she wasn't a woman. She—he—was a man, a young guy in a dress and expertly applied makeup.

Shake had thought, now that he considered it, that the members of the turban battalion had seemed awfully tall.

"Hola," the turbaned transvestite said warily.

Shake checked the leather day pack slung over his shoulder. It was unzipped. Empty.

Gina was gone, and so were, no coincidence, $5 million worth of foreskins.

"I don't believe this," Shake said, though he knew he really should have.

"You speak English?" the turbaned transvestite said. "I speak English, too. I know! I don't believe this either. It is maybe like fate, yes?"

Shake noticed that the turbaned transvestite was holding a straight razor in one hand.

He saw Shake looking at the straight razor and quickly tucked it away into the folds of his dress. He shrugged an embarrassed apology.

"One can't be too careful, no?" he said.

"No," Shake agreed.

THE TRANSVESTITE IN THE TURBAN, who'd introduced himself as Ramón, pointed out the stop that Shake wanted. Up ahead.

"Thanks," Shake told him. "Sorry about the mix-up."

"No problem," Ramón said. "But still, if you need a place to stay tonight . . ."

"I'm pretty sure I've got an empty hotel room waiting for me," Shake said.

Ramón nodded wisely. "This *chica* of yours, she sounds . . . how do you say? Like a trouble with a capital *T*?"

He handed Shake a flask. Shake took a swallow. Rum. Pretty strong stuff.

"You could say that," he said.

Ramón nodded wisely again. "But she is worth it, yes?"

Shake took another long draw from the flask and didn't answer.

Chapter 36

The desk clerk recognized Shake when he returned to the hotel.

"*Buenas noches,* Señor Boxman," he said.

Shake paused on his way to the elevator.

"Any messages?" he asked. "From Señora Boxman?"

The desk clerk looked puzzled. "No, sir, I am afraid not."

Shake crossed to the elevator and took it upstairs. He unlocked the door to the room, stepped inside, looked around.

Both beds were empty. The chair by the door was empty. The other chair was empty. There was no one on the balcony. The full moonlight from the windows was bright enough so he could see what he needed to see; he didn't even bother turning the lights on.

"Gina?" he called.

There was no answer. Shake hadn't expected one.

He let the empty leather day pack slide from his shoulder onto the floor and dropped worn out into the chair by the door. But he stood up again right away, because he wasn't in the mood, right now, to be reminded of what almost happened in this same chair last night.

Then he heard what sounded like the soft thrum of running water.

He turned and saw, beneath the closed bathroom door, a thin ribbon of light.

The bathroom door was unlocked. He pushed it open and saw Gina in the big antique claw-foot tub, up to her neck in bubbles. She was sipping from a can of Diet Coke.

"Surprised to see me?" she asked.

"Yes and no," he lied.

"I figured it was smarter to split up in case one of us got pinch-arooed." She tapped her temple with the lip of the Coke can. "Always thinking."

Shake crossed his arms and leaned back against the wall. He hoped it wasn't too obvious, how happy he was to see her. He hoped as well it wasn't too obvious that he was also considering, seriously, dragging her out of that tub, tying her up with the phone cord, and calling Lexy to tell her where to find her.

"And you thought the foreskins would be safer with you, of course."

"If I'm gonna screw you over, Shake, I'm gonna wait till we have the cash."

"I'm useful for the time being."

She blew some bubbles his way. "You're earning your keep so far."

"So where are the foreskins?"

She pointed behind him. He turned. The padded envelope sat on a stack of towels, on the counter next to the sink.

"You realize," Shake said, "I could take those right now, walk out the door, disappear forever, and you'd have absolutely no foundation for complaint?"

"But if you did that, you wouldn't be able to come take a bath with me, then, would you?"

He considered. She smiled.

"Your choice," she said.

He wanted to make her wonder about the outcome for a minute, but who was he fooling? He started taking his clothes off.

"I'm so glad," she said, "you picked curtain number two."

"The foreskins aren't even in the envelope anymore, are they?"

She smiled, and he slid into the tub with her. He kissed her, then kissed her again. The second time their front teeth clicked together hard.

"They're under the bed," she said, just before he kissed her a third time. "I'm not a total moron."

THEY DIDN'T ATTEMPT SEX IN THE TUB—they'd both been around the block enough times to know that would be better in romantic theory than actual practice. So they dried off in a hurry and headed for her bed, the one by the window. They made it only as far as his bed, the closer one, and barely there.

The first time was nice but unspectacular, rushed and awkward, like a handshake with someone you don't know if you should be hugging instead. Or vice versa.

"Sheesh!" Gina said when she rolled off him. "Is that the best we can do, you think?"

He rested for a few minutes and then they did it again.

The second time lasted a lot longer. It was not unspectacular.

THE SOFT PINK GLOW OF SUNRISE spreading over her woke Gina. They were in her bed by the window. She didn't remember exactly how they'd gotten from Shake's bed to hers. She didn't remember at all how she'd ended up with four small dark bruises on her inner thigh, like fingerprints. Oh, well. Never mind. She sighed happily. She remembered.

She wanted a cigarette, but her pack was on the dresser, a mile away, and she was too lazy. It felt too nice just to lie here with her head on Shake's shoulder, one of her cheeks warm against his skin and the other early-morning cool.

"You awake?" she asked.

"Mmmm," he said, drowsy.

"You're an old guy, I know. You need your rest."

"I need my rest after last night. That's for sure."

"Do you think he'll call?" she asked.

She felt his chest shift a little under her cheek.

"Ziegler?" he asked.

"Who else?"

"If he wants those foreskins, he will."

"You should go into politics."

"Yes. I think he'll call."

"Risky."

"I think he wants those foreskins."

"How do you think Moby got them in the first place?"

Shake shrugged. "Deadbeat trying to pay off a debt. Or an unexpected windfall from an unrelated score. Maybe left behind at lost and found."

"Then he did his due diligence and found out what they were worth." She thought about this. "He was willing to give up millions of dollars just so he could kill me himself."

"Do you feel flattered or scared?"

She ignored the question.

"I like Panama so far, too," she mused. "I'm newly all about Central America."

"Well. San Salvador is a shithole. At least it was twenty years ago."

"Shake?"

"Gina?"

"You want me to let you go back to sleep, don't you?"

"If you want me fully rested."

"I want you every which way I can have you."

She felt him kiss the top of her head. He held his lips pressed there for an extra second, and she knew he was thinking about something. She knew it wouldn't do any good to ask about what.

She propped herself up on her elbow and kissed him on the lips. With more gusto than she'd originally intended.

"Gina?" he said after they came up for air.

"Shake?"

He smiled and drifted off again. She watched him sleep. She thought about everything that had happened, everything that now might, then laid her head back against his shoulder and closed her eyes.

Chapter 37

When Shake woke up the second time, the light streaming through the windows had turned hard and bright—middle-of-the-day bright. Gina was on the balcony—bare feet propped on the rail, reading the Panama guidebook, smoking a cigarette—and the phone on the nightstand was ringing.

"You gonna answer that, buttercup?" she called, without glancing up from the book.

The question on her end was rhetorical, but Shake was giving it some serious thought.

If he answered the phone, he realized, a new door opened. It might lead somewhere interesting—$5 million, for example—or it might lead to a room filled with even more trouble, capital *T,* than the one he was in right now.

Thing was, Shake liked the room he was in right now. He liked who was in the room with him.

But, come on: $5 million?

He sat up and ached in odd places. Normally Shake had no desire to wind the clock back—he was content with the trade-off of youth for wisdom—but right now, aching, watching Gina paint her toes, he did wish for some of the supernatural stamina and elasticity of his dumb-ass nineteen-year-old self.

And just exactly how much wisdom, he wondered, had he traded his youth for? It was debatable. He picked up the phone.

"Yeah?"

"Five o'clock today," said a man's voice, American. "Soberania National Park."

"Want to be a little more specific?"

"Take the SACA bus from Plaza Cinco de Mayo to Gamboa. Tell the driver to drop you at the entrance to the Canopy Tower."

"We'll be there."

"Take the marked path that begins in front of the observation tower. Walk into the jungle for approximately one quarter of a mile."

Was this guy serious?

"Take a bus, not a taxi. Come alone. You'll be watched."

"Do you want us to wear our state-of-the-art hidden recording devices?" Shake asked, amused.

"Don't be late."

The phone clicked and went dead.

Gina had returned to the room, walking awkwardly on the sides of her feet so as not, apparently, to smudge the toenails she'd painted bright red while he was still asleep.

"Have you heard there are places in Panama where the sun sets in the Atlantic and rises in the Pacific?"

He shook his head. He hadn't heard that and wasn't sure he believed it.

"I really want to see a three-toed sloth," she said. "So? We in business?"

"We've got a few hours before we have to leave," Shake said.

"Not much time, but let's make some hay." She tossed the book away and jumped back into bed with him.

"Gentle," he said. "If it falls off, I'm out of luck."

She straddled him and, with more enthusiasm than gentleness—not that he could complain—arranged the sum of their parts into a much nicer whole.

"You and me both, buster," she said.

ON THE WAY OUT OF THE HOTEL, they stopped at the front desk and asked to see the hotel manager. The desk clerk made a call. A few minutes later, a nervous young man with expressive eyebrows appeared. He couldn't have been much older then twenty or twenty-one.

He explained to Shake and Gina, with apologetic eyebrows, that he was only the assistant hotel manager. So that there might be no unfortunate misunderstandings. The hotel manager himself was out of town, on something called a benchmarking trip to London, during which he would visit top hotels and return to Panama with ideas on how to improve the Bradley.

"This is not a problem, Señor Boxman?" the assistant manager asked nervously. "Señora Boxman?"

"Not a problem," Shake assured him.

Gina set the padded envelope on the counter. Back in the room, Shake had placed the glass case, with foreskins, safely inside once more. Gina had watched him. He'd watched Gina watch him.

"We'd like to put something in the hotel safe," Shake explained.

"With pleasure," the assistant manager said. "I will take care of it at once."

He reached for the padded envelope. Gina intercepted his hand.

"My elderly husband said *we'd* like to put something in the hotel safe?"

The assistant manager's eyebrows bounced and curtsied and begged forgiveness.

"With pleasure," he said.

He led them to the safe in back. Shake wasn't sure what he'd been expecting. A massive vault, antique, big brass wheel. It was just a normal safe, though, big but nondescript, with a digital keypad. It seemed sturdy enough, at least.

Shake and Gina looked politely away as the assistant hotel manager punched in his code and unlocked the safe. Then he took a small key from a ring of small keys attached to his belt and unlocked one of the deposit trays. He slid it out. Gina placed the padded envelope inside.

The assistant manager slid the tray shut and locked it. He swung the door of the safe shut. A red light beeped.

"Voilà!" he said.

"When we want to make a withdrawal?" Shake asked.

"Quite simple. One of you will merely notify me and—"

"No," Shake said.

"Nope," Gina said.

"I am very sorry?" the assistant hotel manager said.

"Do not," Shake said, "open that safe for me unless my wife is also present."

"I am not certain, I apologize, that I understand this instruction. If—"

"Do not," Gina said, "open that safe for me unless my husband is also present."

"Under no circumstances," Shake said. "I might beg. . . ."

"I might wheedle and cajole. . . ." Gina said.

"But under no circumstances."

"The safe stays shut unless we're both here."

"Both of us."

"Alert, awake, and capable of reasoned consent."

"Or the safe stays shut."

"Got it?" Gina asked.

The young assistant manager's eyebrows expressed acrobatically nervous confusion. Gina reached out, took his chin between her thumb and forefinger, slowly nodded his head for him.

"You'll understand someday, sweetie," she assured him. "When you're married."

Chapter 38

They took the bus from Plaza Cinco de Mayo north toward Gamboa. It was real jungle a lot of the way. Shake was impressed. He thought he understood now what people meant when they called something "primeval." Every now and then, they'd catch a jarring glimpse, through a gap in the trees, of a giant cargo ship working its way up, or down, the canal.

"I always thought it would just be like a giant concrete ditch filled with water," Shake said. The canal, what he was seeing of it at least, was much more like an exotic, snaking river, crowded on both sides by green, squawking wildness.

"The word 'canal' is misleading," Gina agreed. "It makes you think, ugh, boring. Artificial. Where *cholos* in L.A. race their tricked-out cars when it dries up during the summer."

The bus wheezed and hissed to a stop. The entrance to the Canopy Tower Ecolodge. They walked up the road, up the hill, until they reached the observation tower—what used to be an observation tower and was now the Ecolodge itself; they found the marked path that led into the jungle.

Shake looked at his watch. It was a few minutes before five. The sun had dipped behind mountains to the west (or was it the east?) and the rain forest ahead looked darkly menacing, darkly inviting. Birds screamed and trilled and whooped. Birds and/or monkeys. And/or God knew what.

They started walking. The jungle closed in around them and the light; it felt like they were walking across the bottom of a lake. Strange, but peaceful, too. The screaming and trilling and whooping increased in volume and intensity.

"Scared?" Shake asked Gina.

"I'm looking for a sloth," she said. "They're supposed to have the cutest faces."

They came to a sort of small clearing and stopped. Shake checked his watch again.

"This is probably about a quarter of a mile," he said.

"You think Ziegler lives out here?"

"I think he has a sense of theater," Shake said. "Or thinks he does."

"This isn't a safe place to be when it gets dark," a voice behind them said.

They turned. A guy in a lemon-colored guayabera shirt smirked at them from the edge of the clearing. He was American, about forty, soft around the edges, holding a big flashlight. He flicked the flashlight beam across Shake, let it linger on Gina.

"So why are we here?" Shake asked.

"I'm Mr. Ziegler's executive assistant," the guy said. "Ronald. At your service."

"We're the Boxmans."

"Of course you are." The guy smirked. "Did you bring the items Señor Cornejo mentioned?"

"Did you bring Señor Ziegler's cash?"

"Touché." The assistant flicked the flashlight beam toward the jungle behind him. "Come with me, please."

They followed him down a narrow path that zigged, zagged, climbed, plunged, and disappeared beneath the undergrowth for long stretches. After about fifteen minutes—it was almost dark now—they came to a second, smaller clearing where a muddy four-by-four was parked.

"Vehicles aren't allowed in this part of the park," the assistant explained, "but Mr. Ziegler has certain . . . influence."

Shake and Gina climbed into the backseat of the four-by-four. Ziegler's assistant settled behind the wheel. He bounced through the jungle for a few hundred yards, then cut onto a paved road. It led, eventually, to what Shake recognized as the highway they'd come up on from Panama City.

Theater.

"You could have just picked us up at the bus stop, you know," Shake said.

The assistant didn't answer.

"So tell us about this boss of yours," Gina said.

"My— Ziegler?"

Shake gave Gina a look.

"Well," the assistant said, "I guess I'd say he's just a down-to-earth guy who happened to hit it big."

"Smart?" Shake asked.

"You'd have to think so."

"Would I?"

"Guy made his first hundred million before he was thirty."

"Stole it, you mean."

Shake noticed the assistant's eyes dart over to the rearview mirror, then quickly away.

"How about you two?" the assistant asked.

"Are we smart?" Gina asked.

"Are you having a good time in Panama?"

"I think I speak for both of us," Shake said, "when I say it's not what we expected."

"He speaks for both of us," Gina said.

They drove north, all the way up to the Caribbean, then east along the coast. Their headlights flashed, along the side of the muddy road, on piles of garbage and birds of paradise and schoolgirls in immaculate plaid uniforms making the long walk home from school.

Just before they reached the town of Portobelo, Ziegler's assistant stopped the four-by-four. He pointed to a bluff strung with the crumbling stone remains of an old fort, overlooking the moonlit water.

"Enjoy your dinner," he told them.

Shake and Gina got out. The assistant drove off with a crunch of shell gravel.

In the center of the ruins, on a carpet of green grass, framed by rows of rusted iron cannons, a table had been set for three. There were candles, flowers, and a starched white tablecloth. Two dark-skinned Panamanian waiters in starched white uniforms stood at attention next to the table.

Shake pulled a chair out for Gina. The view from up here, the moon just a night past full, was spectacular.

One of the waiters placed napkins in their laps. The other one poured them each a glass of champagne.

"Mr. Ziegler will join you shortly," he said. Then both waiters melted away into the shadows.

Shake tasted the champagne. "Good stuff."

"I read you can go scuba diving in the Pacific in the morning, the Caribbean in the afternoon," Gina said.

"I'll put that on my list of amazing things to do before I die," he said.

"Now that you can take me off it, huh, sport?"

Shake only smiled. He sipped the champagne and watched the play of glittering moonlight on the water below and just let the sheer sensual pleasure of the moment pulse through him. Gina had kicked off a shoe and propped a bare foot on his knee. She was flexing her toes in a contemplative way. She smelled like the sea. Or the sea smelled like her. Either way, equally nice.

Live in the moment? Shake knew, now, *this* was a moment he wouldn't mind living in for a long time.

He thought Gina might be thinking the same thing, but, truthfully, he had no fucking clue. He hoped that's what she was thinking; he hoped that was part, at least, of what she was thinking.

"This doesn't suck," she said.

"No."

She continued to flex her toes in a contemplative way. "You sniff a hink with the assistant, too?" she asked.

Shake nodded. He finished his glass of champagne and lifted his chin to point behind her. She turned. A man was strolling toward them. It was Ronald, the assistant, who'd changed out of the guayabera shirt and into a tailored linen suit.

"Welcome," he said, grinning.

"Let me guess," Shake said. "Roland Ziegler."

"Gotcha, didn't I?"

"Sure did," Shake lied.

"You know how hard it is to get good help these days." Ziegler laughed. He sat down and put too much effort into it, pretending not to be knocked completely out by Gina. "Seriously, though, no hard feelings, okay?"

"None at all," Shake said.

"Then let's eat!"

GINA WOULDN'T HAVE CALLED ZIEGLER attractive, not exactly. Well, actually, not at all. He was doughy, his features sort of pale and unbaked, and his eyes were a tiny bit on the beady side, set just a tiny bit too close together. Hair the color of a dead lawn in winter, cropped short. But he had good teeth and a larger-than-life self-confidence Gina found almost mesmerizing.

That and—uh, Gina?—the fact that he had a couple of hundred million dollars to his name. Definitely mesmerizing. He'd just told them all about two private islands he owned, one off the Pacific coast of Panama, the other off the Caribbean.

So the guy's a little doughy, eyes a bit beady. Gina warned herself not to be a superficial kind of person.

Shake had just asked Ziegler why he'd decided to move to Panama.

"This used to be a fort to protect the coast from pirates," Ziegler said. He speared a shrimp with his fork.

He did that a lot—not answering the question he'd been asked, or at least not right off, or at least not in a straightforward way most people would answer a question. Shake, Gina could tell, hated it. But Shake nonetheless kept asking questions. Probably because he hated how Ziegler evaded them. Gina shook her head. *Boys,* she thought.

"For a couple of hundred years," Ziegler went on, "more gold passed across this isthmus than all the gold in the rest of the world combined. All the gold from the New World, on its way back to Spain. Incan gold. Aztec gold. Pirates—could you blame them?—they couldn't resist. Pirates and people who wouldn't have even thought of themselves as pirates, but all that gold just lying around, these guys weren't fools."

"I suppose you consider yourself a modern-day pirate," Shake said.

Ziegler grinned and speared another shrimp and prepared to not answer the question. Gina felt Shake clench his jaw.

"A pirate wasn't a common crook. You have to understand that. A pirate wasn't some grimy lowlife who broke into the mansion through the cellar window and made off with the family silver. Wasn't some cracked-out jig, pardon me, who holds up the check-cashing joint on the corner with a Phillips-head screwdriver and a do-rag for a mask. To put it in modern terms. Right? A pirate made his living with skill, brains, audacity. Imagination."

"That what it takes to cheat old people out of their life savings?" Shake asked.

"You only rob the rich, Shake?" Ziegler said. "Give it all to the poor?"

They smiled pleasantly at each other with intense dislike.

Gina watched them. If she had to have sex with just one person for, say, the rest of the month—as horrifying as that concept was—she would of course pick Shake over Ziegler in a second. All things being equal, she'd pick both the waiters over Ziegler, she'd pick the jangly bracelet girl back at the antique shop for sure, the debonair owner of the shop, too. All things being equal. But things, in life, rarely were that.

It was odd, though. When Gina thought about it more carefully—when she thought about having sex with just Shake and nobody else for the rest of the month, for the rest of the year, even—she didn't feel horrified at all. Neither freaked nor claustrophobic. She could actually imagine the two of them a year or three from now. Hanging out together and hatching interesting business plans over breakfast together and scuba-diving both oceans in a single day.

Was it really that much of a stretch? To think that someday she might be a wife and a mom? She'd still be herself, after all, just a wife and a mom, too. Doing wife things and mom things in her own way, not somebody else's.

Okay, she admitted, it *was* kind of a stretch. But that wasn't necessarily a bad thing. She liked stretches; she liked surprising herself and making herself think, *Wow, I can't believe I just did that.*

Gina imagined it would take a *long* time for the sex with Shake to get dull. And she didn't think the conversation ever would. Shake, like few people she'd ever met, knew how to keep her on her toes.

All this made for interesting musing. Gina didn't know if it was useful, though.

She was certain Shake would get it right away, her idea for the chain of high-end dry-cleaning places.

"So, Gina," Ziegler said, turning to her with a big smile. He knew he had good teeth and worked them like a stripper with perfectly shaped nipples. In your face, in other words. "Did I tell you, Gina, about the condo I have in Manhattan? Top floor of the building, with the best view of Central Park in the city."

Gina was surprised. "I thought fleeing the country meant fleeing the country."

"The feds?" Ziegler smirked. "They're idiots. Field agents are basically one rung up the evolutionary ladder from the people who snap your picture at the DMV."

Gina felt Shake clench his jaw again. He was cracking her up. "Is that right?" she asked, pretending, just to make Shake clench his jaw some more, to be breathless with interest.

Shake figured out what she was doing, though. He gave her a look, then made a big point of ignoring her to concentrate on the plate of fish the waiter had set in front of him.

"I've got fake passports," Ziegler went on, "the best, I've got tinted lenses and prosthetic nose attachments and shoes with special heels so I walk differently, but—and I'll tell you, I've come up with some pretty cunning shit—I mean, that's what I *do* for a living, I have to use my brain, my imagination, I'm always having to figure out ways to beat the . . ." He paused and played with his glass of wine. Which, counting the champagne, was his fourth. Gina always kept count. It was almost always useful information. "What was I saying?"

"How cunning you are," Shake said, without looking up from his fish.

"Right," Ziegler said. "Even so. I could probably move back to New York City full-time. Put my real name on the mailbox. They still wouldn't be able to get me."

"But you don't do that," Gina said, flirting, "because you like your islands too much."

"You might like them, too, Gina," Ziegler said.

"Lots of old people with money in Panama," Shake said. Then, "This sea bass isn't bad."

Ziegler leaned back in his chair and chuckled.

"You're right," he said. "Guilty as charged. I didn't pick Panama with a dart and a blindfold. There are certain . . . *opportunities* . . . here, for a guy with my skill set. A few years ago, *Forbes* named it one of the top places in the world to retire. Warm climate, inexpensive, top-notch medical care. A lot of the natives speak English."

"The natives?" Shake said.

"Think about it," Ziegler said, ignoring him, "you're a front-edge Boomer about to hit sixty-two in, what, Philadelphia. A school administrator, for example. Kids all growed up and moved away. You've got a decent pension, some money in the house, but who knows will it be enough. You want two things out of life right now."

He held up a finger. "Financial security." He held up another finger. "Adventure."

"A paradox," Gina suggested helpfully.

"Not in Panama," Ziegler said. "Here, you can have it all. And wait, a third thing, too. A live-in maid to cook and clean. Two hundred and fifty bucks a month. That's a powerful lure, even for someone who listens to NPR and buys, what, carbon-offset credits when they take their ecotour of wherever, wherever. You should see up around Boquete. The highlands? There are gated communities springing up on every hillside. It looks like Boca Raton."

'"The best way to overcome temptation is to succumb to it,'" Gina said. "Oscar Wilde."

Both Shake and Ziegler looked at her.

"What?" she said. "I went to college."

"You did?" Shake said.

"Sort of," Gina said. It was a long story.

Shake finished his fish. Which Gina had found fishy.

"So the sheep come to you now," Shake said. "Not a bad setup."

Ziegler motioned to one of the waiters, who topped off his wineglass.

"That's not the only iron I've got in the fire," Ziegler said. "You kidding me? Medical tourism, for example. That's taking off. And the IMB."

"Where you can look up movies on the Internet?" Gina said.

"International marriage business. Crazy money, and it's just going to get crazier and crazier. Lonely loser schmucks looking for women who won't realize they're dating lonely loser schmucks. Or'll at least pretend they don't realize it, if it means a chance to escape the *precaristas,* the shantytowns. The website fees alone triple my nut, then we bring tour groups in from the States and mix them up with the single girls here."

"The natives," Shake said.

Ziegler let the jab slide. Or, Gina considered, missed it entirely. He shook his head. "The problem is, Panamanian girls, pound for pound they're some of the homeliest girls you've ever seen. Friendly yes, but. At least the ones we can get for the mixers. It's a drawback of the good economy down here. You don't have your motivated labor supply, you know?"

"So the solution is?" Gina asked. A guy like Ziegler didn't say, "The problem is . . ." without already having a "The solution is . . ." all prepped and ready to fire.

"The solution is," Ziegler said, leaning close and showing her his good teeth again, "Cartagena. An hour away by plane, four by boat. And *Colombian* women, wow. Hot, poor, and cheap to transport. Trifecta."

"Huh," Gina said. This was intriguing stuff. She liked learning new things.

"What happens," Shake said, "when these girls, who I'm guessing don't speak much English. Who I'm guessing have some other issues, too, being hot and poor and cheap to transport. What happens when they go up to El Norte and marry lonely losers who couldn't find, on an entire continent of their own, a girl willing to marry them?"

"Who cares?" Ziegler said, with what seemed to Gina genuine bafflement. She realized it was the first time he'd directly answered a question.

The waiters brought dessert and a pinkish dessert wine.

"Let's talk some business, boys," Gina said.

SHAKE WASN'T WORRIED ABOUT GINA'S flirting with Ziegler. It's just what she did. Like, if you were good at math, you doodled equations probably without even thinking about it. It was her way of having fun, of taking the arrogant prick's measure, of softening Ziegler up and making him even more stupid than he already was. Plus, Gina could tell, and it didn't take a mind reader in this case, how much Shake couldn't stand the arrogant prick. That made the flirting even more fun for her.

So why was Shake worried?

Because he knew that if he'd figured out four of the reasons Gina was flirting with Ziegler, that meant there were probably four more he hadn't figured out yet. And probably a couple of others Gina herself didn't know about yet.

And yes, Shake suspected that in the same way the best lies always have a seed of truth, no one could flirt this convincingly without meaning it just a little.

Jesus, Shake thought, annoyed with himself. *Am I thirteen years old here, or what?*

He looked over at Ziegler. Who was pale and plump, with shifty eyes like dull, dark, plastic buttons. A cartoon of an arrogant, stupid prick.

How did a guy like that end up with millions and millions of dollars, two private islands, and enough whatever it was, in addition to the millions and the islands, to get a girl like Gina to flirt with him?

Why wasn't it Shake sitting on the other side of that table?

He'd read a book in prison about why certain civilizations (the Europeans in Columbus's time, for example) had conquered other civilizations (the Incas and the Aztecs, with all that gold Ziegler had mentioned). And not vice versa. Even though the author of the book said the Incas and the Aztecs were just as smart as the Europeans, had balls just as big.

What it came down to were the particular natural resources of the particular continent on which a particular civilization developed. Shake couldn't remember all the details, but basically it had to do with the Europeans and the Asians getting oxen and horses to domesticate. And the Incas, on the other hand, getting stuck with llamas and guinea pigs, which weren't so great for pulling plows or riding into battle.

Ziegler, Shake knew, had been born into money. He'd gone to private schools and Harvard and Wharton. Probably he'd gotten into some trouble as a kid—most kids did—but Ziegler would have never gone to juvie or jail for it; his parents would have put the family lawyers on the local D.A. like white on rice.

Shake frowned at himself. Maybe the theory worked for continents but not for people. His line of work, Shake had met plenty of people who'd started out with nothing and ended up conquering their share of Incas. Alexandra, for example. He'd also met plenty of people who became fuckups no matter what neighborhood they grew up in, who liked to blame their fuckups on everyone and everything but the one who was really responsible. They raised martyred self-pity to an art.

Shake decided to not join them.

"So, kids," Ziegler said, "just guessing here, but—those foreskins don't belong to you, do they?"

"Now, Roland," Gina said, "what in the world would make you think such a thing?"

She had one hand on Shake's knee and the other hand on the table, next to her dessert plate. Although, wait—Shake wondered where Gina's other hand had disappeared to, the one that just a second ago had been resting next to her dessert plate.

Shake, thoroughly disgusted with himself now, looked away. Out at the water down below, glittering in the moonlight. He could make out a small island in the distance—a thin strip of pale sand and a patch of dark jungle, like a hole in the bright, moon-glow sky.

"Why would I think those foreskins don't belong to you?" Ziegler said. The one time out of a hundred he answered a question straight, without bobbing and weaving, he had to repeat it for you first. "Well, because I happen to know a nice Russian lady in Los Angeles and a not-so-nice Whale in Vegas."

"She's Armenian," Shake said. "And she's not so nice either."

"So I wonder," Ziegler went on. Ignoring him. "Do I make my deal with the freelancers? Or be a good corporate citizen and whistle in my original partner?"

"The freelancers," Gina pointed out, "are the ones with the foreskins in hand, don't forget. So to speak. And who might be willing to sell said foreskins at a friend-of-the-family discount."

Ziegler pursed his lips and tipped back in his chair and pretended to mull this over. If this prick ever had to do time, Shake thought, he'd last about a minute, or as long as it takes to suffocate with your head jammed in a pan of rehydrated prison-mess breakfast grits, however long that would take.

"Seven?" Ziegler said finally.

Seven million. Holy shit. Shake knew that Gina wouldn't blow it. He kept gazing out at the water to make sure *he* didn't.

"Nine," Gina said without missing a beat. "We're not running a charity here, you know."

Ziegler laughed and snapped his fingers to summon the waiter. Of course the prick wasn't going to give his answer until it suited him.

"Let's go for a drive before we crunch the numbers," he said. "I've got something special to show you."

Chapter 39

Ziegler drove them into town. Portobelo was no longer so *bello,* just a cluster of cement-block buildings with corrugated iron roofs, muddy, half-paved streets, furtive-browed dogs slinking from garbage can to garbage can, a knockout view of the sea. The town was only a couple of hours' drive from Panama City, but it seemed centuries even further away than that.

They pulled up outside an old colonial church and parked. The stonework was similar to that of the coastal fortifications above, but the church had been repaired and restored over the years, probably several times. It wasn't crumbling; it just looked like it was about to.

The massive wooden doors to the church were closed and locked. Ziegler grinned and told them to be patient, patient, even though neither Shake nor Gina had shown any sign of being anything but. A few minutes later, Shake heard a key scraping inside, the iron lock clanking.

A kid in his late teens, his white shirt buttoned to the top, swung the doors open. He looked just about as furtive-browed as the dogs Shake had seen prowling the streets. He gave Ziegler a quick bow as they entered, then quickly closed the doors behind them and melted away into the shadows.

The interior of the church was lit with dozens, maybe hundreds, of flickering candles.

Ziegler checked their reactions. Shake didn't have much of one. He'd been an altar boy back in New Orleans and served at more than his share of predawn weekday Masses. Gina, though, indulged Ziegler by making an "oooh" face.

"Just imagine," Ziegler whispered. "The stone, the candlelight. All the same. This could be four hundred years ago. Pirates cruising in the bay. Cannons booming from the fort. Your only hope of salvation—right here."

He led them up behind the altar. Shake, former altar boy, felt the jump of boyhood nerves. You weren't supposed to be up here unless you were the priest. Get caught and you'd go to hell. Or at least get a shoe thrown at you back in the sacristy by Father Voisinet, who had one hell of a temper.

"Are you coming?" Gina whispered.

Shake nodded. He waited till they'd both turned, then quickly crossed himself and followed. If a childhood under the guidance of the Catholic Church taught you anything, it was to cover all your bets and keep them so.

"Take a look at this," Ziegler whispered. He lifted back a corner of the sacred cloth and pointed to the center of the altar. A small square, about the size of a cigar box, had been cut from the marble and covered with glass. Inside this compartment were the bones of a human hand. They were the color, in the candlelight, of soft yellow butter.

"St. Terwin of Cappadocia," Ziegler whispered. "Martyred in the ninth century. In what's now Turkey. Before most people had even dreamed there was a New World."

Gina peered at the skeleton hand. "It's real?"

"Even better," Ziegler said. "It's the fourteenth century now, okay?

The Black Death spreading across Europe. People panicking. Peasants starting to wonder, hey, our priests and bishops, they're supposed to have God's ear, right? So why are they rich and why is my, you know, *wife* covered with stinking pustules and dying? The church was worried. Bad PR. So this one priest, guy in a village in northern Spain, he figures he better try to do *something.* So he cuts off his own hand. Discovers, quote-unquote, the bones of the hand of St. Terwin of Cappadocia. Obscure saint at the time—smart priest, he knows he won't run into infringement issues. And then, get this, the Black Death, in northern Spain at least, at least for a while, it goes away. Thanks to the hand of St. Terwin."

"No one noticed that the guy who discovered the hand of St. Terwin was suddenly missing a hand?" Shake asked.

Ziegler scoffed, as if the answer were obvious, which Shake figured meant he didn't have any idea what it was, the answer.

"So how'd the digits in question end up here?" Gina asked.

"The Spaniards brought them over," Shake said, because he knew it would take the prick Ziegler half an hour to get around to answering the question. "When they colonized the Americas, every church they built, they needed a sacred relic to sanctify it."

"It was a dangerous world out here," said Ziegler, who seemed only mildly peeved that Shake had stolen his thunder. He seemed genuinely fascinated as he gazed down at the fake St. Terwin's skeleton hand. "Disease and pirates and wild animals and Indians. You needed protection. Relics were just as important to the Spanish as gunpowder. They took their faith very seriously. This was the crowd, remember, that brought us the Inquisition."

"And that's why you collect fake relics," Shake suggested. "Because you take your faith very seriously."

Ziegler was more than mildly peeved this time but did a fairly good job of covering with a chuckle.

"When I was a kid, the other kids collected, what, baseball cards? *Star Wars* figurines? I could never see the point. If you're gonna collect something, it should be rare. It should be almost impossible to get. And it should have a *history,* it should tell part of the story *of* history. The story should be as fascinating as the thing. The *story* is what you're collecting."

It was first time Shake had come remotely close to not despising the guy. That feeling lasted about three seconds, until Shake noticed Ziegler smirking smugly.

Ziegler tilted his head toward the altar. "But those aren't the bones the Spaniards brought over in the sixteenth century." He smirked some more.

"You stole those," Shake guessed.

"Oh, no!" Ziegler said, as if affronted. "I paid a very fair price for them. Of course, the good gentleman I purchased them from—a novitiate of this very church, what a coincidence—I'm sure I have no idea how they came into *his* possession."

"Maybe someday," Shake said, "the new fake in there will be more valuable than your old fake."

Ziegler gave Shake a blank look. Then rebooted and grinned again.

"The Black Death hand of St. Terwin, at the moment, is the number-one sparkling jewel of my collection. I'd like to make it the number-*two* sparkling jewel of my collection. Yes? If we can arrive at mutually agreeable terms."

"The one hundred foreskins," Gina said. "Speaking of which."

"Eight million," Ziegler said. "Take it or leave it. And word to the wise? I never bluff."

Shake looked at Gina. Gina, just her eyes, told Shake, *Fuck yeah!*

"Eight million it is," Shake said. "I guess we *are* running a charity here."

FUCK YEAH! EIGHT MILLION DOLLARS. Never in Gina's wildest dreams—Well, okay, maybe in her most wild wildest dreams, but still.

Doughboy drove them farther up the coast. To, he said, a private airstrip where awaited his private jet to fly them back to PC. Just Gina and Shake, not Ziegler—who, he told them in typically mysterious fashion, needed to remain behind.

On the ride up, Gina let her mind play with interesting details and implications. What kind of guy paid $8 million for some old fore-skins?

There was only one answer to that question: a guy with more money than sense.

A guy with a couple of private islands and a condo in Manhattan with an incredible view of the park.

Just Gina's type of guy, in other words.

But, seriously—she couldn't be happy with $8 million?

Four million dollars, she reminded herself. That was the deal she'd made with Shake back in Las Vegas.

He gazed out the window. Her partner.

Crazy thing, wasn't it, how long, long ago Las Vegas seemed now?

Shake turned and caught her staring at him. He winked. She wanted to jump him right here, in the back of the four-by-four.

They reached the airstrip. Ziegler walked them to the little jet. The pilot was one of the waiters from dinner, which did not inspire confi-dence.

If I get killed in a plane crash just before I score eight million dollars, Gina thought, *I'm going to be so fucking pissed.*

Four million dollars. It was weird how she had to keep reminding herself she had to split the take.

"I'm going to need some time to put together the cash," Ziegler said. "Why don't we say not tomorrow but the evening after?"

"Fine," Shake said.

"And no offense, I'd like to take certain precautions. Not that I doubt your honesty, but I'd like to bring in my own expert for verifica-tion."

"And we'd like to meet somewhere public next time," Shake said. "Not that we doubt your honesty either."

"Isla Taboga," Ziegler said. "It's just off the coast from Panama City. You take the ferry. There's a church there, at the top of the hill. Iglesias San Pedro. We'll meet in the square outside it. Nine o'clock, evening after next."

"You'll have the money," Shake said.

"You'll have the foreskins," Ziegler said.

The waiter-pilot came forward and opened the door to the little jet.

Ziegler took Gina's hand and kissed it.

"A pleasure," he said, as into her other hand he slipped a piece of paper.

Shake—on his way up the steps to the plane, his back to them—didn't notice.

"Pleasure's mine," she said.

"See you soon," Ziegler told Gina with a smirk.

He started to walk back to his car. Shake, at the top of the steps, had turned back around to watch him go.

"By the way, kids," Ziegler called to them, "I *was* bluffing. I would have gone to ten!"

Then, laughing, he slid into the four-by-four and drove off.

WHEN THEY GOT BACK TO THE HOTEL, they fell into bed and wore each other out. Shake felt both very old and very young. It was a strange sensation, but he wasn't gonna make noise about it.

Afterward, tired as he was, Shake couldn't sleep. He could tell by her breathing that Gina couldn't either.

"So what do you think?" she asked him after a while.

"He's a prick, for one thing."

"A prick who owns two private islands."

"Is still a prick."

"Who owns two private islands."

"Go native with him, then," Shake said.

She giggled. "I didn't take you for the jealous type."

"I'm not."

"Not jealous?" she asked. "Or not the jealous type?"

He chuckled. Like she thought he was really gonna answer that.

"One thing keeps bugging me," he said.

"Yeah?"

"Alexandra mixed up in this."

"Your gray-eyed Armenian lady boss who isn't so nice either."

"I don't see it. Her dealing foreskins to some prick."

"Eight million dollars, buttercup."

"Still. It's not her kind of dance. Moby would have probably paid her that cash for you, straight up. Why dick around with some foreskins?"

"Pun intended?"

"I knew it was a bad one before it even came out."

"Who knows?" Gina didn't seem to find this avenue of exploration as intriguing as Shake did. She asked him did he mind if she turned off the light on the nightstand? After, of course, she'd already turned off the light on the nightstand.

"I don't mind."

"Whatcha gonna do with your split? Your four million?"

"Don't laugh."

She laughed. "Not a little restaurant of your own somewhere?"

"Nothing fancy," he said. "American regional with some flair. Locally grown ingredients."

"Gonna wear one of those big hats?"

"A toque? I just might."

"Were *you* ever her kind of dance?"

"Who?"

"You know who."

He smiled in the darkness. It amazed him, how she could pick up on something like that.

"Lexy and I were never meant to be," he said.

"I see."

"Jealous?"

"I'm not the type either." She leaned over to kiss him.

Chapter 40

Shake woke the next morning to find Gina already dressed, in the bathroom, spraying perfume out in front of her then stepping quickly through the resultant cloud.

"You're a lazy bum," she said when she realized he was awake. "It's almost nine."

"You look like a girl with a plan."

She came back into the room and hopped onto the bed. Had some fun for a minute bouncing Shake around on the mattress.

"I thought I'd get out, look around. Maybe check out that statue, the one the guy at the shop was talking about?"

"Ferdinand de Lesseps," Shake said.

"And whatever else there is to see. As I may have mentioned, I really want to see a sloth. 'Cause really, when am I ever gonna make it back to Panama, right?"

Then, in not the next breath but the one just after:

"You wanna come with me?" she said.

Shake propped himself up on one elbow and studied her. Was the invitation sincere? Or was it calculated to forestall his suspicion? Or was it—who knew with this girl?—somehow both?

It wouldn't be in bed, Shake realized, that Gina finally wore him out.

"Sure," he said. "Count me in."

"Cool," she said, without the slightest hint that his answer might have surprised or thrown her. Instead she grabbed the room-service menu from the nightstand and started flipping through. "You want to order breakfast up or go out? I'm not starving, but I could use some coffee and eggs."

"Never mind," Shake said, trying again, watching closely. "Go on without me. I think I'm gonna sleep in, then find somewhere I can get a massage."

Her eyes didn't tell him a thing. " 'Cause you're old," she said. "Poor, poor boy."

"I'm gonna try to find someone to sell me a walker."

She made a tent of the room-service menu and put it on his head like a hat. It fell off after a second.

"Okay, then," she said.

He waited. If she were smart, she'd ask again was he sure he didn't want to come sightseeing with her? If she were smarter, she wouldn't ask, she wouldn't resort to such a naked ploy as that.

"What kind of massage? Better not be the kind with a happy ending."

"What's wrong with a happy ending?" he asked.

"They're never really either," she said, "in my experience."

"Inscrutable aphorisms from the college girl."

"That's a long story. I'll tell it to you sometime if you're nice. I was a Division I track star."

"What?"

"Briefly."

She hopped off the bed again.

"Go back to sleep if you're gonna go back to sleep, or come with me if you're gonna come with me. Sheesh. I like a man who knows what he wants."

She was impossible to read. But it was sure fun trying.

"I know what I want," he said. "Meet here for dinner?"

"Gotcha," she said, and blew him a kiss on her way out the door.

SHAKE WENT TO THE BALCONY and watched her leave the hotel. She strolled out onto the street without a care in the world—and without glancing over her shoulder up at the balcony. Either she didn't consider the possibility that he might be spying or she didn't need to glance up to know he was.

He thought about tailing her, wherever she was headed, but decided against it. That wasn't the sort of behavior a healthy relationship was built on.

And besides, he had work to do.

After Gina turned the corner and disappeared, Shake went inside and quickly put his clothes on.

Chapter 41

Gina turned the corner, and a limo was waiting for her. She got in the backseat. The driver was one of the Panamanian waiters from dinner last night, the one who wasn't a pilot.

Ziegler handed her a Mimosa.

"Where are we going?" she asked.

"You'll see."

"Whatevers." She was in a cranky mood suddenly and didn't know why. Earlier this morning she'd been in a great mood. Getting dressed, getting ready for an adventure, it always gave her such a delicious buzz. It's why, she guessed, she'd never really been much into drugs. Improvising lies on the fly was like flying, like playing jazz, *great* jazz—coke or E couldn't compare to that.

She couldn't remember her first kiss, and there was some uncertainty in her mind about when exactly she'd lost her virginity. She knew to *whom,* of course—she wasn't that bad; she just couldn't precisely remember if it had happened that first night at the beach house, or was it the night after, when his parents were back in town and they took the blanket down to the water? One of those nights, definitely. Or, possibly, the night before the first night at the beach house. It might have been then.

Give a girl a break. It was a long time ago, she'd only been fifteen, and the experience, let's face it, had been less than magical.

But damn, she could vividly remember her first score. Ten years old. A store at the mall called Wet Seal, which her mother called Wet Snatch. Ten years old, Gina didn't get the joke, of course. She'd been looking at a ring. You weren't supposed to touch, so she did. She liked the way that felt. The tingle. She liked the tingle when she picked up the ring and put it in her pocket and walked out the door.

That was the moment—a few minutes later, once a security guard caught up to her at Sbarro and grabbed her by the arm—when Gina discovered she had a natural gift for lying. It was like, to stick with the jazz metaphor, discovering you had perfect pitch or picking up a saxophone and discovering you knew exactly where you needed to put your fingers to make beautiful music.

Gina had convinced the security guard that the ring she'd taken from the store was actually hers, that she'd set it down when she'd tried on another ring and left it behind by mistake. She'd explained that the ring was a birthday present her mother had given her two months ago, a sentimental keepsake that had belonged to her mother's great-aunt. The great-aunt, when she was a child, had played one of the Lollipop Guild Munchkins in *The Wizard of Oz,* but her movie career was cut short when she died young of diabetes. There had been an inflatable moonwalk at the birthday party, but Gina had not been allowed to wear the ring while bouncing in case the ring accidentally punctured the moonwalk or another child.

Where the hell had all that come from? Gina had no idea. But at age ten she'd learned two things for sure: The getting into trouble had been fun; the getting out of it had been narcotic.

"Do you know anyone with perfect pitch?" she asked Ziegler.

"What?" He looked at her blankly. Doughboy didn't like being asked questions that threw him off or made him think or weren't about him. Which was another thing that set him—far—apart from Shake.

"Never mind." She tipped back the rest of her Mimosa. She thought about how, earlier, back in the room, she'd asked Shake if he wanted to come along with her today. She thought about how he'd said yes at first, then no. Watching her the whole time. Gina smiled. She liked lying to Shake almost as much as she liked fucking him. And for the same reasons. He knew how to play; he raised her game.

Was that why she was in a cranky mood right now? Because she'd lied to Shake?

But that didn't make sense. How could something make you feel good and bad at the same time? Because, crankiness aside, she could also feel in her veins right now that familiar hum, the tingle she always got when she did something she wasn't supposed to be doing.

If she was going to be honest with herself, she had to admit that Shake had his share of faults. He was almost *too* easygoing. Zero ambition. Gina knew he'd never have the giddyup to start his own restaurant.

On the other hand, was that so terrible?

There were a lot of tangled paradoxes here, especially for nine-thirty in the morning. Which was, like, six-thirty Vegas time.

"I wasn't sure you'd come," Ziegler said.

"Then I guess you don't know me very well," she said with a big bright smile.

SHAKE WENT DOWNSTAIRS. The nervous young assistant hotel manager with the expressive eyebrows was at the desk. When he saw Shake approaching, his eyebrows tensed.

"Don't panic," Shake assured him, "I'm not going to ask you to open the safe for me."

"Of course not, Señor Boxman," he said.

"Open the safe for me," Shake said.

"What?" The manager was so panicked he actually clapped both hands to his cheeks, like that Edvard Munch painting in Oslo. Shake knew about the painting, *The Scream,* because one of the guys at Mule

Creek claimed to know one of the guys on the crew who stole it a few years back. But then something happened with the crew, Shake couldn't remember what, and they'd ended up ditching the painting. It had been your typical criminal clusterfuck. A bunch of sociopaths with one good idea and nine bad ones.

"I'm just kidding," Shake told the assistant manager. He had not meant to cause such masterpiece-grade panic. "I don't want you to open the safe for me."

The guy's eyebrows expressed great relief. "No, Señor Boxman. Of course not."

"I have a question."

"Please."

"Where's the worst dive bar in the area?"

"Pardon me, señor?"

"Cheapest booze, skankiest hookers?"

The assistant manager straightened the posture of his eyebrows and made a soft guffaw sound through his nostrils.

"Señor Boxman," he said, "I am very sure I would know of no such establishment."

"But you have a brother-in-law," Shake said. "Right?"

The assistant manager nodded warily. "Three. Yes."

"And I bet at least one of them is a major asshole. *Pendejo?* Am I right?"

Shake knew he was right, the way the assistant manager's eyebrows danced and knitted.

"So," Shake said, "where would your *pendejo* brother-in-law hang out?"

AT THE AIRPORT, ZIEGLER'S PANAMANIAN waiter-driver handed them off to his Panamanian waiter-pilot. They flew in the little jet for about an hour, buzzing east to west across practically the entire length of the isthmus. Doughboy still wouldn't tell Gina where they were headed, nor why he'd wanted to meet with her separately from Shake.

She pretty much knew, without asking, the answer to that second question. And since Ziegler wasn't exactly a mystery wrapped in an enigma when it came to his motives, she was pretty sure she knew the answer to the first question, too.

Sure enough: The plane banked around a scatter of several small islands just off the coast, then came in low over water that was impossibly green, impossibly clear, and landed on the island farthest out.

"Welcome to my lair," Ziegler said with a big grin, and Gina pretended like she was surprised and delighted.

Which, actually, she kind of was, delighted, once she got a good look at his house. It was gigantic, right on the pure sugar beach, with a sweeping teak veranda built partly over the water. As they came up the path, a woman in a starched white uniform hurried out of the house and handed Gina a cool, wet towel scented with aloe.

"So," Ziegler said, "surf or turf?"

"For lunch?"

He chuckled. "Want to hike my jungle or snorkel my reefs?"

He has two *of these islands,* Gina reminded herself.

She picked reefs. Already laid out in one of the bedrooms, which was about three times the size of their room back at the hotel, were a half dozen designer bikinis in Gina's size. She changed into one and joined Ziegler on the beach.

They put on their masks and swam out a few hundred feet. Right off, thirty seconds in the water, Gina saw a huge spotted ray, size of a coffee table. It floated toward her, under her, then flicked the tips of its wings and shot away. An hour later she'd seen two more velvety rays, three turtles, more schools of iridescent fish than she could count. On and on and on.

The only other time Gina had been snorkeling had been at Disney World, one of the water parks there, where you paddled across a cramped little artificial lagoon you hoped none of the splashing kids around you had taken a dump in.

"This is freaking awesome," Gina said. She was underwater when she said it, with the snorkel mouthpiece in her mouth, which probably explained Doughboy's puzzled look when he turned his mask toward her, his beady, close-set eyes behind the mask.

"Blah-wab?" he said. She guessed that meant, *What?*

Gina tried again. "This. Is. Freaking. Awesome."

Ziegler wasn't paying attention. He'd grabbed her wrist and was pointing to the left. She followed his finger and saw drifting nonchalantly past—four or five freaking feet long if it was an inch, sleek and beautiful—a shark.

Ziegler pointed at the shark. Then pointed at Gina.

She was confused. Did he want her to, like, catch it? If he thought she was going to try to catch that shark, he was seriously out of his head.

Ziegler pointed at the shark again, then back at Gina, then at himself. He grinned around his snorkel mouthpiece, and Gina finally got it, then, what he was trying to tell her.

THE PLACE WAS CALLED EL PERICO, and if it wasn't the worst dive bar in Panama City, Shake didn't want to go near the one that was. At least not without a hazmat suit and a detachment of riot police.

It was only noon, but there were already a dozen or so customers—each one sitting by himself, hunched around a drink at the bar or at one of the little tables, silhouetted by the light streaming in through the big doors propped open to catch the breeze. A hard-eyed, acne-pocked stripper was on a small stage. She was doing something, a sort of sluggish shuffle around the pole, that could not by the most generous stretch be called dancing.

Shake waited for his eyes to adjust to the darkness and the haze of cigarette smoke. He hoped his instincts, in this case, were correct. Historically speaking, his instincts were usually correct about half the time, which when you thought about it was probably the worst of all possible past performances. If your instincts were usually wrong, for example, a smart player would learn to ignore them.

His instincts this morning weren't wrong. He spotted, at the far end of the bar, Dikran's big, bald, bullet-shaped head. Dikran was hunched around a drink, watching the stripper, his back to Shake.

Shake checked to make sure there was no mirror behind the bar, then moved silently up behind Dikran. He stepped up onto the rung of Dikran's stool for leverage and used his forearm to slam the big, bald, bullet-shaped head against the bar. With his other hand, he grabbed the Glock that was sticking out of Dikran's waistband.

Dikran spun around and swung wildly. Shake ducked the punch and jammed the barrel of the Glock into Dikran's gut.

Shake tried to remember—he was a car guy, not a gun guy—if Glocks had safeties. If this one did, and it was on, and Dikran processed the implications quickly enough, Shake knew he was a dead man.

Dikran, though, didn't move. Unless, of course, you counted the surge of blood that turned his squashed, ugly face even uglier, bruise-purple with rage.

"Calm down, big boy," Shake said. He didn't want Dikran to pop a vessel before Shake extracted the information he needed.

"You mother*fuck,*" Dikran sputtered. "I *kill* you."

The bartender glanced down the bar at them with a bored look. He said something in weary Spanish that Shake guessed probably meant, "Take it outside."

None of the other customers, nor the stripper, had so much as glanced up. Even though Dikran's head had cracked the bar and made the shot glasses jump.

"Is she here in Panama?" Shake asked. It didn't make sense that she would be, but nothing else about Lexy's involvement in this made sense either.

If she wasn't here in Panama, Shake's plan would require some drastic revision, and it wasn't much of a plan to start with.

"Fuck you!" Dikran said. "I tear your head off like onion and use it to—"

"Shut up." Shake dug the barrel of the Glock hard up under Dikran's rib cage and ripped the testosterone patch off Dikran's arm.

"Fuck!"

"Is she here?"

Dikran just glared at him. He knew he was a bad liar and didn't even attempt one.

Shake relaxed. He moved back a few feet in case Dikran in his rage decided to risk a gut shot from the Glock and hammer Shake with a nuclear head butt.

Even odds, Shake figured.

The bartender looked at the gun in Shake's hand, looked at Shake, said the thing in Spanish again. This time he also made a shooing motion toward the door.

"Hay no problema," Shake assured him.

"Take me to her," he told Dikran. "Now."

Chapter 42

They ate lunch on the veranda. Two new Panamanian waiters Gina hadn't seen before. Ziegler drank three glasses of wine and didn't eat much. How you could live on your own private tropical island, one of your own *two* tropical private islands, and still look doughy—it baffled Gina. The bridge of her nose was already starting to burn.

"After a while, you know," Ziegler said, waving his fourth glass of wine out at the water, "it's just adding zeros. Making the money. You start to look for something larger in your life. Some meaning. I think it's why I like it out here. Out here there's something you can believe in. You can smell it, can't you? The . . . I don't know . . ." He sucked in a deep breath. "The *wildness.*"

She could smell something all right, but it wasn't wildness. She'd been on her flirty best behavior all through lunch, sustained by the momentum of the magnificent snorkeling, but had started to feel cranky again. Doughboy liked to listen to himself talk, and she'd been listening along with him for quite some time now.

"This country hasn't been tamed yet. I like things that haven't been tamed."

"Cut to the chase, Roland," she said.

He went to the railing and tossed crumbs from the bread basket to the fish swarming below.

"I don't want to pay eight million for those foreskins, Gina. Not if I can help it."

"That's the price we negotiated."

"That's the price we negotiated when there were *two* sellers."

He let that statement hang portentously in the air, like it would take Gina a second to crack the code and figure out what he was implying. After which he probably expected her to draw her breath in sharply and say:

Wait, are you saying—you mean . . . ?

Please. She'd anticipated this move of Ziegler's even before he'd slipped the piece of paper into her hand last night.

"I was there, Roland, remember?"

"You're in for half, I presume?" he said. "So looking at four million?"

"Go on."

"All I'm saying, I see a way for both of us to improve our cash-flow perspective."

"Cut Shake out."

"Six million. All yours."

"You save two million . . ."

"And you take away an extra two."

"What makes you think I'd consider screwing my partner for an extra two million dollars?"

He turned back around from the railing and smirked at her.

"Your eyes," he said.

THE RESTAURANT WAS ON THE TOP FLOOR of the visitors' center. Alexandra sat outside on the terrace, sipping tea at a table that looked directly down on the Miraflores Locks. When she saw Shake approaching, herding a furious Dikran in front of him, her face betrayed not the slightest hint of surprise.

"Shake," she said pleasantly, "so nice to see you."

"Lexy." Shake sat down across from her.

"Panama City is a lovely city, yes?" she said. "Very cosmopolitan. And I am fascinated by this canal."

Shake looked down. A cargo ship with Russian markings, unbelievably big, like an apartment building laid on its side, was being tugged toward the lock gates by what looked like two toy locomotives running along each side of the canal at a forty-five-degree angle.

"Do you know about the French?" Shake said. "How they tried to build it first?"

"The French," Lexy said in a dismissive way. "Do you know, Shake, the locks, your president at the time, the first Roosevelt, he hired famous men to decide, when these locks were built, how do we make them beautiful? What ornaments and things? He asked famous architects—the man who arranged Central Park in New York City, among one."

"What did they decide?"

"You see for yourself, yes?" she said, sweeping a hand over the view. "They decide the beauty is already there, in the art of the engineering. They advise your president, Do not touch the locks, or they will be ruined."

Shake smiled. "Good advice."

"I think so." She sipped her tea. Without looking at Dikran, who still stood, hulking and fuming, in front of Shake, she said, "I see you have—how do you say?—get the drop on Dikran here."

"I'm afraid so."

"Motherfuck," Dikran said. "Give gun back."

"I think I'm gonna hold on to it for a while, Dikran, if you don't mind."

Dikran filled his eyes to the brim with martyred Armenian suffering and turned to Alexandra for a ruling. She shrugged.

"Finders keepers," she said. "Go get Shake now a nice cup of tea, please."

Dikran recognized that he was in no position to question orders. He stalked off.

"So," Alexandra said.

Shake studied her. Why had he always been attracted to beautiful but dangerous women? Was it some defect of character? Or a strength?

He did the math in his head and imagined, for a second, a little girl, she'd be four years old now, with Lexy's gray eyes and his . . . what? His nose, maybe.

"Just think, Lexy," he said, "if we'd stayed together, maybe we would have settled down, started a family, bought a nice little house in the suburbs."

"Yes." Her gray eyes twinkled. "I think exactly this is what did happen if we stay together."

"You never know."

She started to answer, then didn't. Together they watched the water boil in the lock; they watched the Russian freighter begin its slow, inexorable rise.

"So," Shake said finally, "if trouble was a city, where would I be right now?"

Alexandra sipped her tea and mused. "New York City, I think."

"That's a lot of city."

"It is a lot of trouble."

"I realize, Lexy, we're past the point where I might be able to ask you, for old times' sake, to perhaps—"

"I am afraid so, Shake," she said.

"Thought so," he said.

"The girl," Alexandra said. Surprising him. "Gina? You like this girl?"

"I suppose I do."

"But she is the one who leads you, yes? Into city of trouble?"

"I let myself be led, pretty much."

"Always a stand-up guy, Shake."

He wondered if that and half of $8 million would buy him enough of a head start. To hide from Alexandra. Dick Moby. In Shake's more optimistic moments, he thought it just might, just possibly. For a few years, at least.

"I don't want to spend the rest of my life looking over my shoulder, Lexy," Shake said. "I'd really prefer not to have to do that. I'd like to know—"

"You'd like to know what the price is?"

"Yes. I would."

"To get out of this mess you are in?"

"Yes," he said.

"You are assuming there is a price."

"No. I'm hoping."

Alexandra sipped and mused. "Could be a very high price."

"I'm fully prepared to pay a high price, Lexy," Shake said. "The money, if that's what you're—"

"What if price is not money?" she said.

This stopped him. "The foreskins?"

She waved a dismissive hand.

"I don't understand," Shake said, even though he was starting to. He felt too hot suddenly. Hot and clammy.

"No?" Alexandra asked innocently, indulging Shake his weak attempt at self-deception.

"You want me," Shake said slowly, "to give you Gina."

"Do I?" Alexandra said, her gray eyes twinkling.

Dikran returned with Shake's tea. He set the cup and saucer in front of Shake, then stalked off to sit glowering a few tables away.

Shake turned the handle of his cup from two to three o'clock. Then from three to four, four to five.

He told himself to stand up, say good-bye, walk away, hope for the best.

He told himself to stay seated, shut up, think it through.

He told himself that in life as in cards there was always a smart play and always a dumb play. There was never anything in between.

He stood up. Then he sat back down.

"But why—" he started to say.

Alexandra put a comforting hand on top of his. "Drink your tea, Shake," she said. "We have all lunch for negotiation."

BY THE TIME THEY LANDED BACK in Panama City, it was almost six-thirty. Ziegler offered to have his driver drop her off at the hotel.

"I can manage," she said.

"You're sure?"

"I've got a couple of errands to run first."

He kissed her hand like he'd done last night.

"You'll consider my proposal?"

"I always consider every proposal," she said without being funny.

She started to turn, but Doughboy still had her hand.

"How long have you known him?" he asked. "This Shake guy?"

"Long enough."

"Long enough to be sure he won't try to cut *you* out?"

She shrugged. "He might."

"But you think you're smart enough to see it coming, don't you?"

She started to nod but then thought about it and didn't.

"I can manage," she said. "Thank you for the lovely day."

"I mean it, Gina," he said. "After we're done with this, I want you to come back to the island with me. I'll teach you how to live well."

"You think I need lessons?"

He chuckled but didn't saying anything. Gina guessed Shake would have said something like, *No, but you could use the practice.*

How much was an extra $2 million? An extra $2 million was a *whole* lotta love, is what it was.

"See you tomorrow," Gina said.

The tinted glass of the limo window slid up. When it was halfway, Gina leaned down and gave it a quick flirty smack of a kiss, the glass where Ziegler's mouth would have been. Then she whirled on her heel before he could say anything and headed for the cab stand.

Chapter 43

Gina made it back to the hotel just after eight. Shake was lying on the bed, watching a cooking show in Spanish.

"Have fun today?"

"Did," she said. "Went snorkeling and saw some manta rays."

"But no sloths?"

"I don't think they live underwater, pumpkin."

He smiled.

She went over and kissed him. "How about you?"

"I went to the Miraflores Locks. Learned all about how the canal works."

"Interesting?"

"It was," he said.

He kissed her back. "Big day tomorrow."

"Wanna stay in and order room service? I'm whacked."

"Me, too," Shake said. "We can hit the hay early."

She looked into his eyes. He looked into hers.

"I'm glad you had a good day," he said.

"Right back at you," she said.

Chapter 44

Ted Boxman had never fully understood the phrase "adding insult to injury" until he reached the end of the paperback he was reading. It was a horror novel, one of the only books in English for sale at the hotel gift shop, about a group of young American tourists in Mexico trapped on a hill covered by a giant diabolical bloodsucking tropical vine. The story was much scarier and more nerve-racking than you'd ever guess from the premise, and Ted had been driven forward page after page by curiosity and mounting dread. Then he reached the end of the book and discovered that because of a printing error the last three chapters of the book were missing.

And, of course, the hotel gift shop did not have another copy.

That was the insult. Ted's injuries were both metaphoric and not at all so. On the metaphorically injured side, he'd been trapped in Panama City for the past two days because every flight back to the

United States had been fully booked. Nothing whatsoever available until the day after tomorrow. He'd been trapped in his hotel room the entire time because he had no money (he'd charged the book, and meals, to his room account), and the replacement credit card that Citibank had promised would arrive in less than twenty-four had, of course, not. Not that Ted had been eager to leave his hotel room. He was persona non grata with Frank the Facilitator and all the rest of the Building Bridges guys (who at this very moment were downstairs in one of the ballrooms, at the Day Four Meet-N-Mix). Apparently Nerlides, his "date" from the first night, had filed an official complaint with Building Bridges.

This reflected badly on all of them, Frank told Ted. It was one thing to be maybe a tad too aggressive with a girl—that was part of the traditional courtship process—but when a client of Building Bridges tried to weasel out of a restaurant check . . . well, that made all of them look like poor, desperate losers, which they were most definitely not.

"Yes, uh-huh, you most definitely all are," Ted had said. Which was probably an inadvisable comment, but Ted had been really angry and still aching (see below) from his not-metaphorical injury.

Frank had called Ted a pissant and banned him from all further Building Bridges Panama City events. Even though Ted had already paid a 100-percent-nonrefundable deposit and even though—this was the real irony—Ted wouldn't have gone to another Building Bridges event if Thelonious Monk himself, Ted's hero, had returned from the dead to groove until the wee hours.

Ted had sustained his not-metaphorical injury when he'd been mugged that first night. The young guys on the deserted street had demanded his wallet. Ted explained that his wallet had already been stolen. This information—translated for the others by the middle mugger, the one with the knife, the only one who could speak English—was met with skepticism. Ted didn't need to understand Spanish to pick that up. There was a brief conference in rapid Spanish among the muggers. Then the short mugger said something to the tall mugger and pointed at Ted. The tall mugger seemed outraged by whatever this suggestion was.

"He no want to frisk you," the middle mugger explained helpfully. "He no want to touch your butt."

Ted, needless to say, didn't want that either. His hopes rose, because it seemed that even though the short mugger's Spanish flew fast and furious, the tall mugger refused to budge on his no-butt-touching policy. But then the short mugger suggested what seemed to be an alternative approach—Ted found this ominous—and the tall mugger shrugged.

"Take off your pants," the middle mugger instructed Ted.

That's when Ted decided to make a break for it. It seemed like sound reasoning at the time. They couldn't really throw the knife at him, could they? No, as it turned out, but they could throw one of their almost-full beer cans. And this was the country, remember, that had produced superstar New York Yankees closer Mariano Rivera, the pitcher who'd led Ted to victory in his fantasy baseball league a few seasons ago. Ted had glanced back over his shoulder to see if they were going to throw the knife at him. At that instant the almost-full beer can nailed him, flush in the forehead. Ted staggered and almost ran into a wall. Beer flowed down his face and stung his eyes. Beer and, he realized, blood.

Ted would find out later it was just a small cut on his forehead. He didn't even need stitches. But at the time he didn't know that. And, more important, the muggers didn't know it either. They flipped out when they saw the blood sheeting down his face and dripping off his chin. They gathered around Ted and showered him with nervous apologies, in both Spanish and English. The middle mugger put away the knife and, inexplicably, offered Ted a stick of gum. Ted, inexplicably, took it. Then the muggers bolted and disappeared in the night.

It was the best thing that had happened to Ted all day, getting hit in the head with that beer can. Which pretty much summed up the kind of a day he'd had.

He turned on the TV, then turned it off. It was driving him crazy, that he couldn't finish his book. He was almost certain that things weren't going to end well there on the hillside covered with the blood-sucking vine, but it was the *how,* not the *what,* that made a good book good.

He went downstairs. He had to pass the doors to the banquet hall.

Ted dreaded a chance encounter with Frank the Facilitator or George Pirtle or, God help him, Nerlides. Luckily, though, the doors to the banquet hall were closed. From behind them came laughter and the muffled bass beat of bad eighties pop rock. Ted hurried over to the front desk. The clerk informed him that yes, he did know of a bookstore that sold books in the English language. And no, it was not far, the walk; the walk was not dangerous.

"You're sure?" Ted asked.

"I am sure," the clerk said, "yes."

Ted didn't have any money to buy another copy of the book about the bloodsucking jungle vine, but he'd already devised a workaround. He wouldn't *buy* the book, he'd just stand there at the shelves and *read* the last three chapters. Ha!

He left the hotel in good spirits. As promised, the walk was not far and he encountered no danger along the way. The bookstore was a pleasant place, light and airy, with a small café that spilled out onto the sidewalk in front. The English-language section, next to the café, was a pretty good size. Ted searched the shelves for the book about the bloodsucking vine. He knew that it had to be here. It was an international bestseller; if it was sold in a hotel gift shop, then certainly—

It wasn't here. He checked again. He checked the shelf above and below, in case a careless browser had misplaced the book. The author's other novel was there, but Ted had already read that one. There were no fewer than six copies of that one.

Insult added to insult added to injury, Ted thought with a grimace, even though he knew now he was just feeling sorry for himself.

He turned to leave. And noticed, reading at one of the tables in the café, an attractive Panamanian woman. She had warm, intelligent brown eyes and hair that corkscrewed charmingly every which way. She had what must have been two dozen bracelets on each brown arm and was reading a book by Flannery O'Connor that had been translated into Spanish.

Ted remembered liking Flannery O'Connor, her stories, in college. He checked the stack of books at the woman's elbow. There was the same book by Flannery O'Connor, but in English, and beneath it was—

Shit! The bloodsucking-vine novel he'd been searching for! In English!

Ted hesitated, then made his way over to the woman's table. He hesitated again when she glanced up at him, but her intelligent brown eyes were so warm, so curious—what could it hurt to ask? Probably she'd just laugh, musically, when he explained his predicament; she'd be more than happy to let him borrow her book and quickly skim the last three chapters.

"Excuse me," he said, "this is going to sound really crazy, but can I ask you a favor?"

The woman frowned. Her eyes no longer seemed so warm. She sighed, a great gust of annoyance.

"Fuck," she said, "off."

Ted, startled, took a step backward, bumped into a chair, and sat down without meaning to.

When she saw this, when she misinterpreted that he was not fucking off but doing just the opposite of that, she made a sound like a growl.

"I said fuck *off*," the woman snarled. She scooped up her books, stood, and marched away to the checkout counter, her many bracelets clanking.

MARIANA'S LIFE THESE PAST FEW DAYS had been one giant pain in the ass after another.

There was work: her boss. Cornejo had been flitting in and out of the shop at odd hours for the last two days. "Top-secret business," whatever that meant. What it meant was that she'd had to work late yesterday and missed lunch today.

There was the apartment: her landlord. He insisted that Mariana was violating the terms of her lease by allowing her sister to stay with her for a few weeks. In retaliation for this perceived violation, he refused to fix Mariana's badly leaking refrigerator.

There was family: Mariana's sister. Who had dropped from the blue sky a few days ago and just seemed to assume she could stay with Mariana as long as she wanted. An impression shared by their mother, father, grandmothers, and four brothers, all of whom—the brothers—had apartments and houses much less cramped and more suitable for a lazy, messy, irresponsible sister who had decided to just irresponsibly up and quit her very good job as a bookkeeper for no apparent or rational reason.

And now there was *this.*

Mariana looked around the hotel ballroom in despair. The American men were—*Forgive me, Lord,* she thought, *but no other word will do*—grotesque. Leering and preening, hairless and fat, most of them as old as her father. They murmured sly asides to one another. When they spotted a woman they liked, they moistened their lips greedily with small purple tongues.

Mariana realized, thirty seconds after she arrived at the function, that she'd been recruited to this event under the most blatantly false premises.

You should have known better, her mother would grunt if she ever found out about this.

Yes, Mariana admitted with a cringe, she should have known better. But she'd been bored with her life, with the men in it, with Latin men in general, and the Building Bridges website had been very sleekly, very professionally constructed. So why not? Mariana had thought. It was a lark, an excellent opportunity to practice her English. If anything more came from the afternoon function . . . well, then that was—she paused to remember an English colloquialism she enjoyed—that was *gravy.*

Two of the other women at her table were clearly prostitutes from Colón. The other was a beautiful but skeletal young Colombian girl who could not have been a day over sixteen and could barely speak Spanish. She ate the entire bowl of nuts on the table, then looked around for more.

Mariana slipped the young Colombian girl a ten-dollar bill and told her to run away as fast as she could. The girl just looked at her without comprehension. Mariana sighed and headed for the door.

"Where ya goin', sweetness?" said a man whose hair transplant had gone badly awry. Mariana just shook her head and tried to step around him. He stepped in front of her again, then laughed and swiveled his hips to pretend they were dancing. Mariana waited, burning a hole through his sternum with her eyes, until the man lost interest and wandered away.

Her mother would never, ever find out about this. Mariana planned to take this afternoon to her grave. This afternoon and everything in it.

She left the hotel and walked to the new bookstore off Calle Uruguay, the one with the café. It was quiet there, as she'd hoped, the rustle of paper soothing, the smell of the coffee, the creak of the wooden floor. She picked out a few books to buy, then sat down to read. She'd begun finally to relax, to feel the cautious return of some peace to her mind, when the American approached.

"Excuse me," he said. She looked up, alarmed. Had one of the Americans from the hotel followed her here? How? "I wonder if I could ask you a favor?"

The American had a small bandage on his forehead, a damp pink spot at its center. Mariana did not want to imagine what was beneath that bandage, or why.

Grotesque.

"Fuck off!" she told the bandage, and gathered up her books as quickly as she could.

TED, STUNNED, WATCHED THE WOMAN with the bracelets and the corkscrew hair storm off. And then, before he really realized what he was doing, he was on his feet, too, storming right after her.

He could feel his face flushing, the cut on his forehead throbbing. *What am I doing?* he thought, alarmed. He had no *idea* what he was doing! It was like he was having—it was like an out-of-body experience, except that he was very much in his body right now, too much so. His body was propelling him at great speed, without any input at all from Ted, toward the woman with the bracelets.

She was at the cash register, waiting for a cashier so she could pay for her books. When she saw him, the fierceness in her eyes should have scorched every bit of resolve from Ted's soul. But, strangely, it didn't.

There shouldn't have been any resolve there to start with.

"I *swear* to all that is holy," she said, "if you do not leave me alone, I will have my four brothers—"

"Just one doggone second, please," Ted said. More forcefully than he'd intended; he could tell this by the surprise on the woman's face. "I don't know why you're being so rude, and probably it's none of my business, but I just want you to know that I asked you one polite question, I'm actually a very polite person, and I'm actually one of those people who wish the world were a more polite and civil place in general, and I really debated coming over in the first place, because I didn't want to bother you, I really wasn't trying to 'pick you up,' but I did come over, which maybe was a mistake, but it's not like I should get lethally injected because of it, and all you had to say, all you had to say was, you know, 'Excuse me, I'm reading,' and I would have said, word for word, 'I'm very sorry I bothered you,' and I would have left you alone, not another word, and you wouldn't have had to have your four brothers do to me whatever you want to have them do to me, which—just let me say?—I'm really not that scared of, given everything that *has* happened to me the last few days, you don't have the slightest idea."

He went on to tell her, the words rushing out before he could even think about stopping them, about how his wallet had been stolen, how he'd been talked into this insanely stupid and demeaning Building Bridges tour in the first place, how no convention planner in his or her right mind would choose Oklahoma City over Kansas City or San Antonio, how he'd been held hostage in a cruddy restaurant and charged way too much for a cruddy meal and then mugged and hit on the head with an almost-full beer can, how he had no money, how the final three chapters of his bloodsucking-vine novel were missing, how that had been the absolute last straw, how he was sorry in advance if he offended her with what he was about to say, but he'd really grown to truly despise Panama. He almost told her about losing Vivian but just in time skidded to a stop at the edge of that cliff, heels digging in.

The woman was no longer staring at the bandage on his forehead. She seemed finally to be really looking at Ted. At his eyes, the rest of his face.

She seemed a little surprised by what she found there.

"What is this expression?" she asked. '"Just one *doggone* second'?"

Ted had to take another big breath. He'd really worn himself out.

'"Doggone' is like a kind of emphasis, I guess," he said. "You can use it instead of a curse word."

"You wanted to use a curse word instead?"

"Yes," he admitted. "I did."

"But you were too polite?"

"I'm going to leave now," Ted said. He felt drained; he felt sad and embarrassed; he just wanted to go home to a life he didn't like very much anymore. "I'm very sorry I bothered you."

He was startled when the woman laughed. It wasn't musical—it was more like a nasally honk—but neither was it unkind.

"Don't give up on Panama," she said. "I think Panama has just been having a doggone bad day for everybody."

Chapter 45

They woke up just after nine, which gave them twelve hours until they were supposed to meet Ziegler on Isla Taboga.

"Want to do some homework?" Shake asked Gina.

She nodded. "You read my mind."

They left the foreskins in the hotel safe and chugged across to Isla Taboga in a beat-up little ferry that looked like it had been in business since colonial times. The Pacific was glass-flat but a darker shade of green-blue than the Caribbean up by Portobelo. Standing by the rail, breeze in his face, Shake had a feeling—without even dipping a toe in either one—that the water down here was colder.

There were only a few other people on the ferry. Shake asked about this, and a weathered old man told them Isla Taboga was mostly a weekend destination for day-trippers from Panama City. During the week, the old man said, the island slept. Shake—homework—made a note of this.

The ferry docked across from an abandoned hotel and a sandy beach. A cobbled footpath wound around a hill and up to the main square. Across from the whitewashed stone church, a few more weathered old men sat around playing chess. Flowers were everywhere—growing wild, spilling off the iron balconies of the old buildings that lined the square—hibiscus and oleander and crepe myrtle. The sunlight up here felt to Shake thick and golden, like syrup.

"Why do you think Ziegler picked this place?" Gina asked.

Shake shook his head. "No telling."

He strolled over to the church where they were supposed to meet tonight and tried the door. It was locked. There was one small restaurant on the square. A waiter in a long white apron had begun setting the outdoor tables. A sign said the restaurant was open till ten.

Shake crossed to the other side of the square. From that vantage point, he could see the ferry chugging back across the bay to Panama City. A quarter turn around the island was a row of smaller wooden docks. A few small fishing boats bobbed in the water.

"Public but quiet," Shake said. "Fishing boats we could hire to get back if we missed the ferry or if he tried something hinky on that end. Remote, but not so much so we'd get nervous. He had to know we'd come check it out."

"Seems fine, doesn't it?"

"It does," Shake said. That's what worried him.

Gina strolled over to one of the chess games. As she studied the board, she rested a hand on the shoulder of the old man next to her. It was such a friendly, familiar, casual gesture. Shake doubted that Gina herself was aware she'd done it. He decided right then that if he hadn't already been in danger of falling for this girl, he was now.

And that's just what it was, wasn't it? Danger.

He asked himself to be serious for a second. To be forty-two years old and not seventeen. Because what would life with a girl like Gina really be like?

She strolled back over.

"I want to learn chess," she said.

"God help the world."

"Do you think he'll try to screw us over?" Gina asked.

"Fifty-fifty."

"He's offering a lot more than the foreskins are worth."

"A guy with his kind of money, eight million bucks is probably a rounding error. Why would he want to hassle with a double cross?"

"But his ego."

"On the other hand. Yeah." Finally, for the first time in the ten or fifteen minutes since they'd been here, one of the weathered old chess players moved one of his pieces. "And we know he likes to play games."

"So?"

"So as long as we keep things public, I think we'll be okay." Shake didn't mention the other thing that he thought might increase their chances, at least marginally, of being okay: the Glock 19 he'd lifted off Dikran, which Shake had hidden in the bottom of the leather day pack he was carrying. Gina had wanted to bring along towels and sunscreen in case the beach on Isla Taboga was any good.

A question raised itself: Why had Shake hidden the gun beneath the towels? Why hadn't he told Gina about the gun? Why hadn't he told her about his meeting with Lexy, the deal she had proposed?

That was three questions, he realized. He didn't have an answer to any of them. At least no answers he wanted to admit to himself.

"I'm surprised," he said casually, "that Ziegler hasn't tried to cut a separate deal with one of us."

"He can tell how much we like each other," Gina said, not missing a beat. She never did. She bumped her shoulder affectionately against his. "Wanna get some lunch?"

IT WAS A LITTLE AFTER ONE, but they were the only customers at the restaurant on the square. The waiter in the apron brought them good, simple fried fish, corvina with the head still on, along with arroz con coco and a couple of bottles of ice-cold beer, Atlas, a local brew.

The drowsy, sun-baked plaza, the flowers everywhere. The smell of the flowers, the smell of the Pacific, which was different in subtle ways from the smell of the Caribbean. More citric, cleaner, rowdier. The food and the wine and Gina across from him.

Shake was about to say it when she beat him to the punch.

"I could get used to this," she said. She gazed out at the plaza. "I think this might have been the life I was supposed to have."

"Not the one you ended up with?"

She shook her head and smiled. "There was a mix-up at headquarters. When I was born."

"An in-file in the out-box."

"You know?"

"I do."

He drank the rest of his beer and studied her while he did it.

She turned and caught him. "What?"

"I can't decide," Shake said. "If you're a good girl gone bad, a bad girl going good, or . . ."

"Just a bad girl?"

"That's not exactly what I mean."

"I already warned you, sweetie."

"I know," he said. "No heart of gold."

Her expression became unusually serious, almost melancholy.

"It's just who I am," she said. "Sometimes . . ."

"What?"

"I don't know. What if free will, what if it's just an illusion? I don't mean like there are Greek gods or anything. But what if the way you're born, the way you grow up, by the time you realize what's happened, it's already all wired. You're wired. You think you're making choices, but really you aren't. And the smart play is to recognize that. That you're a certain way and nothing is going to change that, even if . . ."

"Even if?" he asked.

"Even if sometimes you wish you could."

Shake thought about it. "Maybe the wishing is a start," he said.

"Think it works like that?"

"What are the odds?"

They smiled at each other. A long moment passed—a lazy, sunbaked, flower-scented moment that Shake didn't want to pass at all. Or if it must pass, he wanted to take Gina by the hand and follow it, this moment, remain inside its protective flower-scented bubble, wherever it led, leaving the present—or was it the future?—forever behind.

"Nature calls," Gina said. "Which is a polite way of saying I have to pee like a racehorse." She stood up. "Be back in a jumping jack flash."

Shake watched her walk into the restaurant and disappear. Two of the old chess-playing coots on the plaza, he noticed, were studying their game with such intensity, bent so far over their board, that their heads were almost touching each other.

He looked at Gina's beer. Considered the moral implications of the act, then finished it for her.

He glanced at his watch. They had plenty of time to take the ferry to the mainland, grab a nap, pick up the foreskins from the hotel safe, and be back to the island well before nine o'clock. He was pretty sure Ziegler would show up early, and Shake wanted to be here long before he did.

Ziegler wouldn't have needed time to put together the cash. Shake wondered again why he would have lied, why he wanted to push the exchange back a full day more than necessary.

He could think of several reasons. He didn't like any of them.

Gina's purse was on her chair. She'd left it in full view, as if to vividly reassure Shake that she'd be returning from the ladies' room.

He glanced at his watch again.

The waiter in the long apron approached. "Will you and the señora like some coffee?"

Shake sighed.

"The señora's not returning," he said.

Chapter 46

When she was sober, during the workweek, when she was sober and got pissed off about something, Gina's mother used to just *whale* on Gina's ass. The see-stars-and-fireworks kind of getting whaled on. Gina, when she got to high school, turned it into a joke she told people—that she'd learned how to run as fast as she did to keep her mother from catching her.

The other girls on the track team, all of them black except her, they couldn't believe that a white girl like Gina could run so fast. But they did know, a lot of them, about getting whaled on, and her joke cracked them up.

It wasn't entirely a joke. The trick, when you were getting whaled on, was to run fast in your *mind.* Stay a step ahead of whatever bad shit you were feeling. You couldn't let the bad shit catch you until you were somewhere nice. Where, in the sunlight, you'd wonder, "Huh, *that* was the shit that was bringing me down?" As if you'd had a dream that freaked you the night before but in the morning just seemed kind of dumb, like a Chihuahua covered in tinfoil barking at you.

Gina stepped off the boat. She was feeling some bad shit right now, about what she was doing to Shake. But, girlfriend, believe it, was *fast.* Gina, in her mind, was staying a step ahead. Come time, she'd take a breather and let the bad shit she was feeling catch up—when she was $6 million richer and on a plane to somewhere far, far away. Come time, she'd be happy to take the bad shit she was feeling to dinner at a nice place in Dubai, and they could work through their issues then.

She'd come across a quote from Wordsworth, her one year in college, that summed up the philosophy perfectly: Creativity works best when strong emotions are "recollected in tranquillity."

Exactly. Awesome.

She took a cab from the Amador Causeway back to the hotel. She walked into the lobby. The young assistant manager with the eyebrows was bent intently over the computer and didn't notice her. Gina dinged the bell at the front desk, which startled him. Though it was hard to tell how much that had to do with the bell and how much with what seemed his ongoing state of general bestartlement.

"Hi!"

"Señora Boxman," he said nervously.

"Good afternoon, cutie-pie."

"How may I be of—"

"I'd like you to open the safe for me, *por favor.*"

"What? But, señora —I'm afraid that—" He pulled himself together and managed a chuckle. "You are joking," he said. "But of course."

She leaned close. "I've never," she told him in a friendly, conspiratorial whisper, "been more serious in my life."

He tried another chuckle. It failed miserably. What looked like a faint rosy rash appeared on each of his cheeks. Gina felt bad for the poor guy, but she didn't have the time right now to be gentle.

She selected the smile she never liked to use, the one she'd inherited from her mother, the one that used your lips, your teeth, but never your eyes.

"Open the safe for me," she said.

"As you wish," the assistant manager croaked.

SHAKE HAD AN ADVANTAGE: He knew where Gina was headed. He took Dikran's Glock from the leather day pack, stuck it in his waistband, jogged down the hill to the docks on the far side of the island. The next ferry didn't depart for another twenty minutes, which meant Gina would have hired one of the private fishing boats to take her back to the mainland. Shake planned to do the same.

But of course—he should have anticipated this—Gina had paid off all the other fishermen; there wasn't another fucking boat in sight.

You already know how to play chess, don't you? he asked the Gina in his mind. The Gina in his mind just smiled back at him and put a finger over her lips. *Shhhh.*

Shake jogged back to the ferry landing. He still might have just enough time. He calculated that he'd be about forty minutes behind Gina when the ferry docked in Panama City. Half of that he could make up on the drive to the hotel if he could convince a cabdriver—money or gun or both—to let Shake drive. The other half . . . well, he'd have to hope for a little luck breaking his way; he'd have to hope that the assistant manager at the hotel, the one with the combination to the safe, had the grit to stand up to Gina for a few minutes.

Shake didn't bother to hope he might be able to stand up to her longer than that. Not a chance.

Shake reached the landing. The ferry's engines were revving, but the gangway was still down. He started toward it, then felt someone move up on him from behind; he felt something hard shoved against the small of his back.

"Move a muscle and you're a dead man," a voice said.

Shake ceased the movement of all muscles. He tried to place the voice.

"Marvin?" he said finally, surprised. Shake glanced over his shoulder. Sure enough: The man pressing against Shake's back what might be a gun in the pocket of his windbreaker was Marvin Oates, bug-eyed Vegas hock-shop proprietor.

"Keep your mouth shut and do exactly what I say," Marvin ordered.

"I don't have time for this, Marvin." Shake turned calmly, quickly.

"Hey, I told you not to—" Marvin shut up when he realized that Shake had the barrel of the Glock pressed to his forehead. "Oh."

"Finger?" Shake asked.

Marvin nodded and removed his hand from the windbreaker pocket.

"She said you didn't have a gun!" Marvin whined.

"She?"

"I just want a finder's fee. Ten percent. Or fifteen."

"You're working with Gina?"

"She said you'd have the foreskins."

Shake waited. Marvin's bug eyes bugged even wider.

"That liar!"

The ferry had pulled away from the landing. Shake was tempted by the thought of shooting Marvin. Or at least smacking him with the butt of the Glock. Before Shake could succumb to the temptation, Marvin, who'd been stewing, said, "Ha!"

"Ha?"

"I," Marvin announced triumphantly, "know where she is."

"No you don't."

"I do! She told me to meet her, once I had the foreskins, at this place in the old town. I know the exact place! Plaza France, or something like that. At the statue of some French guy. Ziegler was going to be there, and we were going to get the money then. So ha!"

Shake realized that the universe was supposed to be infinite, filled with multitudinous possibility and variation. On some planet somewhere, for example, Shake had his own restaurant; on some other planet, Ferdinand de Lesseps had succeeded in building his sea-level canal through the Panamanian isthmus. But nowhere, not in the darkest, most far-flung corner of the universe, could Shake imagine a Gina so dumb she'd tell Marvin Oates where she was really going to meet Ziegler.

She knew that Marvin would slow him down, but she also had to know he wouldn't slow Shake down for long.

She had to know that Marvin would immediately spill his beans.

She had to know—

Shake smiled. Of course.

"So what do we do now?" Marvin asked eagerly.

"You," Shake said, "are going to walk up the hill. There's a restaurant on the square. You're going to sit down and eat lunch. You're going to find a nice hotel, get a good night's sleep, then take the ferry back to the mainland in the morning."

Marvin nodded, trying to follow all this.

"Then you're going to fly home."

"Fly home? What?"

"Because if you don't," Shake explained, "I'm going to hunt you down and I really will beat you to death with a gravel-filled sock."

Marvin scowled sourly. He looked at the gun in Shake's hand.

"You think just because you have a gun," Marvin said, "you can tell me what to do."

"That's right," Shake said.

Marvin considered this, then wheeled and started trudging angrily up the hill. He paused after a few seconds and turned back around.

"The least you could do is reimburse my expenses," he said. He took a hit off his inhaler. "I'm out almost two grand because of this stupid trip!"

Shake waved the gun toward the top of the hill. Keep moving.

"Check's in the mail," Shake assured him.

Chapter 47

The statue where she was supposed to meet Ziegler was in the center of Plaza de Francia. Gina spotted it right away. A black bust of a guy with a big mustache, near what she was pretty sure was called an obelisk. FERNANDO MARÍA VIZCONDE DE LESSEPS was engraved in the stone column the bust sat on. Gina remembered the name from the story the debonair guy at the antiquities shop had told them. She didn't remember much of the story. Something about the French, and the Panama Canal before it was the Panama Canal. Gina had been distracted, too busy scoping out the cute little tamale of a shopgirl, trying to figure out who she reminded Gina of. The Latina actress on *My Name Is Earl,* maybe? With corkscrew hair instead of straight?

"Well, well, well," Ziegler said. He'd come sneaking up behind her. He was exactly ten minutes early. The sun had just begun to sink. "I'd say I'm surprised to see you, Gina, but I'm not."

His material was thin. It annoyed Gina. "We've already been down that road, Roland," she said. "Let's make a deal, whaddaya say?"

"You have them?"

She jiggled her purse—the real one, which she'd picked up at the hotel. She'd left the dummy back on Isla Taboga to fox Shake.

"You?"

He lifted the small, hard-sided suitcase he was carrying. It didn't look that strange that he was carrying a suitcase. There were a lot of people in the crowded plaza carrying even odder things—like, one guy, a big ceramic goat.

"To complete the transaction," he said, "please step into my office over here."

He nodded toward the doorway of a nearby building.

"What's wrong with right here?" she asked. She liked all the people around; she liked that there was a guy nearby who looked like a cop.

Ziegler pulled an exasperated face. "I'm not going to hand over six million dollars in cash in the middle of a crowded plaza."

"We could stroll to the edge of the crowded plaza," Gina suggested.

Ziegler just looked at her. "Your choice," he said.

Gina knew what choice he meant: Take it or leave it. She hesitated. She knew what Shake would do, but she wasn't about to walk away from 6 million bucks.

"Fine," she said.

Doughboy smiled his good teeth at her. "Follow me."

They entered the building. Ziegler, who had the keys, started to lock the door behind them. Gina put a hand on his to stop him.

"Yeah, right," she said.

He shrugged. He led her down the narrow, dimly lit hallway to a big, dimly lit room. In the center of the room was a gigantic antique scale model of the Panama Canal.

"Wow," Gina said.

"They're storing a few items here while they renovate the main museum on Plaza de la Independencia. I arranged for the security staff to take a nice long siesta so we could have the place to ourselves. Us and our guest, of course."

The hair on the back of Gina's neck prickled as she realized that someone was standing behind her. She turned.

"You remember Señor Cornejo?" Ziegler said.

The debonair owner of the antiquities shop. He bowed. Gina relaxed. Sheesh, she was jumpy.

"He's here to verify the authenticity of the merchandise," Ziegler said.

"Just in case there might have been a mix-up?"

"Better safe than sorry."

"How's about I verify the authenticity of that six million dollars first?" Gina said.

"Not here."

He led her and Cornejo past the scale model of the Panama Canal, down another corridor, up a staircase, into a smaller, stone-walled room furnished with a couple of plush sofas and lit by about a thousand candles.

"Very romantic," Gina said. What was up with Ziegler and his thing for candles? The guy, no big news flash, definitely had a couple of screws rattling around in that doughy head of his.

He went to the balcony, which overlooked the square, and pulled the curtains open. It was dusk, and the moon was impossibly, beautifully ripe.

"We need the right atmosphere for a transaction of this magnitude," he said. "Don't you think?"

"I think I want to see what you have in that suitcase of yours."

Ziegler set the suitcase on top of the coffee table and opened it.

"You want to count it?"

"You betcha," she said.

Inside the suitcase were stacks and stacks of hundred-dollar bills. Gina thought it would have made her dizzy, looking at all that cash in one place, but it didn't. She felt calm and clearheaded. She picked up a packet of cash at random and riffled through it. Ten grand per packet, just like at Moby's, way back when. She replaced that packet of cash and riffled through several other packets.

Ziegler had been waiting with melodramatic patience. "Well?"

"Okay."

"The foreskins?" Ziegler asked.

"I'll call you in an hour and tell you where you can find them," Gina said.

Ziegler snapped the lid of the suitcase closed, almost catching Gina's fingers.

"Nice try," he said.

"Didn't think you'd fall for that," she said. Although truthfully she thought maybe he might.

She opened her purse and took out the padded envelope she'd retrieved from the hotel safe. Ziegler pointed at Cornejo. Gina handed it to him.

Cornejo opened the padded envelope and very carefully withdrew the glass case with the foreskins. He spent a long time, longer than it had taken Gina to count the money, carefully examining them.

"Oh, my," Cornejo said every few seconds.

Ziegler tapped his foot. He really, Gina realized, wasn't a patient kind of guy. She guessed you kinda had to not be, if you were going to end up making a couple of hundred million bucks by the time you were forty.

"The verdict?" Ziegler said when he just couldn't stand it any longer.

"Well," Cornejo said slowly, "to be *absolutely* certain, of course, I would like to have time for a more extensive examination, but—"

"Genuine?" Ziegler said.

"Genuine," Cornejo pronounced with a little bow.

Ziegler's delight seemed almost childlike. He grabbed for the glass case with both hands and stared at the foreskins for a long time.

"Just think," he whispered, but then didn't finish.

Gina and Cornejo waited. Gina felt embarrassed and a little icked out. Cornejo just seemed embarrassed. He cleared his throat.

"Señor Ziegler," he said. "I wonder . . ."

"Right, yeah," Ziegler said without looking up from the foreskins. "You can show yourself out?"

Cornejo bowed again and glided off through a door on the other side of the room, which Gina hadn't even noticed before.

She reached for the suitcase. "If we're done here?" she said.

Ziegler looked up from the foreskins. It seemed to take a second for his eyes to rack back into focus. He returned the glass case with the foreskins to the padded envelope.

"So wait," he said, "what about my invitation?"

"Thought about it," Gina said. "But islands make me claustrophobic. I'm a gal needs wide open spaces."

She started to slide the suitcase filled with money off the coffee table. The suitcase was heavy. In the best possible way.

"Actually, Gina," Ziegler said, "I've got some good news and some bad news."

Her hand tightened on the handle of the suitcase.

Fuck, she thought. As simple as that: *Fuck*.

Everything had been going so smoothly.

Gina should have known better. She *had* known better.

Fuck.

"Good news," Ziegler said, "I'm now the proud owner of the one hundred extraordinarily rare, extraordinarily valuable foreskins. The most prized religious relic in the world."

He waited, smirking. She refused to give him the satisfaction.

"Want to know what the bad news is?" he finally asked.

"You're a doughy asshole who can't get a girl like me even though he has a hundred million dollars and two private islands? How heartbreaking is that?"

One corner of Ziegler's smirk took a hit but then recovered.

He turned toward the door through which Cornejo had exited.

"Gentlemen?" he called out.

Gina closed her eyes. *Fuck*.

When she opened her eyes again, Dick Moby and Jasper had stepped into the room. Both had guns drawn.

"You *fucker*," Gina told Ziegler.

"Imagine Mr. Moby's delight when I called to tell him I'd found his missing vixen." He pried Gina's fingers one by one off the handle of the suitcase. "Sorry, babe, you're a peach, but you're not worth six million bucks."

Gina tried to distance herself from the moment and appreciate, in an objective sort of way, the sturdy architecture of Ziegler's double cross.

"You keep the foreskins and the money . . ."

"And your pals here get their carnival prize." Ziegler grinned. "Everybody wins."

The Whale stared at Gina with his cold, dead eyes.

"I'm going to skin you alive," he told her, "you fucking cunt."

"Oops." Ziegler chuckled. "I guess not *every*body wins."

Gina was good in situations like this. She stayed cool. She didn't panic or puke or pee her pants like most girls would have.

"Let's all go for a ride," Ziegler said. "Somewhere with more privacy—and soundproofing."

Gina *felt* like panicking, puking, and peeing her pants. She just didn't do it. She assured herself that that was an important distinction; she tried to believe that staying cool right now might make a difference.

"Why don't we stroll instead?" she said. "It's such a pleasant evening out."

"Get her," Moby told Jasper.

"It is you!" a voice said.

Gina turned. The Whale and Ziegler and Jasper turned.

"Who the fuck are you?" Moby asked the guy who'd appeared in the doorway Gina and Ziegler had come through.

"It is you!" the guy said again, excited. He stared kind of wild-eyed at Gina and didn't seem even to notice that there was anyone else in the room. "I knew it was you! When I saw you out on the plaza!"

The guy was tall, with reddish hair and an open, friendly face, and Gina had never seen him before in her life. She had no idea what he was talking about. Given her current predicament, though, and the strong sense that her luck had nowhere to go but up, she wasn't about to split hairs.

"Hi!" she said, delighted. "Ohmygod! How have you been?"

The guy frowned. "You don't remember me, do you?"

Gina laughed. "Of course I do!"

"Get rid of this fucking turd," the Whale snarled at Ziegler.

"How did you get in here?" Ziegler demanded. "This is a private . . . function."

"The side door was unlocked," the guy told Ziegler. Without taking his eyes off Gina. She still had no idea why he thought he knew her.

"I'm not Sienna Miller," Gina said, "if that's what you're thinking. The actress? I get that every now and then."

"You stole my wallet!" the guy said.

Gina blinked. Tried to think. His— Shit!

The airplane; the airport; the baggage-claim area when they'd landed in Panama City.

"The Cocksman?" she said.

He winced. "I wish you wouldn't call me that. My name is Ted Boxman."

"Let's go!" the Whale snarled.

"We're leaving," Ziegler said. He set the suitcase full of money on the floor so he could grab the Cocksman's arm. So he could move the Cocksman away from the doorway. The Cocksman wrenched his arm free.

"No!" he said. "I want to explain to her the repercussions of her actions."

"Take your time," Gina encouraged him. Her processors were humming, white-hot. Door number one to her left, the door she and Ziegler had come through, was blocked by the Cocksman. Door number two, to her right, was blocked by Jasper and the Whale. Her best shot was probably the balcony, straight ahead, a more or less clear shot, but the balcony would involve a twenty-foot drop to the cobblestones below and maybe breaking some key bones, the prospect of which Gina wasn't crazy about.

On the other hand, when you compared that to getting skinned alive, hey, not much of a dilemma.

"I've had the worst three days of my life, thanks to you," the

Cocksman said. "And I really actually do, I want to thank you for that."

Gina cocked her head, curious despite herself. "Really? Why?"

Ziegler had grabbed the Cocksman's arm again, but he seemed curious, too.

"It was the kick in the pants I needed," the Cocksman said, "and I needed one, because I'd spent the last eighteen months just sort of feeling sorry for myself. If you hadn't stolen my wallet, if everything that happened to me hadn't happened to me, and I'm not saying that stuff was fun, but I would never in a million years have—"

"Yo, Ted," Jasper said quietly.

The Cocksman stopped talking and looked over at Jasper. Jasper turned his gun up and to the side, sort of a backward L, so the Cocksman would be sure not to miss it.

"You've got a gun," the Cocksman said, surprised.

"That's right," Jasper said.

"Oh," the Cocksman said. He saw Moby's gun then, too. He saw the suitcase on the floor. He seemed to realize, finally, that the worst three days of his life weren't over yet. "Oh."

Ziegler set the padded envelope with the foreskins on the coffee table so he could use both hands now to pull the Cocksman away from the door. The Cocksman allowed himself this time to be pulled, then shoved onto the couch.

"Sit there," Ziegler said. "Don't move. You understand? You call the police, anything like that, you're a dead man."

"Yes," the Cocksman said. "I understand."

"No," Jasper said.

"He's seen us," the Whale said.

The Cocksman, Gina could tell, didn't understand the implications of this. He looked to Gina for an explanation. She felt a sharp pinprick pang at the base of her throat.

"Leave him out of this, why don't you," she said.

"You want me to leave your friend out of this?" the Whale asked. Gina realized she'd just made a terrible mistake. Not the day's first.

"Fine," Ziegler said. "Let's all go for a ride."

Gina tensed. But then Moby—like he knew what she was planning, the fat, poisonous lizard—took two steps to his right and cut off her clear angle on the balcony.

"Get her and let's go," the Whale told Jasper.

"Not so fast," a new voice said, and Gina felt such a rush of relief she almost really did, this time, pee her pants.

Chapter 48

Shake stepped into the room, the Glock drawn. He was still breathing hard—from the sprint across the plaza, through the building, back through the building till he found the stairs, up the stairs, down a hallway, finally here—but tried not to show it.

Ziegler was to his immediate left. To Ziegler's left, a redheaded guy Shake didn't recognize was seated on the couch. Continuing clockwise, Moby with a gun stood by the balcony, Jasper with a gun against the wall, Gina to Shake's right.

"Who the fuck is *this*?" Moby said. He moved his gun from Gina to Shake. Jasper kept his gun on Gina. Shake put his gun on Jasper.

"Hey, Jasper," Shake said.

"Shake."

"How's the nose?"

"Hurts."

Shake glanced at Gina. "You didn't want dessert?"

"Boy," she said, "am I glad to see you."

"Maybe I should have gone with 'Think again'?"

She considered. '"Not so fast' was okay."

"I'll come up with something really good in about an hour. That's what always happens."

"I know," she agreed. "What took you so long?"

Dick Moby put the pieces together and turned to Jasper. "This the dickhead ripped me off at the motel?"

"This the one," Jasper said. "The one fucked everything up."

The way Jasper said that, quiet and hard—Shake got the sense that there was more to the "everything" in Jasper's mind now than Shake just slamming him in the head with a phone book or nailing him in the nose with a hotel-room door.

Shake glanced at Gina again. "What took me so long?"

"Don't tell me you didn't figure it out," she said. "I'll be gravely disappointed."

"I was your backup plan."

"That makes it sound so . . . I don't know."

"Calculating and cold-blooded?"

"See what I mean?"

Shake had worked out the details on the ferry making the return trip to the mainland. Gina hadn't wanted to lose him back on Isla Taboga, she'd just wanted to *delay* him. That had been Marvin's dual function—to slow Shake down *and* at the same time tell him where Gina was headed. That way if the exchange with Ziegler went down without a hitch, Gina would be gone—with all the money—before Shake showed up. In the event there *was* a hitch . . . well, then—here he was to bail her out.

"It was a pretty good plan," Shake told her, "except for the part where you weren't at the statue like you were supposed to be."

"Doughboy wanted to go somewhere more private."

"What did I tell you about that?"

She grimaced. "I know, I know."

When Shake arrived at the de Lesseps statue, he guessed that's what had happened; he also guessed that Ziegler—the arrogant, impatient prick—wouldn't have wanted to go far before he got his mitts on the foreskins. Shake had searched the windows of every building on the square, without really knowing what he was looking for until he saw the window aglow with candlelight.

Ziegler had inched over to the coffee table. He reached for the padded envelope.

"If no one minds," he said, "I'll just grab these and mosey off while you folks—"

Shake, Moby, and Jasper all swung their guns to Ziegler, who froze.

"Looks like everyone minds, Doughboy," Shake said.

Shake swung his gun back to Jasper. Jasper swung his gun back to Gina. Moby swung his gun back to Shake.

"You think you're gonna live through this," Moby told Shake, "you're even more of a half-wit than I thought you were."

Shake decided to ignore this. He'd made some questionable decisions, he had to admit, over the past week.

"So, gentlemen," he said, "I'm sure you've noticed that the walls are made of stone. How we gonna resolve this situation without an undue withering hail of ricocheting bullets that's more than likely to take us all out?"

Jasper, despite whatever new ax he had to grind with Shake, seemed to be wondering the same thing.

The Whale, on the other hand, stared at Gina with pure malice.

"Think your little girlfriend," he hissed at her, "that Hidalgo bitch, think she'll recognize you tonight when you show up in hell? When you don't have no skin?"

It was the first time, Shake realized, he'd ever seen Gina's mind stop working. Her face just went blank. For an instant he thought it was because of the no-skin threat, but then he realized she was trembling with fury, not fear.

"You killed Lucy?" Gina asked Moby. She looked like she was about to spring across the room at Moby and claw his throat out.

"Gina," Shake said. If she heard him, though, she didn't show it.

"She was a bleeder," Moby told Gina. "But I already knew that."

Shake braced himself. In about one second, Gina would pounce at Moby and Shake would discover firsthand just how many shots from a Glock you could get off before being chewed in half yourself. He glanced at Jasper and saw that Jasper was thinking along the same unhappy lines. But short of divine intervention, there was nothing now they could do to stop the inevitable, no way to stop Gina from—

"Lucy ain't dead," Jasper said.

Moby and Gina looked at him.

"What?" Moby said. So did Gina. So did Shake.

Jasper shrugged. He'd said it. What else was there to add?

"You told me that longhair did her," Moby said. "*He* told me. The one used to work the door, then bitched out afterward."

"That was the plan," Jasper said. "I didn't like it."

"She's alive?" Gina said. "She's safe?"

"Who the holy motherfuck," Moby sputtered at Jasper, "ever asked you did you like a plan or not?"

"She's safe," Jasper told Gina. He looked at Shake in a deeply unfriendly way. "She's gone."

"Lucy Hidalgo?" said the guy on the couch. He had a bandage on his forehead and looked vaguely familiar, but Shake couldn't place the face.

"You know her?" Gina asked, surprised.

"Excuse me," Shake said. "Who is this guy?"

"It's the Cocksman," Gina said. "Remember? He prefers to be called Ted, though. He saw me in the plaza and followed me in here to thank me for lifting his wallet."

"To thank you?" Shake said.

"Shoot the bitch," Moby told Jasper. Meaning Gina.

"Say what?" Jasper said.

"Whatever happens," the Whale said, "I want that fucking cunt dead."

"I shoot her," Jasper said, "he's gonna shoot me." Meaning Shake.

"Then I'll shoot him," the Whale said. "That so fucking hard to figure out?"

Shake gave Jasper a few seconds to get the oars in the water, then stepped in to help with the rowing.

"Jasper," he said, "I hope I don't have to point out to you the fundamental flaw in that scenario."

"Fine," Moby said, "we'll both shoot him." He swung his gun from Gina to Shake.

Shake swung his gun from Jasper to the Whale. "Jasper," he said, "let's talk this out. Let's—"

"Be still and let me think," Jasper said to Shake. "Wasn't for you, wouldn't be none of this happened in the first place."

"I'd do it again," Shake said. He looked at Jasper. Jasper looked back at him. Jasper's expression didn't soften, exactly, but at least he didn't pull the trigger and blow Shake out of his socks. That was a start.

Jasper looked at the guy on the couch. "What you mean? You know Lucy?"

"I think I know her," the guy, Ted, said. "I mean, I know *a* Lucy Hidalgo. I just met her last night. At dinner? She's my girlfriend's sister. I mean, she's not really my girlfriend, Mariana's not—that came out completely wrong and presumptuous. But you know how sometimes when you meet someone, and you spend all day with them, and then the next day, and there's this connection that just—"

Ted stopped. He'd realized that Jasper, in his surprised excitement, had swung his gun at him. Jasper realized, too, and swung his gun back to Shake. Shake swung his gun from Moby to Jasper.

"She's here?" Jasper said. "You know where she is?"

"Of course," Ted said. "She's living with my . . . with her sister for a few weeks."

"What are the odds," Shake asked Gina quietly, "it's the same Lucy Hidalgo?"

Gina shook her head. "I have no idea. My brain's about to explode as it is."

"She just quit her job," Ted said. "She was a bookkeeper. She's taking some time off to get her life straightened out."

"Bookkeeper?" Jasper said. He frowned.

Damn, thought Shake. Then, taking a stab, "Hey, Ted, does your girlfriend's sister Lucy *look* like a bookkeeper?"

Ted glanced down at his shoes, embarrassed. "I don't know. I mean, you know, what does a bookkeeper look like, really?"

"Does this bookkeeper," Gina said, "have a bod that belongs in the museum of all-time incredible bods?"

"That's not really for me to say," Ted mumbled. "I didn't notice."

"Jasper," Shake said, "I think you may have a bingo."

"Huh," Jasper said, his round, sleepy-eyed face wide with the wonder of it all.

"Jasper," Moby snarled. "Get your shit together and let's end this."

Shake decided to give it another, cautious try. "You don't want any part of this situation," he said, "do you, Jasper?"

"No," Jasper said.

"What the fuck is wrong with you?" Dick Moby swung his gun from Shake to Jasper.

Shake swung his gun from Jasper to the Whale. The Whale quickly swung his gun back to Shake. Jasper still had his gun on Shake. Ziegler and the Cocksman were both sitting on the couch, trying to make themselves as small as humanly possible. Gina, Shake could tell, was considering the advisability of a break for the door.

"Don't do it," he told her, "please."

"It will just create more problems than it solves?" she asked.

"Yes."

"I thought you were a fucking professional," Moby told Jasper. "Do your fucking job."

"We're two guys," Shake told Jasper, "at a fork in the road. We've got a chance here to start over. Do it right the rest of the way."

"Too late for that shit." Jasper shook his head sadly.

"Me," Shake said, "I'm gonna open up a restaurant. Nothing fancy. Just local ingredients and an attention to detail. You, you're gonna give Lucy a call. Have a cup of coffee with her and see where it goes. Ted here can set it up." He waited. "Ted?"

"Right!" the Cocksman said. "Yes."

"Shoot the motherfucker!" Moby yelled at Jasper, furious.

"Never too late, Jasper," Shake said. "It's not a second chance unless you take it. Your choice."

"Shoot him!" The Whale was practically screaming now. "Shoot him, you dumb fucking blue-gum shine or—"

Jasper turned and fired three shots so quickly that it sounded like one long shot. The Whale's white shirt flared bright red, and he lurched backward. He thudded against the wall, knocking a candle off the shelf, then slid down the wall. He was so fat he didn't really topple but more like melted over sideways.

"Shut the fuck up," Jasper said.

The flame of the candle that had fallen to the stone floor still burned. Jasper stepped over and with the toe of his shoe extinguished it.

Then he swung his gun back to Shake. Shake kept his gun on Jasper.

"That simplifies the equation," Shake said. He could taste the sharp tang of burned gunpowder in the air. "But we're still in a pickle."

"Can I say something here?" Gina asked.

"No," said Shake and Jasper at the same time.

"Sheesh!"

Shake glanced at the suitcase next to the sofa. "How much?"

"Six million," Gina said.

"Six million dollars?" Jasper said.

Shake nodded. "Half of it's yours," he told Jasper.

"Hey!" Gina said.

"Be quiet, please," Shake told her.

"Let's see it," Jasper said.

Shake pointed at Gina, then the suitcase. "Show him, please."

Gina frowned but crossed to the suitcase. She took advantage of her fresh proximity to Ziegler to give him the finger. Then she opened the suitcase.

Shake whistled when he saw all that cash.

"What do you say, Jasper?" Shake asked.

Jasper thought about it.

"I still don't see why—"

"Gina," Shake interrupted.

"I know." She sighed. "*Please.*"

"All right," Jasper said. "You can keep the— What are they?"

"Foreskins with great religious and historical significance," Shake said.

"Hey!" Ziegler said.

"Shut up," Gina told him.

"Foreskins?" Jasper said. "You don't mean like—"

"I'm afraid I do," Shake said. "Long story. On three?"

Jasper nodded.

"One . . ."

Jasper lowered his gun. "Shit," he said. "I trust you."

Shake lowered his gun, too. Took his first breath in about fifteen minutes.

"What a day," he said.

"Freeze!" Ziegler said, his eyes wild. Shake saw that he'd pulled a small revolver out of his pocket. He grabbed Gina's arm and yanked her close, pressed the revolver to her neck. "Back off or I'll blow her—"

Gina kicked backward and nailed Ziegler between the legs. He squeaked and doubled over. The revolver clunked to the floor.

"You didn't let him finish his colorful threat," Shake said.

"Fucker," Gina hissed at Ziegler.

Ziegler lunged. But not for the revolver. Not for Gina. For, instead, the padded envelope on the coffee table. The foreskins. But he'd overestimated, Shake saw, his capacity to locomote in the aftermath of a kick to the nuts. Ziegler squeaked and doubled over again. Gina picked up the revolver and pointed it at Ziegler's head.

"Don't do it," Shake said.

She considered. "I'm gonna need at least two good reasons."

"You're not a killer, killer," Shake said. "And you don't want to be."

"I could just shoot his dingle off, how about that for a compromise?" But after a second she tossed the revolver away.

Shake stuffed the Glock into his waistband. "Jasper," he said, "you have something we can tie this fucker up with?"

Jasper thought for a second. Then he went to the balcony, found the draw cords for the curtains, yanked them free. He tossed them to Shake.

Shake lashed Ziegler's hands together, his feet, his hands to his feet. With the remaining cord, Shake tied the whole package to a thick stone column, against which Ziegler could struggle to the end of time for all the good it would do him.

"There," he said when he'd finished.

"Foreskins with great religious and historical significance?" the Cocksman asked. "Gee. Interesting. I find that interesting. This will all be a funny story I can tell people back at home." It appeared to Shake as if the poor guy had formally entered a state of official shock. Eyes glazed, movements robotic, he'd taken the slender glass case from the padded envelope and was examining it carefully.

"Don't open that!" Shake yelled, and Ziegler yelled, and Gina yelled.

Ted looked up, startled, but it was too late. He'd already unsnapped the latch and lifted the glass lid.

For a second, nothing happened and Shake had to wonder—were these fake foreskins actually fake *fake* foreskins, not ancient and fragile at all?

But then, one by one, the foreskins began to lift gently off the glass. One by one by one, they wafted upward until the room was thick with them, a hundred pale ghost moths that fluttered and danced in the drafts from all the candle flames. Fluttered and danced, Shake realized, *toward* the candle flames.

"Noooo!" Ziegler let rip a low, throaty moan of animal despair. At the same instant, the first fluttering foreskin touched candle flame. It flared, a single orange spark, then vanished, leaving behind a thin coiled thread of smoke.

"Nooooo!"

A couple more foreskins flared, a few more, then suddenly, like fireworks, like an enormous school of fish turning as one and catching the light, the whole room flashed and popped with orange sparks.

Smoke curled and settled. There wasn't a smell. Shake was glad of that.

"No, no, no," Ziegler said. He was sobbing now.

Shake was looking around for something to use as a gag when he heard the scrape of metal on stone. Heard what sounded like a wet bubbling breath, sucked in hard. He looked over and saw the Whale—still alive after all, just barely—dragging his gun off the floor and pointing it at Jasper.

Before Shake could react, Moby fired. Jasper fired back, putting the Whale down for good. Then Jasper sank slowly to the floor.

Shake hurried over and knelt next to Jasper.

"Jasper, buddy, where y'at?" Shake said. "Talk to me."

Jasper grimaced. "Damn," he said.

"Where'd he get you?"

"Fat cracker shot my knee," Jasper said. "My good one."

Shake looked down and saw the dark, wet mess. He laughed with relief. "Not anymore it ain't, champ."

"Never working again for no fat evil cracker," Jasper said through teeth clenched in pain.

"You won't have to," Shake reminded him. "You're now officially a rich man. You can buy a battalion of fat crackers to carry you around all day in a big, comfortable recliner."

Shake's eyes had started to water. The room was filled with smoke. From candles, from gunshots, from toasted foreskins. Ziegler was still sobbing. The Cocksman had squeezed his eyes shut and was whispering to himself—Shake laid even odds he was whispering something along the lines of, "This is just a dream, this is just a dream." And Gina . . .

Shake looked around the smoky room.

Gina was gone.

The suitcase with the cash was gone.

Shake leaped up. He went straight to the balcony and tore the drapes aside. He gripped the iron railing hard and searched the plaza below.

There—just a quick glimpse of blond head—Gina, disappearing into the Carnaval crowd below.

Jasper struggled to sit up. "What's the trouble?"

"You mean," Shake said with a sigh, "*who.*"

Chapter 49

Shake tore up the drapes, and they bandaged Jasper's knee as best they could. With what was left over, he gagged Ziegler, who'd stopped sobbing but started cursing and threatening and swearing that he'd use every penny of his fortune to hunt Shake down and torture him and so on.

The Cocksman, Ted, had found a wrought-iron candlestick that was just about the perfect length for a cane and brought it to Jasper. Ted had calmed down a little when Shake explained that he, Shake, was a DEA agent working for the United States government and Jasper was an undercover field operative for the ATF, and Ted had just done his country a great service in helping take down a couple of bad, bad men.

Shake didn't know if Ted really bought it all, but he knew that Ted *wanted* to. That was the important thing. And Shake knew Ted was pretty sure that the last part—about the bad, bad men—was absolutely true at least.

Shake and Ted helped Jasper hobble down the hallway to the elevator. Shake pushed the button, and they waited for the iron arrow to inch along from One to Two to Three.

"You gonna be cool?" Shake asked Jasper.

"Shit." Jasper gave his shot knee a condescending glance.

"I mean the money."

Jasper smiled, just a little. "Mr. Moby got a safe back in Vegas."

"And you know the combination?"

"Only one does now."

"Good for you."

"First thing, though . . ." Jasper looked a question at Ted.

"Of course," Ted said. "Yes. I guess, though, that . . ."

"If Lucy don't want to see me in person," Jasper said, "I understand. We can talk on the telephone. Tell her I just want to clear a few things up, then I won't bother her no more, that's what she wants."

Ted nodded. "That sounds good. That sounds okay."

"Tell Lucy I said hi," Shake said. "Tell her thanks for help with . . . ah, the investigation in Las Vegas."

"What about him?" Jasper said. He tilted his head back toward the room where Ziegler was tied up.

"He doesn't realize it yet," Shake said, "but his bad day is just beginning."

The elevator dinged, and the door slid open. They got inside and rode down to the ground floor. The bell dinged again, and the door slid back open.

Standing there, when it did, were Alexandra and Dikran.

Alexandra smiled pleasantly at Ted, then Jasper, then Shake.

Dikran glowered at Shake. "Give me fucking gun back."

Shake handed over the Glock. "Third floor. The room down the hall on the left."

Shake, Jasper, and Ted exited the elevator. Alexandra and Dikran entered. After the elevator door closed behind them, Jasper gave Shake a quizzical look.

"That's the lady runs the Armenians in L.A."

"That's right."

"But—"

"Turns out she wasn't after the money. She didn't want to sell the foreskins, she wanted to use them in a different way."

"Get to Ziegler?" Jasper guessed.

Shake nodded. "Bait. The foreskins flush him out, get him out in the open, then Lexy makes the nab."

"So she can turn him over to the feds?"

"High-profile collar for them. Network news, everybody gets a promotion."

"Thanks to her."

A big prize like Ziegler, Shake knew, would buy Lexy a lot of federal goodwill. A few indictments buried at the bottom of the stack. A couple of grand juries released from service. "She's been setting it up with the deputy attorney general for a couple of months."

Ted had been trying to follow the conversation. Without much luck. Without, actually, any luck.

"So," he said, "I guess I'll head back to the hotel now, if that's okay. I can talk to Lucy in the morning. Then I'll call you, and we can set a time to . . ."

Ted stopped, since he was the only one nodding, not Jasper.

"How about right now," Jasper said, without using a question mark of any sort.

"Well," Ted said. "Well . . ."

Now Jasper was the one nodding. After a second, Ted wisely joined in.

"Go get us a cab," Jasper said.

Ted, still nodding, hurried across the plaza to flag down a taxi.

"You better get that knee looked after," Shake told Jasper.

"It can wait." When Jasper was certain that Ted really was going to flag down a taxi and not try to make a break for it, he turned back to Shake. "You really gonna open that restaurant of yours?"

"Last week I would've had to tell you no fucking way. I was just bullshitting myself and everyone in the neighborhood. But now . . ."

Shake shrugged. "You never know, right? If you're ever looking for a good investment, all that Whale money, look me up."

"Yeah you right."

Jasper was smiling more now. He shook hands with Shake and hobbled off.

Chapter 50

Shake used the last of his cash to take a cab back to the hotel. He waited outside the door to the room for a long time, maybe half an hour. Until roused by a maintenance guy who walked down the hallway and looked at him strangely.

Turn around and leave, Shake told himself. *Don't go inside. It's just going to make it harder, this little sliver of dumb blind hope you won't let go of.*

He unlocked the door and went inside. The room was empty. The bathroom was empty. The bathtub was empty.

No Gina.

Sure enough, going inside made him feel even worse.

He drank a couple of miniature bottles of rum from the minibar, more than a couple, and fell into a queasy, dream-filled sleep. He was a pale ghost moth, fluttering and flaring. A guy with the head of a lion and Dr. Gorsch's voice was demanding his foreskin. It was one of the most fucked-up dreams he'd ever had.

Chapter 51

Jasper stood outside the door to the apartment with Ted and waited. Listened to the locks rattling open on the other side. Seemed like a lot of locks for one door, but Jasper wasn't sure if he minded. He wasn't sure right now if he was in a hurry or just the exact opposite.

Tell the truth, wasn't a damn thing he was sure about right now. All what he'd been planning to say to Lucy when he saw her, all what he'd worked out on the taxi ride over here, it had turned slippery in his mind and slithered out between his fingers.

They hadn't been able to call ahead, since Jasper's cell phone was out of battery.

"Listen here," Jasper said to Ted, thinking now maybe they should wait till morning after all, but the door to Lucy's sister's apartment was already swinging open.

The pretty Panamanian girl who opened the door, Lucy's sister, had more hair than she knew what to do with, and twice as many bracelets.

She smiled big when she saw Ted. When she saw Jasper, she kept smiling, but in a perplexed sort of way.

"*Hola,* Mariana!" Ted said. "This is Jasper. He's a friend of Lucy's?"

Mariana took this in. A girl's voice behind her called out something in Spanish. Mariana called something back in Spanish. Jasper heard the footsteps. That was something he literally heard—Lucy inside coming to the door in her high heels—but it was also a metaphorical expression from his football days. When a quarterback heard the footsteps, it meant he was thinking too much about the hammering he was about to take and not enough about the pass he had to throw.

Jasper was usually the one making the footsteps that made the quarterback lose his nerve. This was the first time it'd been the other way around.

Mariana opened the door wide.

"*Hola,* Lucy!" Ted said.

Lucy looked at Jasper. He looked at her.

"Who are you?" she asked.

"My name's Jasper," he said. He took a deep breath to make up for all the ones he hadn't taken in the last few minutes. "I thought you was a different Lucy."

This Lucy didn't look like his Lucy at all. She was taller, less round, had darker skin. Some body like his Lucy's, but a bitty nose and a turn to her mouth that was nothing like the one he'd been thinking about kissing for the last hour and a half.

Ted was looking at him with genuine sympathy, which Jasper appreciated. Jasper was glad he hadn't shot him.

"I'm really sorry about this, Jasper," Ted said.

Funny thing was, Jasper felt all right. His knee ached like a son of a bitch, and he needed a glass of water, a place to sit for a spell, but the feeling that had started flapping in his chest when he thought he'd found his Lucy, thought she was here in Panama—it was still flapping.

Because he *would* find her. Simple as that. He'd find her and explain why events had unfolded the way they had, and then he'd ask could he kiss that mouth of hers.

This certainty of the future filled him with a powerful kind of peacefulness, one he hadn't known in a long time. Though his knee still ached like a son of a bitch.

"Y'all mind if I have a glass of water," Jasper asked this Lucy and Mariana and Ted. "And sit for a spell?"

Chapter 52

In the morning Shake woke to bright slanted sunlight and the sound of a door lock snapping, the door opening.

He sat up in bed. Too fast, but he didn't care.

A housekeeper rolled her cart into the room. Not Gina. When the housekeeper saw Shake, she fired off a stream of apologetic Spanish.

"It's okay, no problem," he assured her. He lay back down, then rose again, more slowly this time.

"You want I to go?" the housekeeper said.

"No, it's okay. No problem."

She nodded the question: *You sure?*

Shake nodded the answer: *I'm sure.*

The housekeeper began to dust, and Shake shuffled to the shower. The hot water revived him in certain ways, but none of the important ones. He shaved, got dressed, returned to the room. The housekeeper had turned the TV to CNN, to keep her company while she dry-mopped the marble floor.

Shake didn't really have anything to pack. He took one last, long look around the room, even though he knew that this—remembering everything that had happened in this room—would make the moment worse. It did.

"You have fun at the Carnaval, yes?" the housekeeper asked.

Shake considered. "Yes," he said. "Expensive but fun."

Though it wasn't the millions of dollars he was talking about, of course.

". . . California State Penitentiary at Mule Creek," a grave voice said.

Shake looked over at the TV. On-screen was a wide-angle shot of a low-desert landscape he knew all too well: squat gray buildings, fence line topped with coils of razor wire.

"The three men escaped," the reporter's grave voice continued, "by cutting through a cinder-block wall and overpowering two guards. One man—"

The screen cut from a shot of the prison to a mug shot of one mean-looking motherfucker in an orange jump. Vader Wallace. Glaring out at the world. Glaring right at Shake.

Shake winced and didn't bother listening to the rest of the news report. He took the elevator to the lobby. When the assistant hotel manager behind the desk saw him, he went pale.

"Señor Boxman." His eyebrows prostrated themselves abjectly, begged for forgiveness. "I am so sorry. The señora, she— I tried to— But the safe . . . and—"

"Don't worry about it," Shake said. "We were both out of our league."

"Yes, señor." The assistant manager contemplated this fact with sadness.

"About the bill," Shake said.

"The señora, of course," the assistant manager said. "She has taken care of it. Yesterday?"

Shake remembered the hotel in Vegas, right before he blacked out.

"She owed me one," he told the assistant manager. "But I'm still gonna kill her if I ever find her."

"Ah," the assistant manager said. He nodded knowingly. He seemed to understand that Shake wasn't really going to do that, find Gina or kill her, either one, no matter how much he might want to do both.

Shake left the hotel and walked until he ran out of room to walk. He found himself on the causeway. He took a seat on a bench and gazed out over the sparkling water and the prospect, less sparkling, of his own future.

What the hell, he thought, it *had* been fun. And the trend, when you averaged it all together, the sharp spikes and dips, was upward. A week ago, for example, he'd been living in a six-by-nine cell; a good day for him was when the mess served banana pudding instead of butterscotch. He'd never dreamed he'd get to eat fresh fish on a Pacific island with a girl like Gina.

He'd never dreamed a girl like Gina existed. That was for sure.

Maybe there was something to be said, after all, for making your own decisions. For not letting the current of life carry you along at its whim.

He dug in his pocket and found a coin stamped with a bird perched on a royal shield on one side and the sharp-beaked profile of a man who resembled a bird on the other. The paper money here was U.S., but the coins were Panamanian balboas.

He flipped the coin, slapped it on his forearm, started to call it. But then he heard the putter of an engine behind him and turned.

Gina, astride a battered orange Yamaha, took off her helmet and smiled at him.

"Three million dollars says it's tails," she proposed.

Shake tried to play it cool, but who was he fooling? He smiled, too.

"Where'd you get the ride?"

"Borrowed it from a friend of mine," she said.

"This friend meet the generally accepted definition of friend? The borrowing meet the generally accepted definition of borrowing?"

She patted the seat behind her. "Might be enough room for two, sport."

He stood, flipped her the coin. She caught it. Looked at it.

"Heads. How do you like that? You win."

"Why'd you decide to cut me back in?"

"Who says I've decided?" she asked. "Come on if you're coming on."

He hesitated for a second—once again, who did he think he was fooling?—then went around and started to climb aboard the Yamaha. Gina goosed the throttle, and the bike's seat squirted out from beneath him. Gina stopped a few yards away.

"Whoops," she said.

"Sure. Now that you've got my last balboa."

"Come on. I was just teasing."

He walked over and tried again to climb aboard. Again she zoomed away at the last second.

He stood where he was and crossed his arms. Gina smiled her sweetest smile. "I'm sorry. I really am. Come on."

"How do I know you're not gonna screw me over again?" Shake asked.

Gina revved her engine and winked.

Acknowledgments

I HAVE TRIED, WITH THIS BOOK, to get my facts straight and keep them so. As a reader, I like novels that are grounded in careful, meticulous research and historical accuracy. That said, I did take certain small liberties and would like to point them out now.

Philippe Bunau-Varilla, the Frenchman responsible in large part for convincing the Americans to build their canal in Panama, not Nicaragua, comes across in this novel as something of a bullshitter and con man. This is the impression one draws from reading David McCullough's masterful and massively entertaining book, *The Path Between the Seas,* but other historians do take a kinder view of Bunau-Varilla's wheelings and dealings (*French* historians, as you probably guessed, but hey).

As for the one hundred foreskins at the center of this novel, they did in fact disappear during the final days of World War II, but in East Prussia, not Belgium. Experts now surmise, based on documents released after the collapse of the Soviet Union, that the defrocked Belgian Jesuit in whose possession the foreskins were last confirmed may have bartered the foreskins to Red Army officers in exchange for safe passage the hell out of East Prussia. Our best guess, at this point, is that the foreskins are in the hands of a private collector who may not appreciate the full value and significance of what he or she has in his or her hands. For help with the complex history of the foreskins, I am indebted to Professor Tom Cooney, director of the Institut d'antiquités génitales in Oakland, California.

I have never heard either Rilo Kiley's "Smoke Detector" or "Turn It On" by the Flaming Lips played in a strip club in Las Vegas. I have, however, heard Prince's "Kiss" lots of times (careful, meticulous research; see above), and one time the dancer was wearing exactly what Gina wears during that scene in the novel.

Readers in Panama are probably still scoffing in disbelief at Gina's lack of success in spotting a sloth, and rightly so. It's ridiculously easy to spot sloths in the jungles of Panama, especially when you have a crack naturalist guide, as did I, like Mario Bernal Greco. Mario claimed, or at least I thought he did, that a sloth will only come down from its tree once every five days to have a bowel movement. I did not put this in the novel because I could not verify it, and my copy editor would have totally busted me on it (see below).

I'd like to thank some of the people who made this book possible. I'm going to keep the list short because I suspect that the longer the list, the more pissed the people left off it will be.

I'm incredibly grateful to Richard Parks, Marjorie Braman, and Peggy Hageman.

I also have to thank my copy editor, Maureen Sugden, who pointed out that methamphetamine users tend to urinate less often than normal and that, according to statistics, the average act of "adequate" sexual intercourse lasts only between three and seven minutes(!)

Finally, several people were generous enough to read a very early version of this story and give notes: Teena Booth, Dede Gardner, Jonathan Hludzinski, Jeff Hoffman, Rachel Long, Mark Poirier, Ed Rugoff, Will Strouse, and Joanne Wolf.